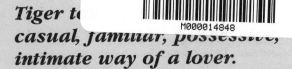

Tiger t... casual, familiar, possessive, intimate way of a lover.

Light caresses on her hand, her arm, her cheek; a finger drawn lingeringly along her collarbone; a touch on the lips as he emphasized a point; a tap on the tip of her nose as he laughed at something she said. Hope didn't know if Tiger was aware of what he did, but she was deeply aware of the electric jolts of need that flashed through her with each brief contact. They took her breath away and comforted her fears at the same time. Made her feel cherished, wanted. Made this whole situation feel real.

Tiger, she reminded herself sternly, was a man who lived undercover; he was used to playing a role. Whatever he did or said, it wasn't real. It was hard to remember that, but she had to.

Then he looked into her eyes with that teasing smile on his face, and all Hope's stern intentions disappeared.

Dear Reader,

Once again, Silhouette Intimate Moments brings you an irresistible lineup of books, perfect for curling up with on a winter's day. Start with Sharon Sala's *A Place To Call Home,* featuring a tough city cop who gets away to the Wyoming high country looking for some peace and quiet. Instead he finds a woman in mortal danger and realizes he has to help her—because, without her, his heart will never be whole.

For all you TALL, DARK AND DANGEROUS fans, Suzanne Brockmann is back with *Identity: Unknown.* Navy SEAL Mitchell Shaw has no memory of who—or what—he is when he shows up at the Lazy 8 Ranch. And ranch manager Becca Keyes can't help him answer those questions, though she certainly raises another: How can he have a future without her in it? Judith Duncan is back with *Marriage of Agreement,* a green-card marriage story filled with wonderful characters and all the genuine emotion any romance reader could want. In *His Last Best Hope,* veteran author Susan Sizemore tells a suspenseful tale in which nothing is quite what it seems but everything turns out just the way you want. With her very first book, New Zealander Fiona Brand caught readers' attention. *Heart of Midnight* brings back Gray Lombard and reunites him with the only woman strong enough to be his partner for life. Finally, welcome Yours Truly author Karen Templeton to the line. *Anything for His Children* is an opposites-attract story featuring three irresistible kids who manage to teach both the hero and the heroine something about the nature of love.

Enjoy every one of these terrific novels, and then come back next month for six more of the best and most exciting romances around.

Yours,

Leslie J. Wainger
Executive Senior Editor

Please address questions and book requests to:
Silhouette Reader Service
U.S.: 3010 Walden Ave., P.O. Box 1325, Buffalo, NY 14269
Canadian: P.O. Box 609, Fort Erie, Ont. L2A 5X3

HIS LAST BEST HOPE

SUSAN SIZEMORE

Silhouette®

INTIMATE™MOMENTS®

Published by Silhouette Books

America's Publisher of Contemporary Romance

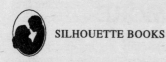

SILHOUETTE BOOKS

ISBN 0-373-07976-1

HIS LAST BEST HOPE

Visit us at www.romance.net

Printed in U.S.A.

SUSAN SIZEMORE

hates winter, but lives in Minnesota anyway. She can't remember a time when she wasn't making up stories. The only things she loves nearly as much as writing are reading and movies. All sorts of books and movies. Her hobbies include collecting art glass and traveling whenever she gets a chance. (Especially getting away from those cold Minnesota winters!) Her first effort at writing romance was a story she wrote as a present for a romance-reading friend. That effort led to the discovery that she loved writing romance, a Romance Writers of America Golden Heart Award and a career as a professional writer.

Chapter 1

"**O**h, God, now what?"

It was another boat, wasn't it? Rescue? Hope pounded a clenched fist against her thigh, and briefly closed her eyes, begging for a miracle.

"Please! I need help!"

She hadn't meant to speak, though the strangled whisper was as much a prayer as a frantic question. She also prayed that her words were drowned by the sound of the boat's approaching engines. It cut powerfully across the water, reaching into Hope's hiding place, and into her dazed awareness. She stayed very still, listening, trying to think, trying to get herself under control.

Hope hated that all she could do was hide. She hated the fear. She hated the knowledge that her uncle, aunt and the yacht's four-man crew were all dead. They had to be dead. She'd heard the pleas, and her aunt's assurances to the invaders that there was no one else onboard. Then had come the shots, the screams, the thud of falling bodies.

There'd been the laughter of strangers along with the sounds of gunfire and death. She heard it all from her hiding spot in the head. She should have done something to help, but it had all happened so fast, a minute or two of hell at most. A minute or two and everyone she loved in the world was gone.

Now she listened to the invaders moving around overhead, talking, and commenting on the approach of another vessel. Soon they'd search the boat, and she'd be dead, too. She didn't know whether to be thankful or not as the deep roar of the newcomer's engine reverberated around her. Her heart thudded hard against her chest; her stomach was curdled with terror. She guessed, from the changing tone of the invaders' voices, that things were about to get worse. Her urge was to stay where she was, frozen with terror, praying not to be found by anybody. But her very active mind raced as she dashed away blinding tears. This was no time to cry, no time for panic. There had to be something she could do! Maybe she was going to die, but she didn't have to cower in a toilet any longer, waiting for it. Her own life wasn't all that important, but maybe she could live long enough to find some justice for the ones so needlessly dead. She had to do something.

After all, it was her fault they were dead.

Cautiously, very slowly, she pushed open the head door. The tiny cubicle was at the bottom of a short, steep stairway that led up to the main deck. Beyond the stairs a narrow hallway led to the yacht's luxurious living quarters. Hope considered hiding in one of the bedrooms, but didn't suppose that would do her any more good than hiding in the head once a search began. She hesitated by the stairs, toying with a wild idea of sneaking up on deck and stealing one of the invaders' boats. She knew nothing about driving a powerboat, less about navigation, but getting lost on open water was better than being murdered. Not seeing anyone at the top of the stairs, she forced herself to take two cautious steps up. Only to fold into a shaking ball on the third step, ducking at the sound of nearby voices.

"*Tigre,*" someone called out. "You're early."

"I make it a habit, Santiago," came the cool reply. "What happened here?"

Hope lifted her head at the sound of the man called *Tigre's* calm voice. She responded to the controlled precision of his tone. She heard the air of command and a good deal of arrogance from this Tiger, though he'd only spoken a few words. His voice might sound fascinating, but what difference did that make? He wasn't an angel come to rescue her, but another modern-day pirate, someone who knew her family's murderers, did business with them. She hated him already.

"The boat was here peacefully fishing when we arrived. We liked what we saw," she heard Santiago continue. "So we took it. I have a plan."

"Something you needed a bigger boat for?"

"That's right, *Tigre.* We're changing the rules."

"Cardenas makes the rules."

Tiger sounded annoyed, contemptuous, and more than a little suspicious. Santiago sounded expansively cheerful. The dangerous undercurrents in every word they spoke sent shivers down Hope's spine. Tension hung in the hot air. Something awful—something else awful—was about to happen.

"Forget Cardenas. You deal with us, *Tigre.*"

"I don't think so."

"Fine. Then we'll take your cargo, just like we took this boat, and keep the money. We're in business for ourselves now."

"*Take* my cargo?"

"That's right."

Tiger laughed, it was a very dangerous sound.

Another voice shouted, "Look out, Tiger!"

Then the shooting started again.

Hope covered her ears, and pressed her body as close as she could to the stairwell while shots and shouts raged above her. After a few moments the determination to escape overcame the fear.

The roar of a boat engine brought her head up.

"Santiago and his men are getting away!"

"Let them!" Tiger shouted above the noise.

There was more gunfire, and the sounds of running feet thudding across the deck.

Hope knew that the chaos on deck might provide her only chance to escape. In the end, the decision to dash up the stairs was governed by the knowledge that she was in no more danger trying to dodge through a firefight than she was waiting to be found.

No one noticed her when she found flimsy shelter hiding behind a canvas deck chair. As the shooting lessened she crawled toward the outside edge of the deck, heading for the large boat tied up near the stern. As she stood she caught a glimpse of a sleek red boat moving through the water away from the yacht, and the chiseled features of a dark-haired man as he glanced back for one long look at the people on the deck of the yacht before speeding away.

She didn't look back when she began to run. She'd almost made it to the railing when a knife flew past her to bury itself in the mahogany deck in front of her. She tripped as she stumbled over the hilt. Hope fell, rolled, and grabbed the knife haft without thinking. She had no idea what to do with a weapon, especially a knife against guns, but she automatically grabbed at any slim chance to survive. However, having the knife did her no good because the moment she jumped back to her feet it was kicked out of her hand, landing far across the deck.

She was trapped, defenseless, quickly surrounded by at least a half dozen armed men. Hope found herself staring into the icy blue eyes of the man who'd disarmed her. He was a very tall man, lean but broad-shouldered, tautly muscled and dressed all in black, bringing midnight into the bright Caribbean day. He had a long face, with high, broad cheekbones and a wide mouth, but it was his predator's eyes that caught and held her attention. He was the leader. A tiger in truth.

Even knowing what sort of man he had to be, Hope couldn't stop herself from reaching a hand toward him. She just barely managed to keep from begging him not to hurt her or help her, though she had to bite her tongue to do it. She couldn't look away from him, though, and knew he read her weakness in her eyes.

The man called Tiger slipped a large gun into a shoulder holster, and the knife back into a sheath on his belt. The movement drew Hope's gaze down his chest and to his lean hips and the hard-muscled thighs outlined by his tight black jeans. Awareness of his body sang shockingly through her, confused her. The sudden spark in his eyes reminded her that all she was wearing was a bright red bikini. She had to fight the urge to cover herself with her hands. Shame raced along with the unexpected heat in her blood, and Hope closed her eyes briefly. When she did grief flooded in, memory of her aunt's last words and the sound of gunfire filled her mind.

"Maybe they aren't dead!" The thought and the words came at the same time. Hope would have raced away to search for her family, but the Tiger in black blocked her from moving.

"They're dead." He said the cold, hard words without

sympathy or compassion. The rest of his men had gathered around them by now. He took his gaze off her to speak to them. "What about Santiago's men, Brant?"

"They all got away," Brant responded.

"Looks like we spoiled their party, though," one of the others said. "Party time for us now."

Hope heard their laughter and terror shot through her grief. She had the impression that these renegades were circling her like starving sharks. They were all staring hungrily.

Tiger laughed, a low dangerous sound. "What makes you think there's going to be a party, Rick?"

The men exchanged smirking glances. Rick said, "She's got a body to kill for, with an angel's face."

"Not going to be an angel long," someone else said.

"Sure she is," Brant said. "One bullet's all it'll take when we're done with her."

There was more laughter, but Tiger's voice cut through it. "The purpose of this meeting in the middle of nowhere was to deliver a shipment to Cardenas. We still have a shipment to deliver. No extracurricular activities will be involved. Understood?" He looked around slowly, forcing each man to drop his gaze before he moved on. One by one, his men backed away from Hope as well. "Good."

While he watched them, she couldn't take her eyes off him. He was the most dangerous thing she'd ever seen. She was actually thankful that his men thought so, too. At least she was thankful that he saved her from rape and murder. Despite the noonday sun broiling down on the nightmare scene, Hope had never been so cold. Cold from the inside out, cold as the death she'd seen staring at her from the men's eyes before Tiger made them back off.

The only heat in the world came from the hand that slipped around her waist suddenly, from the hard-muscled body that touched hers when Tiger pulled her close. It was the sultry heat of flesh against flesh. She didn't understand how he could warm her when his words and actions were so frightening.

Tiger kept his arm around her as he gave orders. Once he seemed satisfied with his men's compliance, he pushed her ahead of him down the stairs to the lower deck. "Your room," he said as they reached the private cabins.

Hope hesitated, giving him a quick, defiant glance over her shoulder, and then she opened the first door on the right. He pushed her into the closet-size cabin and closed the door behind them.

He leaned against the door. "Get dressed."

Hope's initial reaction was that she couldn't possibly have heard her captor correctly. She found the hard expression on his face anything but reassuring, and a kind of banked fire burned in his light-blue eyes. She could feel that fire spread all over her and into her, as his glance moved slowly up the length of her body. The dark heat that filled her robbed her of her voice. It threatened to take away her wits as well. If the man called Tiger hadn't been blocking the door, she might have tried to bolt from the cabin.

She might want to run, but this brown-haired Tiger had a gun, a knife and all the cards. She hated it, and him, but if she wanted to survive she didn't have any choice but to do exactly what he said. After a few seconds her tense shoulders sagged, and she tore her gaze from his. She then awkwardly changed into a pair of shorts, a pastel T-shirt and a pair of canvas deck shoes.

He must have read her angry body language, because he said, in his quiet, deadly voice, "Anger is good. If you keep it under control it'll help you survive."

She whirled to confront him, only to wince at the sound of a splash as a body was tossed overboard. Hope fought down anguish; told herself this was no time to give in to grief.

"Who were they? Your parents?"

The look she turned on him was full of scalding hatred. "That's none of your business!"

"I didn't kill them," he reminded her. He took a step toward her. That brought them close together in the small, narrow cabin. He tilted her chin up. Once she had gone very still, he said, "When I ask a question, answer. I give an order, obey. Understand?"

She took a deep breath, let it out slowly. His gaze burned into hers, making her feel as if she were being stabbed by a pair of blue lasers. "Okay."

"Who were they?"

She fought off devastated sadness and swallowed back tears. "My uncle and aunt."

"What's your name?"

Her head was spinning, but she remembered that he wanted answers to his questions. "Hope Harrison."

She was grateful when he didn't make any stupid jokes about Hope in a hopeless situation, though from the brief, amused sparkle in his eyes she could practically hear him think it. He gestured toward the door. "Let's go."

Hope felt an unreasonable urge to hide behind the man as they came up into the sunlight. She was aware of the heat of her skin where Tiger touched her more than she was of the burning light that poured down onto the mahogany deck. She could imagine what his men thought had gone on in her cabin. It made her stomach curdle with disgust and dread, and she found herself looking thoughtfully at her captor. Why hadn't he touched her? Why wasn't she dead?

"You sure we can't—" one of the other men began.

Tiger cut the other man off with a curt, "No. There's

plenty of women on Isla Sebastian.'' He smiled, showing deeply incised dimples. ''And I'm buying.''

Isla Sebastian? Hope had heard of the tiny island nation—at least she'd seen a television show about undercover cops posing as drug dealers on the island. The island's only town was supposed to be a wide-open, wild haven for outlaws. The island was run by a corrupt government that few other nations even recognized diplomatically. Most tourists didn't go there, but on one side of the island were some expensive resorts for the adventurous and very wealthy who traveled there by yacht. She didn't want to go to Isla Sebastian. She especially didn't want to go to a jungle with this man called Tiger.

''Isla Sebastian?'' Another man asked. ''What about Ibarra?''

Tiger shrugged. ''He was somewhere in South America the last I heard.''

Someone laughed derisively. ''He wants you dead, man.''

''People he wants dead generally end up that way,'' another added.

''We need to make contact with Cardenas,'' was Tiger's cold answer. He swept his gaze around the deck. Hope felt the temperature go down as he froze the argument out of the men. ''We still have a delivery to make. I didn't want to deal with his errand boys in the first place. This time we deal with Cardenas himself. Tiger Rafferty's an honest man.''

So that was his full name, Tiger Rafferty. For some reason knowing it was important to her. Shock shot through her along with the thought, leaving her indignantly surprised that he was important to her. Hope eyed Tiger Rafferty up while he talked quietly with his men. She took in every lean, dangerous line of his body, the darkness of the mink-brown hair that framed his long, sharply angled face while all the time a heat flowed through her that had nothing to do with the burning Caribbean sunlight.

What was the matter with her? What was she thinking? She wasn't. She was just feeling. Responding to an overwhelming male presence on some instinctual, gut level. Weak female turning to strong male for protection? God, how disgusting! Guilt added to her confusion. Not an hour ago the only family she had in the world had been murdered while she'd hidden to save her own skin. Maybe if she hadn't been such a coward she could have done something to help them. She was still being a coward. It was cowardly to look to this Tiger Rafferty as some sort of savior, protector—hero. He was no better than the men who had killed her family.

Tiger Rafferty wasn't an honest man. He was just another callous thug. When she would have moved back, he was instantly by her side. Hope wondered if he was called Tiger because he moved with such dangerous feline speed and grace. Or because he was a killer.

She didn't have time to dwell on it as he grabbed her arm once more and pushed her ahead of him across the deck toward the fast-looking boat tied up against the side of the yacht.

"No! I'm not going—!" Hope balked, but he grabbed her around the waist and swung her across to the other boat before she was able to fight, or find words to express her sudden fury. In fact, all she could manage to say about his casual attitude toward kidnapping her was a coldly sarcastic, "Thanks."

His response was a smile. A smile so genuine and bright that it sent a dazzling rush of sensation all the way through her. For a moment Tiger Rafferty strongly resembled a rescuing angel. Its passing left her blinking in confusion. He was a monster. How could she—?

"You're welcome," Tiger said. Then he took her below and locked her in his cabin.

"You ought to get some sleep, Tiger."

Tiger could tell by Rick's leering tone that his second in command wasn't thinking about sleep.

"Yeah," Tiger agreed reluctantly. He checked the navigational unit before running his hands through his hair. It was a clear night, the calm water lit by a full moon. There was a storm out there according to the radar and the weather service, but they were well ahead of the unseasonable weather. They were making good time. Brant paced the deck on watch, everyone but Tiger and Rick were sacked out. Tiger hadn't slept much in the past couple of days. The thought of going below was more than tempting. A yawn he couldn't stop decided him.

The laughter that followed Tiger as he went down to his cabin told him that Rick didn't believe he had any intention of sleeping. He stopped in front of the cabin door, to prepare himself for the fact that the young woman locked inside wouldn't believe anything he might tell her, either. She had less reason to believe him than Rick. He didn't have much energy to deal with a frightened, resentful prisoner. As much as he wanted to fall into bed, he didn't want to open the door.

Tiger closed his eyes, listened to the sea and the sound of the *Rani*'s engines while he gathered some reserve of energy to do what he had to. The sounds soothed as nothing else could, though not for long. He loved being at sea. He loved the sleek, fast boat. It was about the only thing about this smuggling job he enjoyed. Sometimes Tiger had to remind himself that possession of the *Rani* was just part of his cover.

While the *Rani* wasn't as large or luxurious as the yacht where he'd found Hope Harrison, it had a big hold, room for his small crew, and was far faster than it looked. It got the job done. So did he. He'd worked hard to build a reputation as a ruthless, pragmatic, hard-eyed professional since he'd talked his boss into letting him take on the field assignment his best friend's death had left uncompleted. Bringing Hope onboard was going to cut into the believability of his growing rep if it was thought he did it just to rescue her. Good deeds were dangerous in this world where he walked. Better for it to look like he was keeping her as his woman until he could get her safely away. Keeping from turning the illusion into reality would be the hard part. Keeping illusion from turning into reality was always the hard part. Tomorrow he'd be rid of Hope, and his reputation would be safely intact.

Tiger ran his hands tiredly across his face, rubbing the grit out of his eyes with the heels of his hands, then rolled his shoulders, too aware of the aches. "Hell of a way to make a living."

After he muttered the words into the darkness, he stopped stalling and unlocked his cabin door. Inside was something he wanted but couldn't have. It was crazy, he knew, but he'd wanted her from the instant she'd turned on him, holding his knife in her hand. He'd reacted to the threat, and just barely managed to keep from shooting, but his body tightened with lust at the same time. A dark, primal part of his mind took in the sight of her and loudly announced, *Mine!* He'd had to fight that wild longing from that moment on. Made no sense, did him no good.

Think of her like you do your sister, he told himself, missing the young woman due to be married soon. He missed the world he'd left behind, and the man he used to be. That man wouldn't be lusting after a helpless prisoner. Try to imagine that it's Julie in there, grieving and scared, he told himself. That ought to be enough to at least get you through the night. He told himself that all he needed was a good night's sleep even though his body told him he needed something else.

Hope pretended to be asleep when the door opened. She felt stupid. Like some scared rabbit frozen under a bush in the futile belief that a predator wouldn't see her. She wished she hadn't given in to exhaustion and lay down on the bed after hours of pacing across the rocking deck. She wished a lot of things. Things like being able to turn off the images that wouldn't leave her brain, or just dying, or wishing for the fear and anger and pain and blame that cut through her to stop.

Hope knew that her family and the crew wouldn't be dead if she hadn't wanted so badly to have an "adventure" for once in her dull, quiet life. Oh, she'd been concerned for Uncle Bradley's health, and Aunt April's worry that her and Uncle Bradley's marriage was languishing because he worked so much. Hope had wrapped her real, selfish, reason for the family trip in a layer of concern, in a longing to do something different.

Hope knew that she'd mostly wanted to get away from what Mark called "their situation." As though his leaving her for another, more exciting woman, but asking if he could see her occasionally was just another business deal to him! She was nothing but a convenience to the man she'd thought she loved. She'd never meant anything to him. What was worse, every member of her family was now dead. She kept surviving. What did she have to live for? And why?

Though she kept still and her eyes tightly closed she was utterly aware of Tiger Rafferty being in the little cabin. She knew without seeing that he watched, with his back against the door, no more than three feet away. Over the noise of the boat, over the sounds of the water, she heard when he moved. The only place to go in the room was toward the bed.

She'd been aware of him even when he hadn't been anywhere near her, even when he'd been up on the deck. This was his den, the place where he lived. How could she not be aware of him when she was locked inside the place where her captor slept? She'd feared he'd come, anticipated it, almost hoped for it just to get it over with. She didn't know what to do about it.

Hope sat up as she heard him move toward the bed. There was no use trying to hide. She glared at Tiger. "What are you doing here?"

It was an incredibly stupid question. She expected to see mockery in his eyes. He smiled all right, but his expression wasn't anything she could read. "I live here. Move over."

He turned off the light, then sat down beside her before she could leap out of the bed. A hard shove pushed Hope closer to the wall. He swung his legs onto the mattress and forced her onto her back with an arm across her chest. Suddenly she was in darkness with a hard, hot body on one side and a cold, hard bulkhead on the other. She was aware of the heat and the cold and the hardness—especially the taut, rigid muscles of her captor.

She wanted to demand to be let up, wanted to ask what he was going to do. She wanted, but she couldn't make any words form on her tongue.

"It doesn't matter," he said, as though he knew she hunted for something to say. His arm still pinned her on her back. "Go to sleep."

His arm was like a band of iron just below her breasts. She felt his thigh pressing against hers, and the bare skin of his torso all along her side. "How am I supposed to sleep with you—here?"

He yawned loudly, and took his arm off her. "Curb your impulses. If I can do it, so can you."

She struggled to rise. "My impulses—! You—!"

He didn't let her move. He turned onto his side, catching her wrist just as she struck out. "Quiet."

The word was a fierce whisper in her ear. His breath was on her cheek. A shiver went through her as she saw the glitter of his predator's eyes even in the near darkness. The temptation to scream was stopped as he put a hand over her mouth.

"The agreement is that you do what I tell you. Right now I want you to shut up and go to sleep. It's my bunk, but I'm going to be a gentleman and not make you sleep on the floor."

The sensation of his fingers against her lips was more than Hope could stand. It wasn't that he was hurting her, it wasn't that at all, but it was something like pain that shot through her. Something like fear. Something very like fire sizzled in her blood. She managed to nod, in anticipation that her response would be enough to make him stop touching her mouth. When he did move his hand away, she bit her lips to keep a moan from escaping. And in punishment for the wild, evil emotions Tiger Rafferty stirred in her.

He still held her wrist. She didn't dare ask him to let her go. He didn't move, and neither did she. Her mind raced and spun, and she listened. To the water, and the sound of the engines as the boat sped them toward an island beyond the boundaries of law and civilization. She listened to the man beside her breathe, experiencing every breath as he slowly relaxed against her. She knew the exact instant he went to sleep.

It was only when Tiger's breathing became deep and steady, when his weight rested against her, warming and somehow comforting, that she finally let herself cry for the first time all day. It wasn't until she let herself cry that she was able to fall asleep.

Chapter 2

Hair brushed across his chest, a soft cheek rested over his heart. His arm was across a slender back, his leg was thrown over hers, as they tangled closely together in the small bed. His body was alive with sensation, hardly able to tell where he began and she started. It felt like they'd slept together for years. Half aroused, and only half awake, he drifted on the edge of consciousness, enjoying the touch of supple female flesh for a while. He didn't want to do anything, just lie here and enjoy. She smelled so good. Felt so good. Maybe, in a minute, he'd roll over, put her under him, kiss her awake. Then they could—

The loud knock on the door shattered Tiger's pleasant drifting, dreaming state. He was on his feet instantly, arousal switched to alert tension, aware of the woman only because of the indignant noise she made when he pushed her away to jump up. His attention centered on the door.

The knock came again. ''Tiger?''

Brant. Tiger shook his head to clear it further. Sunlight

poured in through the small window over the bed. Daylight. "What?" he answered.

"We're in," Brant called back. "Docking in ten minutes."

Tiger felt the changes in the *Rani*'s speed and position through the soles of his bare feet as the engines throttled down. He listened. Heard the cries of gulls, the sounds of other boats, human voices carrying across the water. He should have noticed earlier. He threw Hope an annoyed look, blaming her for his getting caught up in some peaceful fantasy when he should have been paying attention. He couldn't let it happen again. Not if he wanted to get them both away from Isla Sebastian alive.

Hope shook hair out of her face and glared back at her captor. She'd been sound asleep a moment ago. Now she had to live with the disgust at having slept in that detestable thug's arms. Peacefully.

She centered her animosity on Tiger Rafferty. "What are you looking at?"

"Nothing. Get dressed."

"I am dressed."

Tiger ignored that he'd said something stupid. He went to the door and opened it just wide enough to see Brant.

Hope watched Tiger warily while he spoke quietly to the man in the corridor. Tousled hair and a day's growth of beard didn't make him look any less dangerous. Certainly more disreputable. Disreputable suited him far too well. He's a murderer, she reminded herself, ashamed that she could look at him with anything but disgust. She was aware that she hadn't actually seen him murder anyone, but considering how she'd ended up sharing this cabin, she figured it was a safe assumption.

"What about Santiago?" the other man asked. "Think he ran back to Cardenas? What do we do about Santiago?"

Hope listened closely, waiting for Tiger's answer. People like Rafferty spent their short, violent lives double-crossing each other, killing anyone that got in their way. *He hasn't killed you yet* a small voice from her heart reminded her.

"It's Cardenas we need to get to. If I have to negotiate with Santiago to do it, fine."

Just business, Hope concluded. *Another businessman,* she thought bitterly. *Just like Mark, but with a gun.*

"Can't Cardenas wait? What about the party you promised first?" the other man asked. "What about the woman?"

Tiger didn't even look at her. He swore, yanked the door opened, and slammed it behind him on the way out. The men continued their conversation up on the deck. Hope could hear shouting, but she couldn't make out any words.

After a while, it occurred to her that it didn't matter what Tiger Rafferty intended to do to her. It was up to her to take control of her own life. She'd always been too passive, too pragmatic, and what good had it ever done her? She had nothing to lose, nothing to return to, no one to care. Maybe it was time for a little reckless abandon in her life. After all, it could only get her killed, and that was likely to happen anyway.

"Are you going to kill me right away, or do I have time to pick up a toothbrush?"

Tiger wasn't sure what to make of Hope's sudden bravado. He decided to ignore it. In another half hour at most they'd be at the Church of St. Cecilia. The priest there, Father Felipe, was one of his few civilian contacts. A smart, ingenious, good man who knew who he was and would be happy to take Hope under his protective wing.

They were on a narrow street that led steeply up from the docks. San Sebastian was a small town, built almost vertically on the sides of a dormant volcano that loomed up over the harbor. From the looks of some of the buildings they passed, it appeared that a storm had been through since his last visit to the island.

He kept walking, with his hand firmly around her wrist. He was bigger and a lot stronger. She went where he wanted her to go. He didn't tell her the destination he had in mind. He didn't pay any attention to the street vendors that thrust their wares in their way.

"Excuse me, but could we—"

"No."

"You don't know what I was going to ask."

"Didn't I tell you to be quiet?"

"No. You told me to get dressed."

"That was an hour ago. Be quiet."

"I'm not scared of you."

If he hadn't felt her gaze on him, hot and defiant, if her steps hadn't lagged until he was practically dragging her up the hill, he wouldn't have finally looked at her. "Yes, you are."

Their gazes locked, held. He stopped thinking, and pulled her closer, until there was no more than an inch between them. He had one hand on her shoulder, one locked around her left wrist. The flat of her hand came up to touch his chest just over his heart, whether to fend him off or for some more intimate purpose he couldn't tell. He felt the heat of her touch through the thin cotton of his shirt, and it was like it was her racing heartbeat he was sensing. Her eyes widened, the color deepened. They were so blue he thought he was going to drown in them.

There was a crowd around them in the congested street. Low, flat-roofed buildings with faded pastel paint and shuttered windows bunched up against the sides of the road. Shaded alleys darted off in all directions from the main street. Tropical flowers in window boxes and on pushcarts and piles of fruit added scent and color to the scene. Flies buzzed, there was a lot of shouting, and the sun was hot as hell overhead.

For a long, painful, delicious, confusing moment Tiger didn't notice any of the riot around him. All he was aware of, for what couldn't have been more than a stolen second, was the sight, scent and feel of Hope Harrison. He was aware that all she was aware of was him. His hand slipped from her shoulder to circle her waist. Her hand moved up to circle the back of his neck. He felt her fingers in his hair.

Just as he was about to kiss her, she shook her head violently, and tried to push away. He felt like he'd just been slapped awake. He almost let her go.

"Stop looking at me!"

He kept a tight grip on her wrist. "I was going to do a lot more than look." He turned and began hurrying them up the street again.

"No, you're not."

"I said *was*. The mood's past."

"Good. Keep it that way."

"You weren't exactly fighting it." This time his reply bought him the silence he wanted. He could still feel Hope's glare as he shouldered a path for them through the crowd.

He couldn't afford to be reckless, or away from his men for very long. As he'd promised, he'd given the men twenty-four hours and a cash bonus to spend carousing. He hated the waste of time, but a deal was a deal, even if he did half blame his hapless prisoner for causing the delay. In twenty-four hours Father Felipe would have arranged to have Hope off the island. No matter what went down she wouldn't be a part of it. But even getting her to the priest still forced him to spend more time in her tempting company than he liked. She was making him act soft and stupid. Like a horny teenager.

Now, here they were at Isla Sebastian, and he was no closer to completing his assignment for Naval Intelligence than he had been twenty-four hours before. Less. He damned Santiago, since it wasn't fair to curse a group of innocent bystanders who'd gotten killed due to Santiago's greed. He damned himself. And he damned Hope Harrison just because she existed in this time and place. Because he wanted her. Because she'd never know the Naval Intelligence officer even existed. She'd only have painful memories of a very bad man who went by the ridiculous nickname of Tiger.

"What kind of name is Tiger, anyway?" Hope asked.

She was growing tired of Rafferty's fierce determination to ignore her as he hurried her up the steep, narrow street. He was correct, she was scared of him, and not just because he held her life in his hands. She was more scared of how he made her feel when he shouldn't make her feel anything but loathing. She did loathe him. He disgusted her, but loathing and disgust didn't seem to be enough to shake off the other things he made her feel. "Where are we going?"

He just kept walking, with her bouncing along behind him like a balloon on a string. When he continued to ignore her, Hope dug her heels into the dried mud of the street, leaned her weight back and refused to move any farther up the hill.

Tiger was forced to turn around and say, "Do you want me to carry you?"

"No."

"Then come on."

"No."

"You're a spoiled, rich, brat, you know that?"

Hope took a shaky breath as the pain of loss stabbed hard through her. "You don't know that," she snapped back. "You don't know anything about me. Just because my family's rich—because my family... Damn!" She turned her head away, refusing to explain anything to him. She hugged her grief to herself, concentrated on it because it was the only emotion she could bear to look at. Everything else was terrifying, shameful, wrong and centered on Tiger Rafferty. He couldn't have her grief, too.

She made herself look at him again. Hope focused on the important thing rather than imagining it was remorse she saw in his eyes. "Where are you taking me?"

Tiger decided he might as well tell her.

But the shot came from behind them before he could answer. It was loud even in the noisy street. People screamed, scattered, ducked.

Tiger grabbed Hope around the waist. He spun them around, forced her to run with him toward the nearest alley. Just as they reached it, a second bullet gouged plaster off the corner of a building a foot above his head.

The third bullet came even closer. Tiger wore a light denim jacket in the tropical heat for the single purpose of concealing his shoulder holster. The temptation was strong to pull his own weapon and return fire, but he didn't do it. He wouldn't risk taking innocent lives in a firefight on the street. His first responsibility was to protect Hope, and if that meant running away, running away was fine with him.

Several seconds elapsed with no shots being fired, though he could hear footsteps running behind them. Tiger grabbed Hope and pulled her around one corner, then another. He paused long enough to look back from the cover of a building. Hope pressed up behind him. He didn't know if she was trying for comfort, using him as a shield or trying to get a look at their pursuers herself. Her breath brushed the back of his neck. He put a finger over her mouth, and waited until she nodded her understanding. After they waited for a few more moments in tense silence, he nodded and took his hand away from her lips. He eased her backward, risked another quick look the way they'd come, then they headed up a narrow alley between rows of rickety fences. A black cat squalled and flashed away as they passed one whitewashed gate, but there were no people around.

The latch on the next gate they passed turned beneath his touch. The gate opened onto a small, neatly tended vegetable garden. Beyond the garden was the concrete back porch of a salmon-pink, two-story house. Laundry dangled listlessly in the humid air from a clothesline hung between a palm tree and the porch. A lazy old black dog lifted its head from the stoop, but didn't bother with barking a warning. Tiger relaxed when the animal slowly lowered its muzzle back onto its crossed paws.

Tiger maneuvered them so that the laundry as well as the fence shielded them from the alley. Being six foot six, he had to bend carefully to conceal himself. When Hope ducked as well, he noticed for the first time that she was not a short woman. He took a chance and released his hold on her. He also finally drew his gun.

Hope rubbed her aching wrist as she looked between the armed man and the garden gate. She tugged on Tiger's sleeve and mouthed one word, "Santiago?"

His eyes narrowed, as though he were annoyed at her knowing any of his business. "Maybe," he mouthed back after hesitating a moment.

"Maybe?" She whispered this time. A sense of outrage overrode her more sensible fear response. "How many people do you have trying to kill you?" He gestured for her to keep quiet. She didn't have it in her to obey at this point.

'Right. There's Ibarra, too. You don't have a lot of friends, to you?''

"I don't need friends." The words came out a low, dangerous growl.

The look in his eyes hinted at something different, but Hope supposed that was her imagination. She spun slowly around, looking for something, she didn't know what. A weapon? What would she do if she found one? Defend herself against whoever was chasing them? Use it to escape from Tiger? She eyed him speculatively as the notion struck her. Why not run? Strike out on her own? Surely there had to be someone, somewhere on Isla Sebastian who would help her if she got away from Tiger.

"Don't even think about it."

Maybe her expression and body language gave too much away. Maybe they were somehow connected. When he grabbed her arm it was like an electric current sparked between them. He pulled her against him. She was aware that he held a gun in one hand and her in the other, but the threat didn't come from the weapon. It came from the sizzle that passed between them where they touched. It came from the flash in his eyes as he looked at her. How could she have considered those blue eyes to be ice cold?

He put his lips very close to her ear and whispered, 'You're not going anywhere but with me. Understood?''

His eyes might not be cold, but his voice was. It sent a shiver of fear through her. Hope blinked, too aware of the heated hardness of his body and the softness of his hair against her cheek.

Hope screwed up her courage and tried to make a joke of her answer to his threat. "Sounds like you're asking for a date." She was immediately sorry—of all the stupid things to come out with!

He chuckled, and the low sound in his throat sent a shiver through her.

"Sweetheart, we're aren't dating, we're going steady." There were people after them, and here he was hiding behind someone's laundry holding Hope Harrison and mouthing nonsense. The last time they'd been in this position—only a few minutes ago—someone began shooting at them.

He forced his attention back to the situation. He made himself move away from Hope, something that should have been easy, but wasn't. "Stay right here," he ordered, and moved to the fence.

Who is it? he wondered as he peered cautiously up and down the alley. Had to be Santiago, he guessed. He hoped Ibarra was crazy, and mad for revenge for something Tiger hadn't done. Tiger had heard that Ibarra was in Colombia. If he'd thought otherwise he wouldn't have brought an innocent woman to the island Ibarra made his home. Could it be one of Ibarra's men who'd spotted him and was looking to make points with the boss? No, he rejected the thought. Ibarra was a loose cannon since his brother's death, but his new second in command had publicly stated that Ibarra's feud with Rafferty was none of his business, that he was only interested in the business. Besides, it was well-known that Ibarra had stated that the "Tiger Hunt" was his own personal affair, a *mano a mano macho* thing.

Tiger didn't see anyone, but he thought he heard movement—maybe an alley cat, maybe an assassin. He waited, still, patient and professional once more. He made himself be aware of the woman behind him, but only enough to make sure she did as she was told.

Hope settled down cross-legged on the ground and waited. She was dizzy from being afraid, being helpless and out of control. Or maybe it was hunger, she decided, as the warm tangy scent of a tomato ripening on staked-up vine drew her attention. She couldn't remember the last time she'd eaten. Looking at the plant, she had a moment's guilt as she remembered how much Aunt April loved fresh tomatoes. She got up and cautiously approached the dog on the steps.

If it barked she supposed they'd be in trouble, since it would alert both the homeowner of their intrusion and the gunman of their location. It seemed to her, though, that the best escape route would be for them to go through the house, and to do that, they needed to get by the big, black dog.

The dog stood up as she reached it, came down the steps, and leaned against her, looking up with pleading eyes. Hope automatically began rubbing the animal's big head. She was close enough to the open back door of the house to peer inside. There was a silence and stillness about the place that made her think no one was home. Maybe she could sneak up the steps and through and out without Tiger taking any notice that she was gone. Leave him to face the danger alone? Why not? And why did the question send a twinge of guilt through her?

Tiger had his hand around her wrist again before she could think of an answer. "Let's go."

He pulled her past the dog and up the porch steps. The dog made no protest as they went into the house, but she heard it barking loudly a moment later. She also heard someone running through the garden as Tiger hurried her through the house and outside once more. Tiger slammed the front door, pushed a porch chair in front of it with his foot. He slipped his gun back in its shoulder holster, and then they ran again.

She eventually lost track of where they went. Hope did notice that some of the areas they traveled through looked to have heavy storm damage. Others were just slums. She knew she was lost, hoped he wasn't. Then, she hadn't known where they were going in the first place. Going up and down the steep mountainside streets for what seemed like hours in the hot midday sunlight didn't help her growing disorientation any. Tiger carefully kept checking behind them, especially whenever they entered an open area. She watched Tiger watching the people in the streets and loitering in the plazas. People got out of their way after one look at Tiger's hard expression. It was disturbing to think that the natives of Isla Sebastian were used to staying out of dangerous men's ways. No one shot at them, which she supposed was a blessing. On the other hand, she was getting winded. More than winded, she was getting sick.

The next square they entered contained a large, open-air market. They were near the water now. The air smelled of sea salt and fish, and the sky was full of gulls. Their raucous calls stabbed into Hope's head, making her realize for the first time that she had a headache. She put her free hand to her temple, and dug her heels in, refusing to be pulled along like a toy anymore.

"Enough," she proclaimed when Tiger turned his dark, angry look on her. "I won't go another step." Couldn't was more like it, but she refused to show weakness to this man. "We must have lost the guy by now," she added, trying to make him see reason. "Unless everybody on the island is out to get you."

Tiger was not at all certain they'd lost their pursuer when he rounded on the stubborn woman. She was wide-eyed and pale beneath her tan. Pale with a hint of green. He frowned and took her by the shoulders. "What's wrong with you, woman?"

"Wrong?" she spluttered. "Oh, nothing—apart from the kidnapping and the current chase scene we're involved in."

She pushed ineffectually against his chest. "Let go of me! And let me go!"

He shook her. "Hush." His voice and actions were harsher than he intended.

Her wide eyes grew even wider, but she kept quiet. She set her jaw, trying to mask weakness and fear with a stubborn show of belligerence. At another time he might have admired her attempt to stand up to bullying, but not when the bullying was from him. Trouble was, it would be easy to feel more than just admiration for this woman—better not to feel anything at all.

"You agreed to do what I told you," he reminded her. "You're not being given a chance to back out on that deal." He glared at her until her gaze dropped from his and her shoulders slumped beneath his hands. He didn't blame her for hating him. "Good," he said when he was certain the fight had gone out of her.

As they set off, he put his arm around her shoulders and they looked like a happy strolling couple. The market was a familiar place, with rows of stalls full of fresh fish and produce. There were some cafés and shops in the building around the plaza. He told himself it was less conspicuous walking with her this way, and tried not to think about how right it felt to hold her in the curve of his arm.

"I'm taking you to a friend," he told her, finally realizing that it might do some good if he gave her some reassurance

She wasn't sure which sensation was worse, the growing nausea, or the dread that she supposed was causing her light-headed dizziness. The scene they passed through was growing harder to focus on with each step. Each step, in fact, was growing more difficult to take. The crowd's noise hurt her ears, the colors and the bright light hurt her eyes, the smells—the smells were the worst part.

No, the worst part was his telling her that he was taking her to a "friend." What did he mean by that? This Tiger person could be planning on selling her to this "friend" for all she knew. She should ask him just what he meant.

She tried to stop walking, tried to get Tiger's attention, but the next stall they passed held a barrel of pickles and a pile of very dead fish. The combination of aromas hit her nose and her empty stomach before she could open her mouth. Hope did stop in her tracks; that was all she could do, as her eyes rolled up in her head and she fell into Tiger Rafferty's arms in a dead faint.

Chapter 3

"This is lovely," Tiger muttered darkly. "Just lovely. Now I've got a fainting maiden on my hands." He eased open the curtain on the French door of the upstairs bedroom and looked cautiously down to the bustling square below. The building he'd carried Hope to served food and beverages on the ground floor, and rented the upstairs rooms out by the hour. Carrying Hope across the plaza had drawn attention. Their pursuer would have no trouble finding the two tall Americans if he asked anyone in the market about them.

Tiger swore softly, and glanced back at the long-legged young woman stretched out on a pink chenille bedspread. A sheen of sweat glistened on her lightly tanned skin in the stifling heat of the upstairs room. She moaned occasionally, but hadn't moved. He couldn't tell if she had a fever or not, not in this heat.

Outside, the market traffic had died down as the locals sensibly found ways to escape the midday sun. There was a ceiling fan overhead, but he'd been told that the power in this part of town had been out for days. There were candles set in colored glass votive holders set around the room if he wanted light, but the dimness with the sheer curtains drawn was fine with Tiger.

The phone lines were out on the island, as well. Oh, his cell phone would have worked for calling Felipe, since the satellite service used by the resorts, the outlaws and the offshore bankers who served their financial needs, was in working order. But the priest didn't have the luxury of answering Tiger on a cellular telephone if Tiger tried to call. Tiger thought that maybe he'd contribute something to help communications to his friend's church in exchange for help with Hope Harrison.

Tiger took a seat in the rickety chair beside the bed and rubbed the back of his neck. He watched her sleep; he wasn't sure for how long. There was something oddly pleasant about just watching her sleep. It didn't make sense, but nothing had since the first moment he saw her.

"You're driving me crazy, woman," he murmured, and discovered that he was holding her hand. Even worse, he was patting it comfortingly. It was her left hand, he noticed, and there was a faint pale line on her ring finger showing that she had worn a ring on it not so long ago. Wedding ring? He wondered. Engagement? How old was she? Still in her twenties, he guessed as he looked at her. Where was she from? Her rich contralto voice blended a Southern and East Coast accent that made him think of Maryland. And who was the man whose ring she'd worn? Why wasn't she wearing it anymore?

And why was he thinking such questions? She didn't have a "Need to Know" about his business, he certainly didn't "Need to Know" about hers. All he had to do was to make sure she was safe. That was all. Period. End of

story. What he had to do didn't stop him from wanting—
wanting to know about her. Wanting her. He swore under
his breath, both with frustration at the sheer physical ache
of desiring someone he couldn't touch, and with annoyance
for letting the presence of a woman get to him in any way.
Don't trust her, he reminded himself. Don't trust yourself
to trust her.

Hope's eyes fluttered open. He didn't let go of her hand
as she bolted upright with a shocked gasp. The gasp turned
into a groan. Then she blinked, and said, "Where am I?"

"In a brothel."

The words were meant as some sort of joke, but the
terrified look she turned on him was anything but amusing.
"I knew it!" she cried before he could say another word.
She snatched her hand out of his. She turned a defiant glare
on him. "Is this your *friend's* place?"

"No."

"You're going to leave me here to—"

"This isn't my friend's place. I'll take you there when
you're feeling better."

Hope didn't know why a smile lifted the corner of Tiger's lips, but there was something annoyingly reassuring
in the gesture. Something disturbingly attractive, as well.
The effect was dizzying.

"No," she said, putting her hand to her forehead.
"That's not why I'm dizzy." And she was, very. Her stomach twisted in a painful knot, and the oppressive heat made
her want to throw up. "What is the matter with me?"

The man who held her prisoner—the tall one with the
dimples—stood up. "When was the last time you had anything to eat?"

Was that it? Was that all that was wrong with her? Hope
swung her legs over the side of the sagging bed and curled
her hands around the edge of the mattress for support. The

bedspread bunched under her tense fingers. She looked up, fighting dizziness. It was a long way to tilt her head to meet the surprisingly concerned gaze of the man standing in front of her. She wanted to ask him why he cared. Instead, she answered, "I don't know." She blinked hard as she tried to remember. Visions of the attack on the yacht came back to haunt her, making her never care if she ate anything again. Everything that mattered was gone. She had no right to—

"How long?" he persisted.

"Yesterday morning, maybe."

He shook his head, and moved toward the door. Before he went out he growled, "Stay put."

Hope did as she'd been told, at least for a few minutes. It took her that long to gather enough strength to get to her feet. Once she was up, she soon discovered that he'd left her in a second-floor bedroom that had a small balcony facing the market square. She considered jumping to the ground, but went looking for a bathroom first. Sometimes other needs had priority over escape attempts. She was happy to discover that a doorway led from the bedroom into a small bathroom. The electricity wasn't working, but a small window let in light, and the plumbing did work. After using the facilities and splashing water onto her hot face, she began to feel a little better.

A loud rumbling from her stomach informed her that she was indeed very hungry as she walked back into the bedroom. A moment later the door opened and Tiger came in, carrying a laden tray. The spicy aroma that hit her made her mouth water.

"Hope you like spicy food," he said as he kicked the door shut behind him. "Because that's all you can get on Isla Sebastian. The local cuisine isn't so much piquant as it is downright hostile."

Was that a joke? Hope eyed the man suspiciously. "Tiger Rafferty," she said. "Gunrunner and food critic."

"Yeah," he answered, putting the tray down on the bedside table. "I write the food and wine column in *Mercenary's Monthly*."

Hope laughed, and sat down hard on the bed as she did. A few moments ago she'd looked at her gaunt reflection in the bathroom mirror and been convinced she'd never feel anything but empty pain again. Now, she didn't know if it was the promise of her first meal in days that made her feel better, or if Tiger's light attitude was infectious.

Just because he isn't threatening your life at the moment is no reason to be reassured, she reminded herself as she tried hard to concentrate on anything but looking at him. His dimples were showing again, and she definitely didn't want to look at them. A smiling Tiger Rafferty confused her. Just because he could crack a joke and had brought her a meal didn't change what he was—which was a gunrunner that somebody was actively trying to kill. It was not good to be around this man.

There was a part of her that denied her last thought, but she ignored it, and concentrated on the food. "What is that?" she asked, pointing at a bowl. The thick soup in it was a creamy saffron yellow, with bits of meat and vegetables floating in it.

"Squash soup," he answered. "Power's out, but Remy has a cook fire going out back with a big pot of this stuff simmering away. That's how he cooks it most of the time anyway. Local delicacy. You'll like it. Try the bread first, though, to line your stomach."

There were several wedges of chewy-looking flatbread on the tray, and a large glass of water. Hope had been too well trained in polite behavior to keep from saying, "Thank you,'' before she dug in, but she resented being grateful and dependant.

Maybe because she was so good at it. Mark had said that, told her that she was too passive and retiring, dull, with no sense of adventure. So far her attempt to change her personality had gotten people killed, and made her dependent on yet another man. She wondered what Mark would have to say if he knew she was currently in a bedroom on a tropical island with a sexily dangerous male called Tiger.

''Who is he?''

Hope looked up quickly, heart racing at the hard tone of Tiger's voice. There was nothing gentle in his expression, but there was something—compelling—in his eyes just the same. Something that sent a wave of heat flashing through her. She blinked, and dragged air into her lungs. ''What?''

He pointed at her hand. ''You're rubbing your ring finger.'' And looking pissed off, he added to himself. He wondered why her expression made him feel both annoyed and pleased. And—jealous? That didn't bear thinking about. He asked, ''Who is he?''

The room felt smaller, he seemed bigger. The atmosphere around them was charged with primal tension. For a moment the awareness that she was sitting on a bed, and that he was only a few feet away was all that she could think about. She forced herself to concentrate, to deny there was anything going on between them. At least long enough to lift her head haughtily and demand, ''Is that any of your business?''

''No. Who *was* he?''

''Somebody who wanted somebody more exciting,'' she heard herself answer. The words just came out.

She clapped a hand over her mouth after the damage was done, and told herself she'd only responded because of Ti-

ger's insistence the day before that she answer his questions
and do as she was told. When he threw back his head and
laughed she tried hard not to imagine masculine triumph in
the sound, tried not to admire the strong column of his
throat, or notice the thick sweep of dark hair against his
shoulders. He was far too handsome for her good, though
his looks shouldn't matter at all. What was this feeling
worming its way through her as she looked at him? There
was attraction, but she could deal with having an unwanted
attraction to a vibrant male animal. It was the fact that she
found his curiosity…endearing—yes, that was it, endearing—for even a moment that was truly frightening.

She decided it was safer to stop looking at Tiger Rafferty, safer to stop trying to analyze emotions and concentrate on not feeling any. She picked up a spoon and dug
into the soup. She ignored the fact that it burned like fire
going down and made her sweat. She ate as quickly as she
could, and hoped it would give her enough energy to carry
her through any chance she might get to escape.

He had no right wanting to tell her that she was exciting
enough for him. He heard the desperation in her voice when
she'd answered—answered because he'd threatened her if
she didn't cooperate. Of course she wanted to be left alone.
Just do your job, Rafferty, and keep your emotions out of
it. No female entanglements. He was good at avoiding
those. Had been good at it, at least, until his first sight of
Hope Harrison yesterday.

"We've got to get out of here," he muttered and turned
back to Hope. It wasn't safe outside, but it was safer than
being alone with her. "Finished?" She turned those bright-
blue eyes up to him again, and nodded. "Good. Let's go."
He gestured toward the door. "And no more fainting.
That's an order."

"Yes, sir, Captain Rafferty," was her tart response.

He was just barely able to keep from replying that he was a long way from making the promotion to captain. Oh, yeah, it was definitely safer for his cover to be away from this woman.

Hope proceeded Tiger down a narrow, rickety staircase then through a room crowded with shadows and mostly empty tables. The aromas of a wood fire and simmering spicy soup drifted in along with heat and sunlight from a doorway at the back of the building. The front door opened as they approached it. A young woman entered, and smiled as she saw Tiger. At the same time a man spoke from the doorway of the outside cooking area.

"You going, *Tigre?*" the man asked.

The young woman said. "Welcome back, *Tigre.*"

Tiger turned his head to speak to the man as the woman squeezed between Hope and Tiger. Hope saw her chance and bolted for the street door.

For the first few moments Hope's heart pounded so loudly in her ears she couldn't hear if Tiger came after her. The humid heat hit like a blow as she raced into the market plaza. She ran through the crowd, dodged around the back of a row of stalls and concentrated on not looking back. She bent low and kept her head down, letting the impulse to run lead her through the market. She entered the first street she came to, panting as she ran uphill. She passed people and the occasional car, but didn't dare ask for help. Eventually she stumbled into an alley and took a moment to get her breath and bearings.

Now what? she wondered, and risked a cautious look around the corner. Tiger was nowhere in evidence. She didn't know where she was, either, but that was no different than it had been all day. She didn't know where anything was on the island, didn't know who she could ask for aid, or if there were any authorities she could go to. But she was free. Everything else was just details, right? She didn't have to worry about Tiger Rafferty's mysterious plans for her anymore. She didn't have to think about him. Acknowledging that she didn't have to think about him immediately brought an image of him into her mind, long and lean, bright-eyed and dangerous. She could still feel the strength and warmth of his hand imprisoning hers. She pushed the images away, and tried hard to *think*.

"And *not* about him," she warned herself. She leaned her head back against the faded wooden wall and licked her lips. They tasted salty from sweat and sea air.

What to do? What to do? What would Uncle Bradley advise her to do? Or Mark? And what did that matter? They weren't here. "In control of my own life," she reminded herself. "That's what I want." Well, it was what she was stuck with, anyway. "Mistress of my own fate." She shook her head. "Couldn't I hire someone to do this for me? I'm not cut out for adventures, you know," she addressed a passing alley cat. "Not really."

And standing in a filthy alley talking to a stray animal wasn't going to do her any good, now was it? Hope sighed. Fine, she thought. Here's the plan. She stared across the alley at the blank wall opposite her and couldn't think of a thing. She had no money, no passport, didn't know anyone who wasn't a criminal, didn't think Isla Sebastian had so much as an American Consulate.

"Maybe there's an airport," she murmured, rubbing her chin thoughtfully. Maybe she could hire a plane somehow.

She considered heading back toward the port facilities as a more practical solution. There had to be some sort of official customs office down by the docks, right? Despite the lurid reports of the island being run by gangsters there had to be some sort of government bureaucracy in place, didn't there?

"To collect bribes if nothing else," she added cynically.

The port would be the logical place to go looking for these theoretical government officials. The main glitch in this plan was that Tiger's smuggling boat was tied up on the docks she needed to get to. Tiger was also, theoretically, searching for her.

If he was, she reasoned, he wouldn't be expecting her to go anywhere near his boat. The docks would be the last place he'd look for her. Then again, it was possible he'd decided not to bother chasing her since she was more trouble than whatever she'd been worth to him as a prisoner. Maybe he'd gone back to his boat, or joined his men carousing in a bar, and she didn't need to fear that he was looking for her. Hope sneered as she recalled the pleased look and eager tone of the woman who'd spoken to him. The woman's presence had given Hope her chance to escape. She told herself that the notion of Tiger's letting her go so he could spend time with the other woman was a foolish one, and didn't matter to her anyway.

Whatever the case, she couldn't stay in this alley forever, and the port facility was at least a downhill walk. She'd had enough of running up the side of a volcano for one day, thank you very much. Hope cautiously left her hiding place. She'd only gone a few blocks before she caught sight of Tiger Rafferty.

She spotted his tall figure standing at the far side of a cross street. His back was to her as he turned in a slow circle, scanning doorways, pedestrians, parked vehicles and passing traffic. Hope barely managed to duck behind a parked truck as she saw Tiger begin to turn in her direction.

I ought to just let her go, Tiger thought as he continued to hunt through the streets of Isla Sebastian. His conscience wouldn't let him do that. He'd made the decision to get Hope to Father Felipe, and he owed her at least that much.

Help her because you're an officer and a gentleman? he asked himself sarcastically. Just trying to do his duty to an American citizen in distress? Or was he being dutiful because she was sad and beautiful and vulnerable—and he wanted her more than any woman he'd seen?

All of the above, he told himself, and kept on looking even as he cursed himself for letting a woman get to him. It was getting close to nightfall. He needed to find her soon. Isla Sebastian was dangerous enough in the daylight; Hope wouldn't stand a chance on her own from the dangerous two-legged animals who took over the streets at night.

He knew he should calm down, that trying to conduct an assignment from a base of emotions helped ensure that assignment's failure. He was well aware that his reaction to Hope Harrison was a visceral, physical one, but knew he had to keep his emotions out of it. He had to fight attraction and concentrate on duty. He was angry as hell about the way she clouded his motives and judgment—and furious with her for taking off like a scared rabbit when he'd given her no reason to think he meant her harm.

Well, hardly any reason.

This thought caused him to smile, and helped him to calm down. He stopped on a street corner and looked carefully at his surroundings. It was time he used his brains instead of rushing around like an idiot. "Excuse me," he said to a street vendor who sat on the tailgate of a rusted-out pickup piled full of melons. "Have you seen a tall young woman with short blond hair come by in the last few minutes?"

Hope saw Tiger step up to a truck across the street and speak to a young woman. The woman's long dreadlocks swung from side to side as she shook her head in answer. He said something else and the woman smiled widely as she nodded. The charm he exuded during this brief encounter was electrifying. Hope's reaction was almost enough to lure her out of hiding. How ridiculous of her! The man was hunting her—she had no business being drawn to him just because he didn't look angry or threatening at the moment.

She hunkered down in her hiding spot, but trying to make herself smaller wasn't much use when she was still essentially out in the open. A dog came over to sniff curiously at her, and a little boy followed the dog. A man walked past behind her and looked from her to the man searching for her across the street. The passerby hesitated for a moment longer, then decided not to get involved and moved on. The next one might not be so disinterested. She had to get out of here. She gave the dog a pat and the boy a smile, then inched away from the truck. She saw an open doorway in the building behind her. If she made a quick dash for it he might not see her. She took a deep breath, and chanced one more look his way before making her move.

When she saw the gunman she didn't hesitate for a moment to scream, "Tiger! Behind you!"

She didn't see what happened next, because panic made her turn and blindly run once more into the maze of Isla Sebastian's streets. She heard shots behind her, and they gave wings to her fleeing feet. Until the thought *What if he's hurt? Dying? Dead?* brought her to a stumbling halt. For a moment Hope was blind with anguish. When the wave of pain receded she found that she was standing in a dark alley, her arms wrapped around her stomach, her shoulders heaving with painful sobs.

What was wrong with her? Why couldn't she ever do anything right? Tiger could be dead and it would be her fault. He was out on the street, in the open, vulnerable, because he was looking for her. She should have done something, helped him somehow. She was always useless, always—

Wait a minute. A bit of reason finally surfaced out of the flood of recriminations. Tiger's one of the bad guys. It's not my fault someone is trying to kill him. And why couldn't she stop thinking about him? Worrying about him. "Simple solution," she murmured. "I'm crazy."

She scrubbed her hands over her face, wiped away tears and grime, and tried to get her thoughts and emotions in some sort of order.

You have to stop blaming yourself for the things that aren't your fault, Aunt April had told Hope once when she was young. *And only blame yourself for the things that are.* Her aunt had been joking when she'd added those words, but Hope had been ten years old and grieving for her parents' deaths. She'd taken the statement deeply to heart and still lived with the consequences of something that had been meant to lighten a sad moment.

It wasn't blame she tried to deal with these days, but responsibility. Tiger Rafferty's welfare was not her responsibility, but she couldn't quite make herself believe it. For some insane reason he'd become important to her. It would be going too far to say that she cared for him, but—

She sighed as she looked around. Where the devil was she, anyway? The rat that looked back at her didn't offer any answers, but the sight of the creature made her back quickly out of the alley. When she turned around she found herself on a street on the waterfront lined with busy saloons. She could hear the roaring of powerboat engines on the water nearby, drowning out even the strident noise of the gulls. She didn't know how she'd gotten here, but it looked like she'd gotten her wish and made it all the way back to the port.

Now all she had to do was find the Port Authority offices

and put what passed for a plan into effect. Which way should she go? she wondered, and turned slowly around in the effort to decide. By the time she'd made a full circle two men were standing in front of her.

One smiled and put a hand on her shoulder. The other one's first words were a lewd suggestion. The one touching her added a price he was willing to pay for a sexual act she'd never heard of.

Hope took a few steps back. Her ears burned from the words she'd heard. "I think you've mistaken me for a professional lady, and I'm not." She held her hands up before her as the two men moved after her. "Goodbye," she told them.

"If you want to work for free that's fine with me," the larger of the pair said, and lunged for her.

Hope turned and ran back into the alley, only to discover that it dead-ended in a brick wall. Trapped, she heard the men panting up behind her. She found a rock on the ground and heaved it as hard as she could as she turned on her pursuers. It struck the big man in the shoulder. He swore, but came to a halt. His friend came closer, a wide grin splitting his face. Hope snatched up a broken bottle from a refuse heap and held it defensively in front of her.

"Stay back!" she warned. "Just leave me alone!" Her back was quite literally to the wall, her attention focused on the smiling thug who only grinned wider as he kept coming toward her.

"Come on," the big man urged his friend. "Let's go."

"Nah. I want to have some fun."

"I warn you!" she shouted.

The big man backed out of the alley and disappeared into the growing darkness. The other one obviously didn't see her as a threat. She slashed the bottle at him, but he sidestepped easily. "Leave me alone!" she shouted again.

Shadows moved at the head of the alley. Had the big man changed his mind? Hope risked a quick glance over her assailant's shoulder. She didn't know whether to scream with terror or relief at what she saw.

She did, however, scream.

Her attacker turned as Tiger Rafferty said, "You bothering the lady?"

"Uh…" the man grunted.

Tiger gestured with his gun. "Go," was all he needed to say.

He stepped aside to let the man pass, then tucked the gun back in its holster and walked slowly toward Hope. She waited, heart racing, her back pressed against bricks that still held the heat of the day. She couldn't take her gaze from his as he approached.

When he was a few inches away from her, he leaned forward, resting his hands flat on the wall on either side of her head. He put his face close to hers. "Hope Harrison," Tiger Rafferty said, voice soft and intense, "what am I going to do with you?"

The world spun, then focused in on her intense awareness of him. A mix of fear and fire raced through her. The fire settled deep inside her. Some of the same fire sparked in his eyes. He moved closer, his body pressing against hers. She heard the glass shatter as she dropped the bottle to the ground.

"What am I going to do?" His voice was rough with sudden passion. "Anything I want," he answered his own question. And kissed her.

Chapter 4

This is no way to treat a lady, Tiger thought. Then, she didn't taste like a lady, she tasted like a woman. Her mouth was hot on his, clinging. The hands on his shoulders were holding him close, not trying to push him away. What they were doing didn't make any sense, but it felt too good to think about for a long, delicious minute. The kiss happened, there was no stopping it.

He did manage to summon enough self-control not to let it go any further, and damned himself for ten kinds of an undisciplined fool once he managed to pull away from kissing Hope Harrison. He discovered that his hands had slipped around her waist and pulled her close. He could feel her heat, and his own hardness pressed between them. He swore and let her go, turning his back on her while he got himself under control.

He couldn't seem to think around the woman. He was just reacting, and to his worst impulses. He's been warned about letting this happen. That could get them both killed.

Most importantly, it could get her killed. He had to get his duty over with, and keep their time together impersonal. Only, he was too aware of the taste and feel of her. He wanted to apologize for what he'd just done, but an apology would be personal. He knew he should grab her and get her out of the alley. He also didn't trust himself to touch her right now.

"Let's go."

Hope was too stunned to understand at first. All she heard was his angry tone. It only added to her hurt confusion. Emotions were coming too fast for her to process them. She was still angry and fearful at the men who'd backed her into the alley, still elated at knowing Tiger was alive and well, overjoyed at his rescuing her, afraid of him, overwhelmed by his fiery kiss, and fearful of her own powerful response to his demanding, erotic touch. She had no business needing or wanting or responding but couldn't seem to help doing any of those things. She was so overwhelmed by everything boiling through her that all she could do was stare numbly for a moment when he spoke.

He saw that she was too terrified to respond to his order, and cursed himself. The ordeal had clearly gotten to her. The poor woman had probably let him kiss and fondle her simply in an effort to keep him from killing her. You couldn't blame a person for doing anything they had to to stay alive. He couldn't afford to let any compassion for her show.

He had to get her attention, so he took her by the shoulders and shook her a little. "Focus," he demanded. "Right now. You got us into this, now you're going to have to help get us out." Once her expression cleared, and she was actually looking at him, he stepped away. When he did, his arms actually ached from denying his own need to hold and comfort her.

Tiger's touch calmed her, but his words stung, lashing across both fresh wounds and old scars of guilt and blame.

"My fault?" she lashed out shrilly at him. "How is it my fault?"

"You're the one who ran away," he reminded her.

But...but...she was a prisoner! Prisoners were supposed to try to escape. She opened her mouth several times to speak, to defend her actions, before it occurred to her that she didn't have to defend herself to this man. "I saved your life," she pointed out.

"And I just saved yours."

"Then we're even." She couldn't keep her curiosity at bay. "What happened? I ran after I shouted, so I didn't see— I heard shots. Did you—?" She wanted to know, but didn't like the thought that perhaps her warning had gotten the other man killed.

"I shot faster," was Tiger's answer.

She thought she was willing to leave it at that, but heard herself ask, "Was it Santiago?" She'd only gotten the briefest glance at the gunman.

"No."

"Too bad." The cold words just came out. Her hatred of the man surprised her. She knew suddenly that she'd be pleased to hear that the man responsible for yesterday's murders was dead. She felt very much a stranger to herself. Yesterday's Hope Harrison would never crave revenge. She would never want to make love to a wild, dangerous man who called himself Tiger, either. Somehow she was going to have to find her way back to yesterday's Hope. She knew the longer she was with this man the farther she got from the woman she was supposed to be.

"One of his men," Tiger answered her, and gestured toward the mouth of the alley. "Let's go."

Hope shook her head. "I'm not going anywhere with you."

"I'm the one with the gun. That isn't a threat," he added as her breath caught in a gasp. "You need a gun to be in this part of town at night." He gave a mirthless chuckle. "You need a gun to be in any part of this town at night. Do you have a gun?"

Hope realized for the first time that it was night. Somehow she'd just equated the darkness and shadows with the things that had happened. How long had it been since she'd escaped from Tiger? Why had he bothered to come looking for her? She was grateful that he had. She kept being grateful to him, and that made her even more angry at herself than she was at him.

She fought off that gratitude with a snarl, "Maybe you know where I could buy a gun, Mr. Rafferty? Providing them is your profession, as I recall."

"And with what are you planning on making a purchase?" He looked her up and down in a way that made her blush. "I don't accept credit cards, Ms. Harrison."

The way he studied her sent waves of heat through her, made her breasts feel heavy, the tips harden in response. "Stop that!" She wasn't sure if it was him or herself that she snarled angrily at.

"Come on, Hope. Let's get out of here. Stay close," he warned as they headed back into the maze of streets clinging to the mountain. "We move softly and don't make a sound. Understood?" He was satisfied with the nod he received in answer.

He made sure they traveled cautiously once they left the alley. He only briefly considered taking her back to the *Rani,* though it was docked nearby. No, the sooner he got her to the priest, the safer it would be for both their souls, despite the dangers of Isla Sebastian at night.

One of the reasons he was called Tiger, after all, was because he wasn't afraid of walking through the darkest jungles alone. *You're not alone now,* he reminded himself. *Be careful!*

He should have just taken her to the church of St. Cecilia, but it was a long way. A day of chasing around the steep streets mixed with the adrenaline rushes of danger and arousal left Tiger with a mixture of appetites. The hunger for food was the one he chose to satisfy. He supposed Father Felipe would offer them a meal, but it wasn't like Tiger to impose any more than necessary.

He ended up taking her back to Remy's. It was like starting back at square one, but it was a place where he felt relatively safe. The tables were crowded with people eating and drinking by candlelight. There weren't all that many candles, making the place shadowy and mysterious; it was always dangerous and exotic. Cigarette smoke hung in the sultry air, mixing with the scents of candle wax, sweat and hot spices. Tiger's mouth watered as the aroma from Remy's soup cauldron drifted in from out back on the evening breeze. His other senses were alert to any danger as he looked carefully around the shadow-filled room. The few men who looked back dropped their gazes quickly, not ready for the trouble Tiger's glance promised. Tiger still waited just inside the doorway for a few moments before taking Hope to a table. Santiago's man had run off with a bullet in his shoulder, but other danger could be lurking here.

Then again, danger lurked everywhere on the island. His inspection was enough to satisfy his cautious impulses. Now it was time to eat. Crowded though the place was, he spotted a small empty table in a corner near the stairs and took Hope over to it.

Several women looked his way as they walked by, a couple smiled invitations, but the sight of Hope by his side kept the working girls from approaching. Men looked at Hope, eyes glittering with kindling hunger, but his hand on her waist and the hard expression on his face convinced them instantly that it would be more than their lives were worth to approach his woman.

Hope didn't seem to notice any of this macho posturing. Her naive innocence was an encumbrance in this rough world, but it would still be a shame for her to lose that innocence. Though he was having trouble protecting her from himself he was determined to keep her safe from everyone else. Soon he'd have her out of here, away from the danger he posed.

Hope was very uncomfortable with sharing a candlelit table for two with Tiger Rafferty. It was like she was living some insane parody of an intimate relationship. She'd seen the women look at him and felt the oddest mixture of something like jealousy, and an imitation of pride that he was with her. When his hand came around her waist she'd almost given a smug toss of her head. The possessiveness of his touch, and in the look he gave some of the men they passed sent thrills of confused fear and excitement through her. It all left her utterly confused as they took seats facing each other across a space no wider than a chessboard.

Their legs brushed against each other under the table. The memory of his kiss was still fresh on her lips. The gold light thrown up by the candle highlighted his wide cheekbones and the strong lines of his throat, outlined the width of his shoulders and heightened the glow of his tanned skin. The man was not hard to look at, and she wished very much that he was. He didn't look a thing like Mark. She knew that shouldn't add to his appeal, but it did. Mark was tall, but not as tall as Tiger. Well-built, but not in the same rangy, wiry way. Mark was handsome, but there was no hint of danger in the regular lines of his face; no mystery. No—character. Mark was smooth, Tiger was rough. None of this should matter, but it did.

"Hungry?" Tiger asked her.

Very. She refused to put a name to her hunger, not that she had to. She made herself answer his question lightly. "You're going to make me eat more of Remy's soup because I ran away, aren't you?"

He smiled. "Seems like a fit punishment."

The sight of his dimples did not help her ambivalence, nor did his sense of humor. Why couldn't he just be evil and cruel and not have kissed her? Sexual attraction aside, it was very hard to either hate or like someone whose motives weren't clear. He kept saving her from bad situations, yet all indications were that he was a very bad man himself.

"What is with you, Tiger Rafferty?" she demanded as he got a server's attention.

Tiger stiffened at the question, and took his time about ordering their meal. Fortunately the girl waiting tables was happy to flirt a little before going back about her business. What he had to fight off more than anything else was the temptation to tell Hope the truth. Maybe he would soon, when they reached Father Felipe, but telling her he worked for Naval Intelligence in a room full of real bad men was no way to keep either of them alive.

No, no, and damn it, no! He told himself sternly. "Need to Know," remember? Don't go soft because she's a woman. Your assignment is classified. That means you have no right to tell her just because she's vulnerable and wants reassurance. Or because you're attracted to her, and her knowing would make you look better in her eyes. The point wasn't for him to impress a woman he wanted, the point was for him to track down the name of a man who was responsible for stealing high-tech, classified weapons from a Naval facility. People had died already. His best friend had died. His job was to make sure no one else did. He owed it to Pat's memory to get the job done.

Then maybe he could go home and live like a human being again. Maybe then he could tell a woman the truth when she asked him a question. Maybe then the questions would be simpler, like, How are you? How are you feeling? You didn't have to kill anyone at work today, did you, honey? The thought was a cynical one, but he shuddered inwardly at it.

He wasn't going to answer her question, was he? Hope tried to shrug it off, and tell herself it didn't matter. It was only her future she'd inquired about, after all. Actually, she hadn't. If he didn't want to explain about himself, that was his right, even if she did find his reaction oddly disappointing. Maybe she should concentrate on the subject of her future.

"Okay," she said once the waitress was gone. "What's with me? Me and you," she added as he coolly looked at her, stumbling in her attempt to make her question more articulate.

"Me and you?"

The room grew silent around them, utterly still. Something changed in the atmosphere, heated it with pulsing electricity. The noise went on unabated, the hot evening breeze continued to blow in from the open doors, body heat and candle heat and the sultry heat of the tropical night was all the same. But the stillness was there for them, and the electricity.

"I mean—" She shook her head. "I don't know what I mean."

Tiger's head tilted to one side, a thin smile touched his lips. She ran her fingers nervously across the unpainted wooden surface of the table while he looked at her in a way that was devastating, hard to articulate though her bones and blood and nerve endings understood it implicitly.

"Yes, you do." He reached across the tiny width of the table and took one of her hands in his. He turned the open palm up, toward the candlelight. She shivered when he ran his finger across the center of her palm. "You have a long life line, Hope Harrison." He placed his own open hand beside hers. It was much larger than hers, long-fingered. "I don't."

She found herself gazing at the lines crisscrossing his skin. Which one was the life line? What did it matter? What mattered in this moment was the way she felt when he looked at her, when he touched her.

He covered her hand with his, palm to palm, and she was reminded of a line in Shakespeare about saints having hands that pilgrims' hands do touch—which had to do with Romeo seducing Juliet with the touch of their hands—and they'd both ended up dead, which was something one should remember when passion threatened to take the place of sense.

Hope took a deep breath and let it out slowly. She forced herself to be aware of the rest of the room, to hear the loud voices and laughter. She searched for balance, but her senses reeled instead. Someone nearby was playing a guitar and singing. The song had a sort of blues-doused-in-jerk-spices sound. The language wasn't English, but the lyrics were obviously about love. The music was hot and sexy and didn't help. It made her want to dance, and more than dance, with the man whose hand touched hers. There was something exotic and tempting about the glow of many candles; the shadows softened the darkness and urged her to disappear into its sensual depths.

Who was this man and what was happening to her? She

was losing herself just looking at him, from the simple touch of his hand on hers. When had they stopped talking and started—whatever this was? Seduction? No, that wasn't what was happening, not quite. She *knew* his reaction to her was no more deliberate than hers was to him.

Or was it?

Suspicion hit her hard, and she was glad of the jolt that helped bring her back to reality. "Are you trying to distract me?" she asked, jerking her hand from his.

His eyes narrowed dangerously. "Why would I want to do that?"

"How would I know?" she snapped back. "When you won't tell me the reason you do anything. I don't even know why you let me live."

She immediately wished she hadn't spoken those words. She wished they hadn't been followed with the painful thought that maybe she didn't want to live. And the thought that maybe this attraction she was letting herself experience for Tiger Rafferty was her way of distracting herself from facing far too many unpleasant truths.

Tiger leaned closer, candle flame reflected in his eyes. Or, maybe they were just burning with anger. His voice was soft, but the intensity was laser sharp. "If I wanted you dead, you'd be dead."

"But—"

He put his fingers over her lips. She hadn't realized that she'd leaned forward to listen to his quiet voice. "Santiago attacked your family before I even arrived," he reminded her. "Then when I showed up Santiago started the shooting and my men defended themselves. Remember?"

Calm down, Tiger told himself. Cool it. Don't react like an insulted boy because your feelings are hurt. She's been through a traumatic experience—one damn thing after another. She might not remember any of it too clearly no matter how lucid she seems. If he thought that he ought to come off as a rescuing hero to her, he was mistaken, and insane to boot.

She had no reason to trust him, admire him, or save his ass, even though she'd done just that. "Why'd you do that?" he asked as the server showed up with plates of blackened, barbecued chicken and beans in a spicy red sauce. He sat back in his chair, waited until the woman moved off, then asked again, "Why?"

Hope scooped beans onto her fork and tasted them. They were just as explosively hot on her tastebuds as they looked. Her eyes watered, but she chewed, swallowed and took another bite. You got used to the flavor. In fact, it was quite good, in a self-inflicted-wound sort of way.

"Why?" he asked again.

The one small word held a world of curiosity, and other, less easy to discern, emotions. Hope couldn't help but look up, and into eyes that held resentment and anger.

Though her initial response was to accept that she was to blame for whatever angered him, she refused to flinch away from any accusations from this man. "What?"

She didn't realize she was holding her fork like a weapon until he tugged it out of her hand. "Why did you warn me?"

"What? You're angry I saved your butt?"

He was angry at himself—at his wanting to discuss so much when silence would be safer. "I'm angry you ran off, but I'm willing to overlook that bit of idiocy."

"Oh, thank you *so* much, Your King of the Pirate Ship."

Her sarcasm grazed, but didn't wound him. He really shouldn't call her an idiot for taking what seemed like a logical action from her point of view. "You're a feisty one, aren't you?" he asked, in a very bad Long John Silver imitation.

That got a smile out of her, and a proud lift of her chin. "I like to think so."

"Good." She looked surprised at his praise. "But why did you save my life?"

She shrugged. "I don't know. It was the ethical thing to do?"

Tiger knew bad guys shouldn't say thank you, shouldn't show any softness or caring. He took a swig of the warm beer. He glanced around the crowded room, peering carefully into shadows. "Thank you," he said, though he didn't look at her when he spoke, or let himself glance back for her reaction. Her reaction shouldn't be important, to words that shouldn't have been said in the first place.

His words. They confused her, pleased her. She didn't mind Tiger Rafferty confusing her so much, but the prick of happiness that sent unwanted sparks through her made her angry. With herself. With him for daring to occasionally show any positive qualities other than hard-ass toughness and the ability to use a gun. Yesterday she didn't think all that macho stuff positive qualities in a man, but yesterday she hadn't been on Isla Sebastian.

She wondered now if she was ever going to get off Isla Sebastian, or away from him. That a part of her questioned why she would want to get away from Tiger Rafferty was truly frightening. While he searched the room with narrow-eyed intensity, she watched him with equal absorption, and knew part of the answer.

This is not a healthy attachment, she told herself. *And you better stop it right now.* She wasn't the best judge of men, she had to admit. Hadn't she thought Mark was an ethical and trustworthy man? Hadn't he blown all her assumptions about him out of the water with the admission that he'd been seeing another woman almost as long as he and Hope had known each other? Hadn't he made her feel like a fool? A dull, unimaginative, easily manipulated fool at that. She'd wanted to die after that little talk with Mark.

Of course, if she hung out with Tiger Rafferty for any length of time she could get that wish. Then again, an insidious voice inside her added, with Tiger you know exactly what you're getting. He doesn't pretend to be honest and trustworthy. At least he hadn't harmed her—yet. And he was so incredibly gorgeous.

And this is relevant how?

Hope took her gaze off Tiger's lean form, his chiseled, sun-bronzed face and the tantalizing thickness of his long brown hair. She tried to forget the intriguing timbre of his voice, the expressiveness of his smile, to blank out the memory of his touch.

She concentrated on her food, telling herself she had no idea when, or even if, she'd get another meal. Then it occurred to her that Aunt April, Uncle Bradley and the crew of the yacht would never see another meal, or another day. They were gone, dead, their bodies lost at sea. Grief stole her appetite, her own sense of responsibility drove out every other thought and sensation. The hot room aglow with candlelight disappeared around her. Tiger disappeared, though he was barely a foot away. Hope's heart burned, everything was dark, and she was utterly alone.

"It's all my fault."

Tiger heard the strangled, whispered words. Hope's pain stabbed sharply into him. He didn't know what Hope was talking about, but the intensity of her feelings shook him to the core. His gut response was to turn to her, take her in his arms and offer comfort. He couldn't do that, and it had nothing to do with his mission, or protecting his cover. It had to do with the two men who'd just came in the door.

Ibarra's men.

He knew one of them by name, Estaban Quarrels,

Ibarra's new second in command. The other was one of Ibarra's bodyguards, a loyal thug, if not too bright. Quarrels was an unknown factor, the bodyguard was a definite worry. Quarrels advanced with caution, moving just past the doorway before halting and scanning the room. The bodyguard remained just behind him, his bulk blocking the exit. Tiger waited, tense and still, ready to draw a weapon if he had to. He hoped the crowd and the dimness would keep Ibarra's men from noticing them.

He looked cautiously around. He didn't like having to take his attention from Quarrels and the goon, but looking for escape routes was imperative. It was too far to the back door. The front was blocked, but they were near the stairs. Going up might not get them out, but there might be a back staircase. If they could get upstairs before Quarrels spotted them it wouldn't matter if there was an exit up there, they could lay low until Ibarra's men had their dinner and left.

A man going upstairs with a woman was normal behavior in Remy's. If he was careful to keep his face turned away, Tiger could trust the men wouldn't look their way when they moved. He hated dragging Hope through more trouble, hated risking having her seen with him, but it was already too late for that. She would be perceived as belonging to him by every man on the island.

He risked a look at her, and saw the shining tracks of tears on her cheeks in the candlelight. Could he risk getting her up and moving? Trust her in a tight situation?

He leaned close enough to whisper in her ear. "We have to go." His words brought no reaction. He swore under his breath as he slid stealthily to his feet. After leaving money on the table, he pulled Hope out of her chair. He was careful to hunch over and keep his back to the room, even though it made him feel more vulnerable. He hated not being able to see Ibarra's men, but the point was to keep them from noticing him.

With that in mind, he put his arm around Hope's shoulders, hunched further to disguise his distinctive height and walked her toward the nearby stairs. They were hidden by the darkness and thick cigarette smoke, and a large group at one of the tables got up to leave. This wall of people further helped to block his and Hope's retreat.

It was only a few steps, with her warm and soft body against him. It felt almost real, like two lovers going off to be alone. Tiger let out a long, strained breath, and took Hope up the stairs. He managed to find them an empty bedroom; a check didn't find a back staircase on the second floor. Tiger returned quickly after to the room where he'd left Hope. Moonlight filtered through the gauzy curtains pulled across a wide French door. He closed the hall door and locked it after lighting some candles he found on a rickety dresser. The dressing mirror doubled the flickering candlelight, the gold flames adding a warm touch to the silvery glow from the moon.

''Wonder what Remy charges for staying the night?'' he murmured.

Hope remained seated on the edge of the bed and made no response. He brought one of the candles over to the bedside table. He almost wished he'd left the room in complete darkness, as what he saw was not promising. Hope's eyes shone with tears, and her face was wet with them. She didn't look afraid. She looked defeated and in pain, and very, very exhausted. She didn't even seem aware of him. She'd fainted on him once today; he hoped she didn't pass out now. He wouldn't blame her, she had to be exhausted, but having her unconscious wouldn't help if they needed to escape.

Did they need to? How? Jump out the French window,

if necessary, he supposed. They'd probably survive the fall with only a few broken bones. Maybe. Better to take the risk than to end up fatally shot. He knew Quarrels's dangerous reputation. Tiger glanced at the door, then he took a seat beside Hope on the bed. He took her hand in his without even noticing. His mind was on Quarrels, but his impulses responded to her anguish.

Quarrels was dangerous, deadly. He was also a businessman. Cool, calm, unemotional. He had no grudge against Tiger Rafferty, no vendetta. Ibarra was the boss, but Quarrels had recently replaced Ibarra's younger brother as second in command. Tiger had heard that he was trying to keep some sort of rein on Ibarra's violent temper and impulses. Tiger wished Quarrels luck, as much luck as he was willing to wish any drug-dealing maggot. He still wasn't sure Quarrels hadn't seen them, or what he would do if he had.

Tiger cursed himself. His informants had sworn that Ibarra was off the island! Maybe he was, and Quarrels was at home minding the store. Maybe Tiger could still get Hope to safety, make the meeting with Cardenas, and then get the hell away from Isla Sebastian and the undercover operation for good. He didn't need complications.

Hope whimpered. He turned at the pitiful sound, and she put her arms around him. Her head came to rest on his shoulder.

"Speaking of complications." He breathed a sigh into her hair, and held her because she needed it.

She cried, and he let her. He should have been wary and on watch, but lying down with Hope cradled protectively in his arms was more important. Eventually the candles burned out. Tiger didn't know when he slept, because in his dreams he still held her.

Chapter 5

Hope felt better when she woke up. Physically she felt like something the cat had dragged in. Emotionally she felt bruised and tattered, but still better. She tasted salt on her lips, and that was the first thing she noticed as she came up out of a dark, dreamless sleep. The ache in her muscles, especially in her calves, was next. She'd been crying, and she was sweaty. She could really use a shower. And to brush her teeth. She'd said something to somebody yesterday about a toothbrush, hadn't she?

Yesterday. What had happened yesterday? And the day before?

The questions drifted through her mind, but she wasn't quite ready to face answering them yet. All she knew was that she felt better. She still hurt, would always hurt, but it was better. Facing what "it" was could wait for a few more minutes while she luxuriated in being curled up on a soft bed, her arms and legs entangled with a long, hard body. Despite the sultry heat surrounding her, the warmth of his body felt delicious. Made her feel safe. It sent a faint buzz of desire through her, a feeling that was more pleasant anticipation than demanding need.

She didn't let any questions about how and why she shared a bed with a man enter her thoughts yet. She sighed, and took primal comfort from resting her head on the man's shoulder, on having his hair soft against her cheek. Her hand rested on his chest, where she could feel it rise and fall as he breathed. His arm was thrown over her waist, but she felt more protected than pinned down. He was dressed, so was she, and she knew nothing had happened between them last night. Somehow that was both reassuring and disappointing.

Disappointing?

Hope came fully awake on the thought, just as a clap of thunder sounded loud enough to rattle the bedroom walls. It wasn't the harsh noise that caused her body to jerk, her eyes to fly open, or the loud gasp that caught in her throat. Her reaction came when everything flooded back in that instant.

She remembered everything as she turned wide eyes on Tiger Rafferty. The sight of him beside her amazed her. But it didn't frighten her. She knew it should, and maybe it would later. Right now the sight of him was the most beautiful thing she'd ever seen. The most comforting for her aching sorrow. He'd held her while she sobbed, she remembered that now. He'd *been* there.

She wanted to wake him up and demand why, but a voice cautiously warned her not to ask questions, just to accept that he'd done her a kindness, but not to let herself fall into the trap of trusting a man again. Mark had made kind gestures, too, and look at what he'd done to her. But she couldn't stop the wonder—the affection—that sparked through her at the sight of sleep-tousled, in-need-of-a-shave Tiger Rafferty.

While she studied him, he opened his eyes and did the same to her. A spark of interest flashed in his eyes for a moment. It arced between them. Then his expression flattened, and cooled. He slowly took his hand away from her hip.

Hope didn't move; her hand still rested over his heart. When he frowned she heard herself ask, "Do I look that bad?"

She was amazed at her light tone. She'd been able to make jokes with this man almost from the first. She wasn't witty, or quick with words normally, but quipping with Tiger—or maybe it was verbal sniping—was a natural way to express herself. Or maybe to defend herself. After all, he was not exactly looking friendly at the moment.

"You look fine."

She looked more than fine, and the words came out gruff in an effort to hide what he really felt about the sight of her from both of them. The bed was comfortable, it felt good waking up next to her, but he couldn't give in to the dangerous seductiveness of spending a rainy day in bed with a beautiful woman.

They needed to get out of here. Before he succumbed to the urge to take advantage of where they were. It would be so easy, especially because she was looking at him as if he were some kind of hero. He doubted she realized how vulnerable she looked.

"How do you feel?" Her emotional welfare was not his concern, but he wanted to know. Words helped keep him from taking any action, such as kissing her, that might show he cared.

Hope nodded.

"Good." He rolled out of the bed and stretched when

he got to his feet. He walked to the French door and took a cautious look outside. "We have to go," he told her when he was reasonably satisfied that no one waited to ambush them out in the market plaza. The plaza was less crowded than he'd like for the sake of cover, the heavy rain keeping the stall owners and shoppers away. Maybe the storm would keep bad guys as well as normal people inside today. He hated going out into the vile weather himself.

"Maybe I should steal a car," he muttered as sheets of rain sluiced down the glass.

Oh, wouldn't that be just great? Delivering a kidnapped woman he'd spent the night in a brothel with to a priest in a hot car. What would his mother have to say about that, if she were still alive? He could imagine his sister's opinion. He saw Hope reflected in the glass as she sat up in bed. He wanted her to forget they'd ever met. He didn't want to regret that they hadn't met under normal circumstances. They hadn't, and her memories of him weren't going to be good ones.

"I have to get back to the *Rani*," he said, without turning around. He still watched her as she climbed out of bed, and combed her fingers through her short hair. He liked her hair, and the way it showed off the graceful length of her neck.

"Which means what?" A flash of lightning lit the room. She jumped a little as thunder quickly followed.

"Which means we have to leave. Now," he added emphatically as he turned to face her.

She put her hands on her hips. "Could I get a shower first?"

He laughed. "You'll get one as soon as we step outside."

"Yes, but will there be any soap involved? You could use a shave," she added. "And a change of clothes."

"I'll have both. When I get back to the boat."

She arched a sarcastic eyebrow at him. "And this will do me good how?"

"You'll be rid of me," he answered. "I'm taking you to my friend," he continued as fear as intense as the lightning outside flashed across her face. "He's a priest," he explained, damning himself for not explaining sooner—but when had he had the time? Yesterday, he angrily reminded himself. In a bedroom just up the hall. You idiot! And you wondered why she ran away from you? Any woman in her right mind would run away from Tiger Rafferty. "Need to Know" was one thing, so was caution about trusting a woman, but maybe he'd taken it a little too far.

Hope backed a step, wary of the angry look on Tiger's face. She ran into the mattress, and sat down hard. "A priest?" she asked, looking suspiciously up at Tiger. "You're taking me to a priest? You're kidding, right?"

"No. Why would I be?"

"Because—" She gestured helplessly. "Because—"

"Because I'm a gunrunning bastard who gets shot at a lot?"

She nodded slowly. "That about sums it up."

"I have hidden depths. And friends in high places." He shrugged self-deprecatingly. "At least Father Felipe's willing to hear my confession now and then. He'll see that you get home safely."

A priest? The man had been running her all over the island—all right, she'd done some of that running on her own…and whose fault was that?—looking for a priest? No, not looking. He obviously knew where this Father Felipe was, but hadn't felt any need to mention the man's existence or whereabouts to her.

"You mean all this time I thought I was in danger—"

"You were. You are."

Hope rose angrily to her feet. She pointed an accusing finger at Tiger Rafferty. "Not me. You. You're the one Santiago was shooting at."

His eyes glittered dangerously. "You sure about that?"

She sat back down. "No."

"You could be as much a target as I am." He carefully refrained from telling her about seeing Ibarra's men last night.

"Why?"

"You saw him didn't you? And he might have seen you." She nodded. "You're as much a witness to his trying to double-cross his boss as I am. Cardenas won't take kindly to knowing about that."

"You think Santiago actually went back to Cardenas and acted like nothing happened?"

He nodded. "He didn't have much choice. If for no other reason than this is the only port he could reach in his boat."

Hope shuddered as she remembered that Santiago had boarded the yacht to highjack it. "He had big plans," she said bitterly. "And needed a bigger, faster vessel."

Tiger nodded. "That's what he said."

Hope stood. "He tried to kill you."

"One of his men tried to."

He took her by the arm. "We're leaving now."

She tried to shake him off. "I'm not going anywhere with you."

"I'm taking you to Father Felipe."

"I'm not going. Not with you." He looked back at her, cold-eyed and determined. Hope stood her ground. "Why don't you give me your friend's address and I'll find it on my own. Go sell guns to people. Have a nice day at the black market, dear," she mocked. "I'll be fine."

Tiger didn't blame Hope for not wanting to be with him, but he couldn't do as she suggested. Santiago might have men looking for her. It was his responsibility to keep her safe, even if she loathed every moment spent in his company.

He didn't let her argue anymore, but kept a firm grip on her arm and made her come with him. Remy's wife waited at the bottom of the stairs, and they paused only long enough for Tiger to pass a large amount of folded bills into her waiting hand. The woman smiled, and waved them on their way. Tiger could sense Hope weighing whether to ask the woman for aid, but a warning look from him kept her quiet.

They went out into the driving rain, and were soaked to the skin within moments. Moving as quickly as possible in the wind and the rain, Tiger led the way through the maze of streets to the church of St. Cecilia. It was in a poor neighborhood; not surprising, since most neighborhoods in the town were poor. The church was in an area that was not as rough as much of the town. Felipe's parishioners were hardworking people who had little, but did the best they could. In fact, they were far more respectable in many ways than the people who lived on the other side of the island or came to stay at the exclusive resorts that covered acres of tropical land and long stretches of beach. Those secluded properties were patrolled by small private armies, while the people in the neighborhood of St. Cecilia's had to look out for each other.

He glanced at Hope as lightning crackled overhead. Her short hair was plastered to her head, the soaking T-shirt and shorts clung to every curve. She looked more bedraggled than sexy, but he found that charming, and somehow enticing. He flicked a heavy drop of rainwater off the end of her nose. "You look like a half-drowned puppy."

She squinted at him, and shouted over the storm. "What?"

"Nothing." He was being sentimental. No way he could afford that.

It was a good thing there wasn't far to go. St. Cecilia's was only around the next corner. In a few minutes he and Hope Harrison would part company forever. The realization left him with a hollow feeling inside and an ache around his heart. It was odd, stupid and dangerous that a woman he'd known for such a short time, under such harrowing circumstances, should affect him this way. He felt as though he were losing her, and it hurt. She would never know the truth, always remember him as an outlaw, someone who deserved nothing more than her contempt.

Without thinking, Tiger pulled Hope into the shelter of a deep doorway. With his hands on her shoulders he pressed her against the peeling paint of the door, using his body to shield her from the downpour that blew in after them. It was dark in here, he could barely make out her face. That made this easier.

"My name is Michael," he said, bending to put his lips close to her ear. He wanted to make sure she heard him despite the thunder and the wind, and he could barely make himself whisper the truth. He'd been warned to trust no one, especially not a woman. His commander held the firm belief that women talked too much. "I'm a lieutenant, with Naval Intelligence."

He knew he shouldn't even be whispering it, but what could be the harm now? It was important to him that she remember him as he was, or, at least, as he wished he was, instead of the gunrunning criminal called Tiger.

He lifted his head, and their gazes met as a flare of lightning brought an instant's worth of white light into the dim recess of the doorway. Her eyes were wide, her lips parted in astonishment. Raindrops sparkled on her long lashes. She jumped as a clap of thunder boomed after the lightning.

Her hands clutched at his waist, bunched in the material of his shirt, pulled him closer.

He felt the warmth of her skin beneath the cool, slick wetness of her clothing. Her head tilted curiously to one side as the rumble of thunder died.

"Michael?" she asked, a throaty whisper. Curious. Suspicious. And, yet, there was something seductive simply in the way she spoke his name.

He nodded. "Michael. I'd be in trouble if I broke cover anymore." He moved farther into the small shelter as a gust of wind sent a chill across his back. Her warmth drew him. Her nearness was intoxicating.

Lightning showed him her face again, and her beautiful, inviting mouth. He couldn't speak. He couldn't do anything but draw her into his embrace. His self-control was lost somewhere in the storm. Sanity wavered, his need as wild and battering as any hurricane against what was left of his rationality.

Hope didn't know what to think, and after a few moments, when Tiger's mouth hungrily covered hers, she didn't want to think. She was soaking wet, scared to death, alone in the world, and now thoroughly confused, but when Tiger kissed her none of the rest mattered. She was just as hungry. Her tongue danced and played over his. The heat of his mouth drove out everything but need. As if she'd been hit by the lightning, fire sizzled through her. Her hands roamed over his back, down to cup his buttocks. She whimpered, and ground against him, and felt his thumb circle the already hard tip of one breast.

When his head came up and his hand moved away, she was panting, bereaved, aching with hunger, and equal parts ashamed and furious. Her body and emotions were at war with each other. And her brain—the part of her that was supposed to be in control of everything else—her brain was almost useless. She didn't know what to think, and, for a moment, didn't even quite remember how. Back at Remy's place this morning she'd had a few lucid moments. That had all been washed away—by the storm, by his words, by his touch. She struggled desperately to fight through the confusion, the shame, the anger, the aching, shivering, physical reaction, and bring her thinking processes back on line.

The first thing she did was slap the lieutenant who called himself Michael across his face. She'd never struck anyone in her life before now, and found that the impact stung her palm. It rattled the muscles in her arm and shoulder, and sent a pang of guilt all the way to her heart. It didn't make her feel any better, either. It did seem like the appropriate way to respond in this situation.

And the situation was?

Hope wasn't sure, but she was seethingly, boilingly, ter-rifyingly angry. "You lied to me!" she shouted at the man who stood before her, tall and powerful, with the mark of her hand outlined starkly on his cheek by the frequent flashes of lightning. He had kissed her, more than once, made her feel wild things she'd never dreamed she could feel, made her still long for him to kiss her again and had been lying to her all the time!

"I didn't tell you everything. That's not the same thing."

"Yeah, right. I've heard that before." Mark had very carefully not told her everything, and look how he had be-trayed her. "For my own good, I suppose?"

"Yes."

"I've heard that before. Lieutenant." She spat the word out, and very nearly spat on him. She had never felt like this before—this raw and primal and fierce. She hated feel-ing this out of control. Hated that he could bring this *beast* out in her. One that wanted to rip and claw—and mate. "I don't believe you. Why should I believe you?"

"You're not dead."

At another time she would have found his cold, hard words sobering. Now she shook her head wildly. "What's Naval Intelligence have to do with—" She waved a hand, taking in the storm-racked island, the situation with Cardenas, Santiago, Ibarra, weapons deals, smugglers, pirates—everything. Though all she could manage to say was, "This."

"I can't tell you."

"Won't."

"Can't."

"Why bother telling me anything? Why should I believe anything you say?"

He touched his cheek. He was breathing hard, his eyes sparking with emotion. At least for a moment. She watched with a pang of terror as the gaze he turned on her went hard and flat. "Let's go."

"Am I just this *thing* you pull along until you can get rid of it?" she demanded as the driving rain hit her in the face once more.

He glanced back at her for a moment, then marched them resolutely along. "You're my responsibility."

"I'm responsible for myself."

"Not here, you're not. Not now."

She touched her tender lips. Lashed out from her battered psyche. "Is making out with me part of your assignment, Lieutenant?"

He whirled on her. The next thing she knew he'd backed her up against the wall of the nearest building. His hands were tight on her shoulders. His eyes blazed with anger. "Quiet. Not another word."

He held her there, her back pressed against the hard, wet

bricks, his large, angry presence filling her senses, until he'd stared her down. Hope ended up gulping back tears as her courage and outrage faded. Fear of him seeped inexorably into her once more, soaking her spirit the way the rain soaked her clothes and skin. Maybe…maybe…the man was one of the good guys, but that didn't make him less dangerous, any less threatening.

Her words tore at his soul, but what he had to do to force her silence was worse. That was something he did to himself, and to her. If he'd wanted her to fear him he wouldn't have broken the silence that protected his cover. Tiger knew he'd handled it all wrong. He'd been wrong to trust her even a little, but he'd wanted her to forgive him for the past two days, to think well of him after they parted at the priest's house. He hadn't reckoned on her shouting out his true identity in the streets of Isla Sebastian. The problem was, he hadn't thought about what he did, only responded to his need for this woman. Letting himself feel anything for her only increased the danger to both of them. Fool! Idiot!

"It's not far," he said once he was sure she'd be cooperative for a while. "I don't want to hear a word from you until we get there."

As they rounded the last corner the wind whipped Tiger's hair across his face. When he pushed back the soaking strands he saw the church of St. Cecilia across the width of the deserted plaza. Rain streamed down the church steps to pool on the broken brickwork paving the square. One of the church doors was missing, the other twisted precariously on its hinges. The top of the steeple was gone. Glass had been blown from many of the windows. The shell of the church looked like it had survived an explosion—or a severe tropical storm. Many of the other buildings around the plaza looked equally damaged, though details were hard to make out in the driving rain. Tiger glanced slowly around the plaza, a deep sense of foreboding overlaying his already frayed emotions. The priest's house was around the back of the church. Tiger hoped the bulk of the building had sheltered the small house from the last storm.

The storm was getting worse as he hustled Hope across the plaza. They stepped across fallen rubble to get to the narrow path that led between the church and a neighboring building. They had to walk single file, but at least the tight channel between buildings offered protection from the wind. It didn't shelter them from the rain, but any respite from the wild weather was welcome.

"We'll be there soon," he told her, voice loud as the storm howled above them. "You'll be safe with Father Felipe."

She stiffened, but he didn't let her stop. "Safe from you?" she called back.

"Safe from everything on Isla Sebastian." He added. "You wouldn't survive alone, and I wouldn't trust you with anyone else on this godforsaken hellhole."

She glanced back over her shoulder. He saw the effort it took her to be defiant. "I don't trust you."

"I don't care." He tried to sound nonchalant, though pain twisted through him at his tough-guy words. Truth was, her attitude about trust was the right one. "There's the house," he added. "Hurry up."

"Gladly," Hope snarled, and began to run toward the small building in the distance.

Chapter 6

"Not here? What do you mean he's not here?"

Hope stood in the center of the dark living room and looked helplessly at Tiger as he returned from his search of the small house. There was no power, of course, but at least the roof was intact. That meant a lot to her right now. She was shivering, clutching her arms tightly to her sides to stave off the relentless chill. Water dripped off her, forming a puddle on the worn rug. She moved away from one damp spot, only to start dripping where she now stood. Dry clothes and warm skin were a memory. Oddly enough, the temperature of the air wasn't all that cool, especially here out of the fierce wind. She supposed she'd been out in the storm a bit too long, and was suffering a temporary reaction now.

She stopped hugging herself long enough to run her hands through her hair. Then she shook her head like a dog trying to get the water out of its coat. Some of the flying drops hit Tiger in the face. He didn't protest, but wiped the

water away and continued looking around as though expecting the priest to pop out of the shadows.

Maybe he didn't protest her getting him wet because he
was as bedraggled and soaked as she was. She almost felt
sorry for him, except that he was the one who'd dragged
them out into the foul weather. And she had too much to
resent him for. Maybe she wouldn't let herself feel compassion for him, but she fought off any urge to be frightened of him at the moment.

"Maybe your Father Felipe is at the church," she suggested. "Or at a hospital, or shelter."

Tiger nodded. "Yeah. Half the people in the area might
have lost their homes from the look of things out there.
Felipe probably has a shelter organized."

Tiger had grown more frustrated by the minute as he
searched every nook and cranny of the low, three-room
parish house. He went to the living room window and
stood, looking across the small garden toward the back of
St. Cecilia's. Toward the small parish cemetery with its
tilting headstones and crosses to his left. Up at the sky
where the storm was finally showing some indication of
abating. The fierce weather was unseasonable, disturbing,
and was doing nothing to aid his efforts to get an innocent
young woman out of a dangerous situation.

A situation where his lustful reaction to her was proving
to be the most dangerous factor. It was making him stupid,
careless, crazy. He doubted Hope realized how sheer her
clinging wet shirt was over her breasts. How the cloth
molded to her wet skin, leaving nothing at all to his imagination. He fought hard to keep his eyes and his hands off
of her.

*Why the devil hadn't all that rain had the same effect as
a cold shower?* he raged inwardly. *And where the devil is
the priest?* "I'm going looking for him," he told Hope.

"Stay here," he warned before going out into the rain once more. He shot her a stern glance over his shoulder. "I mean it. Promise you'll stay here."

Hope had no trouble answering him. She put her hands on her hips. "My aunt had a saying," she told him. "About how some people were too stupid to come in out of the rain. I'm not stupid." He snarled in response, but for a fleeting second a hint of dimple showed at the corner of his mouth. Hope tried not to see this sign of humanity, and tried not to react at all to this nanosecond of charm. "If you're going to go, go," she said. "I'm going to look for some towels to dry off with."

She didn't tell him to hurry back, but once the door had closed behind him she wanted to. Except for the few hours after she'd escaped yesterday, Tiger had been by her side through every dangerous moment since he'd boarded the yacht in mid-hijack two days ago. She'd gotten used to having him around, and to being dragged around by him wherever he wanted her to go. She was beginning to feel like she was some kind of accessory item for him. Like a charm that dangled helplessly from his wrist as he went about his business. Which was mostly being chased by other bad guys, she conceded. Being Tiger's companion was not a safe occupation for a gently reared young lady, now was it?

Still, once he was gone, she found something—lacking— in her surroundings. "Dryness," she said, dismissing the vague loneliness that assaulted her almost instantly. "That's what's missing. If I don't get dry soon I'm going to mildew."

Hope set determinedly about searching for towels. It wasn't as if the place was gigantic, with a hundred cupboards and closets to look in. She discovered that there was only the living room, a small kitchen, an even smaller bedroom and a bathroom that somehow managed to crowd in the necessary plumbing in the smallest space possible. She found towels in a linen cupboard, and a dry T-shirt in a dresser in the bedroom. Hope held up the sleeveless white cotton garment, and considered her options. She felt odd about putting on the priest's undershirt, but couldn't think of any other way to get warm. In fact, stripping off all her wet clothes sounded like a good idea. She ignored her qualms, kicked off her shoes, and set about taking off her clothes.

After a few minutes the soaked shorts, shirt and underwear had been replaced by the T-shirt and she'd wrapped a beach towel around her hips as a skirt. She took her wet clothes to the kitchen sink, wrung as much water as she could from them, then draped them over kitchen chairs to dry.

The storm had broken by this time, and light spilled through the windows as the tropical sun came out. Hope opened the kitchen window and positioned the clothes-draped chairs to take advantage of the heat and light. With any luck her clothing would be dry soon. She stood in front of the window for a few moments with her eyes closed, letting the sun warm the last of the chill from her.

The sudden heat soaked into her, and reminded her of Tiger's hands caressing her, warming her from the inside out.

"Oh, dear," she murmured, eyes flying open. She fanned herself with her hand. She looked around, guilty for having such thoughts in a priest's house, while wearing the priest's clothes. "Oh, dear," she said again, and then laughed at the notion that she had somehow tainted poor Father Felipe's garments with her lewd and lascivious musing. "Lascivious," she heard herself say, in a voice so sultry she barely recognized it as her own. "What a tasty word that is."

Hope shook her head. There must be something in this excessively tropical atmosphere that was driving her crazy. She didn't normally talk to herself, or think—lascivious—thoughts. Heat, and the exotic setting, combined with the impossible situation, and Tiger's—everything!

"Tiger Rafferty."

It was as though she conjured him when she spoke his name aloud. The kitchen door opened as the words came out.

"What?" he asked as she whirled around.

Tiger stood framed in the doorway, long and rangy, unshaven, his shoulder-length brown hair still damp from the rain. He looked as disreputable as they came. She knew that there was a gun hidden beneath his jacket, and a knife in a sheath somewhere on his person. He was capable of terrifying her, and exciting her. Right now, the sight of him aroused her very active curiosity.

"What kind of name is Tiger?"

"You asked me that once before."

She nodded. "Just before someone shot at us."

"We have a short history together," he said. "But an interesting one."

"Your name," she insisted. "Stop hedging."

He shrugged, and ducked his head sheepishly. The sweet, self-deprecating gesture was almost enough to convince her that he couldn't possibly *really* be a criminal. Fortunately, a cautious voice was there with the reminder that she'd learned the hard way with Mark that appearances were very deceiving. She could not trust what she *wanted* to believe.

"Michael," he said as he came into the room. "I've never liked to be called Mike. Tiger was a nickname my sister and my best friend Pat gave me when we were kids.

My friend—''He shook his head, his expression closing up. ''When I went undercover Pat started calling me Tiger again. It stuck.''

He had a sister. A friend. From the look on his face, something had happened to that friend, and he wasn't prepared to talk about it. He'd been a kid once. He was a person, not a force of nature that appeared fully formed and without a history in a cloud of gunsmoke. He was a man. Possibly one with a girlfriend. Or a wife.

It was a small room, and this man's presence filled it. Hope found herself backing up until she bumped into the sink. Sunlight flooded through the open kitchen window, draping her bare shoulders in warmth. Tiger snagged a chair away from the table and settled his long, lanky frame on it after first shrugging out of his wet jacket. Hope tried not to look at the shoulder holster or at the gun itself. She tried even harder not to notice the breadth of Tiger's chest, or his long, sinewy arms. She'd always had a thing about sexy arms on men, and Tiger's—Michael's—arms were a prime example. His large, capable hands did not bear studying, either.

Maybe the effort to get to know anything about him was stupid. They'd be out of each other's lives soon. She'd worry about him if she came to believe that he really was an undercover agent of some sort. Despite several aberrant episodes in the last forty-eight hours she was a dull, staid, cautious person. She did not have adventures, and didn't have anything to do with anyone who did.

Besides, people with dangerous professions tended to get themselves killed. She'd already had more than enough death of people she cared about. And, knowing her perverse nature, she'd probably find some way to blame herself for any harm that came to him. The less memories of this awful time she had to take with her, the better.

That was what the reasonable part of her said. When she spoke, it was to ask, "How long have you been doing this undercover thing? Why?" He gave her a warning look. Resentment flared, hotter than the tropical sunlight, as she recalled how he'd let her believe he was a real gunrunner. Which maybe he was, and this Naval Intelligence ploy was some head game he'd decided to play with her. Though Lord knew why he would bother.

She shook her head in an attempt to get some of the confusion out of it. She hunted for a reasonable subject to focus on. "What about Father Felipe? Did you find him?"

Tiger looked disgusted. "Found out where he is. There is a shelter set up for people who've lost their homes to the storms. A woman there told me that Felipe managed to catch a plane to Florida between storms. Looking for funds and supplies for a relief effort." He frowned at her. "So it looks like I'm still stuck with you."

"Thank you very much," Hope snapped back, stung by his tone. "I didn't exactly ask for this, Lieutenant!"

He held up a warning finger. "Remember what I told you?"

Hope refused to flinch at his tone, and the hard look in his eyes. "Plane?" she said, keeping her attention on what was really important—which was getting away from Rafferty, whoever he was. "Did you say Father Felipe took a plane?" He nodded. "This island has an airport?"

"A couple," he answered. "Private. Controlled by Ibarra," he added.

That pretty much scotched her next suggestion. "Oh." She leaned back against the kitchen counter, arms folded. "You were expecting Father Felipe to be able to talk my way onto one of Ibarra's planes, right?" He nodded. "And these planes normally do what? Smuggle drugs into the States?" Another nod. "And Father Felipe knows this?"

"Felipe works with what he's got to to help the people here."

That was no answer, but Hope let it go.

"Besides, Ibarra does have legitimate business interests. So does Cardenas," he added. "He owns the resorts on the other side of the island."

"So? What? You're going to try to dump me on Cardenas next?" A look of outrage crossed his face, but before he could respond Hope stormed on. "I've had about enough of this, Rafferty! Stop treating me like some helpless child you have to protect! I can get home on my own." She pointed toward the door. "Get out of my life and leave me alone. Go play spy." She waved her fingers at him. "Have fun at the undercover op, dear. Don't forget to take your gun. Bye." She knew what she sounded like, and that the word rhymed with *witch,* and was ashamed of herself even as she spoke. But...she wasn't a child, even if she felt childish at the moment.

"I'm not taking you to Cardenas," he heard himself say. "I can't ask a man who may think I'm trying to double-cross him for help. I have to convince him I didn't blow off the arms deal first. I need to be in the man's good graces, but there's no way I can risk being in his debt. That's not how the game's played on Isla Sebastian."

"What about Santiago?" she asked. "Isn't he going to try to kill you again? Don't you need to eliminate Santiago? Or expose him to his boss?"

"I don't know what I'm going to do about Santiago," he admitted. All he'd really thought about in the past two days was getting Hope to safety. It had certainly clouded his judgment, and that could get him killed. He still had to worry about her safety. Which meant he couldn't leave her here even though that was what she wanted. She distracted him, slowed him down, reminded him too much of his real identity. He resented her for reminding him who he really was, and he resented her for distracting him, and he knew none of the resentment coursing through him was really her fault. He knew violating his commander's warning about not getting involved with a woman was his own doing. That didn't stop him from glaring at her, though, did it?

She glared back, and the fire that shot through him had nothing to do with anger. It was a wonder steam didn't rise off his damp clothes at his reaction to her. It wasn't her fault that he wanted her, either, even though she was standing there wearing not very much, looking proud and defiant, and incredibly sexy. The attitude, he realized, was an act of will more than her natural tendency. Vulnerability showed through the hard shell she tried to project, and that seduced him as much as her physical appearance.

He had been planning on saying something to her, on giving her some terse order concerning what their next move was, but his mind went blank. All he could do for a long, tense moment was look at her as his body tightened with desire, and a slow, warm flush rose on her lightly tanned skin.

Hope tried to blame the sunlight on her overheated state as she turned away from the hot look Tiger was giving her. And that she had been returning. It took two to tango—that was the saying, wasn't it? And the tango was a very seductive dance indeed. That the two of them had been tangoing since they first saw each other made no sense, but denying the attraction wasn't going to make it go away.

She tried ignoring it for now. "You hungry?" she asked him, and hoped that didn't sound like an invitation to anyone but her. She cleared her throat, and opened a cupboard. "Would it be wrong for us to take food from a priest? It's not like stealing, is it?"

"Felipe won't mind," Tiger told her. She heard him get up from his chair. "If there's anything to eat."

Hope tensed when Tiger came up behind her, holding her breath for a moment as his arm reached around her. He reached up to the cabinet's highest shelf and brought down a can.

"Tuna," he said. "Yum."

While Hope took up breathing again, he tossed her the can and continued to hunt through the cabinets. He brought down another can of tuna, followed by green beans. She reached into the lower shelves and found spaghetti sauce and instant mashed potatoes.

Once the contents of Father Felipe's larder were laid on the counter next to the sink, Tiger said, "Think you can do anything with this stuff?"

Hope eyed the canned goods skeptically, then turned the same look on Tiger. "You're assuming I can cook?"

He grinned, flashing those killer dimples again. "Of course you can," He said heartily, and patted her encouragingly on the shoulder. "Nothing to it."

She grimaced. "Right. All we need's a can opener. An untainted water supply wouldn't hurt." She tapped a finger thoughtfully against her nose, then pointed at Tiger. "Oh, and a stove might come in handy."

He gestured toward the small stove in the middle of the kitchen. "How about that?"

"The power's off."

Tiger took a look at the stove. "I think it's wood burning," he declared after his examination.

"You think?"

He threw his hands up. "Hey, you're the cook. I just drive the boat."

Hope couldn't keep from smiling. She held her hands out toward him, and wiggled her fingers. "You want me to break these nails? To sweat and slave over a hot stove for you? To make tuna-and-green-bean spaghetti sauce over mashed potatoes for your dinner?''

''I have hopes.''

''I am Hope.''

''So you are.''

She found herself smiling as a thought hit her. ''Doesn't that sound lovely? Eating a nice, bland, won't-attack-you-before-you-get-a-chance-to-swallow-it meal straight-out-of-the-can glop?''

He sighed contentedly. ''Oh, yeah.''

She noticed that she was tilting her head up to look at him. Mainly because she had gone from standing by the sink and he had gone from standing by the stove, and now they were in the center of the room, standing very close to each other. When had that happened? The how and the why she had no trouble discerning; it was the fact they'd moved closer without realizing they were doing so that was disturbing.

Hope took a giant step backward. She turned around and opened a drawer. ''I found the can opener!''

''We're saved!''

Stop being cute! She thought angrily. *Just stop it right now!* He's not what he seems, she reminded herself. Few men are. He lied to you, remember that! She warned sternly. She took a deep breath, held on tight to her resentment of the male of the species, and turned back to him.

She found him holding up a full gallon plastic water container. ''Untainted,'' he announced. ''Unopened. You don't want to know what else is in the fridge, though. Power's definitely been off a few days. Fortunately, the storm damage hasn't been that bad over the whole island.''

''How'd you know that?'' she asked as she opened cans.

"The woman I talked to at the shelter told me."

"The last thing I expected at this time of year was bad weather," Hope said. "I never could have talked Uncle Bradley into the trip if we thought—"She took a deep breath as pain surged through her.

Tiger's hand landed softly on her shoulder. His thumb began to make slow, gentle circles on the tense muscles of her back. "If you don't want to talk about them, that's okay."

He probably didn't want to hear about her family, or anything else about her. But he sounded sympathetic, and his touch was comforting. Hope shrugged his hand off, denying herself solace. She couldn't stop herself from talking, though. "I didn't think all the ramifications of the cruise through. All I wanted was to get away from Baltimore. To have an adventure." She gave a small, pitiful laugh. "And look what happened."

"It's not your fault hijackers attacked the boat."

She wanted to tell him that it was his fault for choosing the rendezvous site, but she didn't know that he had. Besides, Tiger hadn't known some innocent bystanders would come sailing by. Or what Santiago would do. In her irrational moments she did blame him, but she knew it wasn't fair.

Hope made herself let the subject go, for now. Tiger couldn't figure out how to get the stove to work. So she poured potato mix and water that was lukewarm from days in a nonworking refrigerator into a bowl and began stirring. She flashed a smile at Tiger. "You know, I think this water may be just warm enough to do the trick."

He licked his lips. "Gourmet delight."

They ended up eating bowls of barely warmed potatoes covered in tuna pasta sauce while sitting in the yard outside the house. They washed it down with glasses of tepid bottled water. Hope sat in the shade of a flowering tree, but Tiger moved into the sunlight, working on his tan, he said, and getting his clothes dry at the same time. When Hope took the empty dishes into the kitchen she changed out of her makeshift outfit back into her now dry shorts and shirt. They were still dirty, stained, torn in places and smelled faintly of sweat, but at least they were dry. Her canvas shoes were still damp, but she slipped them back on anyway. She felt incredibly grubby. However the peculiar, but actually tasty, meal had helped restore a lot of her energy. Oddly enough, the companionable silence she'd shared with Tiger in the quiet churchyard while eating had also been pleasant, restful. It was simple pleasures like being dry and full, she guessed, that made a person happy to be alive. Or at least appreciate being alive.

When she went back outdoors she was once again brooding on the subject of life and death. She was thinking about justice when she came up to Tiger. "What about Santiago?" she demanded. "You're going to arrest him, aren't you?"

Tiger came slowly to his feet, uncoiling his long body with the litheness of the big cat he was named after. "No," he answered her.

She hid her pain at this casual answer with a show of anger. "Why not? Because you're not who you claim to be? Are you one of the good guys or not?"

"Define good guy?" was his cynical response.

She wasn't interested in discussing ambiguities or shades of gray. "Santiago needs to be brought to justice."

"So do a lot of people who live on this island." Tiger hated the suspicion in her eyes, and the hurt. He wanted to look away, to turn his back on her, because her suspicion hurt him. The woman had no faith in him. She had no reason to. What was his problem? She didn't trust him, he shouldn't trust her. That's how it ought to be. But the way she was looking at him made him want to do anything he could to make everything better.

"I'm not here to save the world," he told her.

"What are you here for, then?"

"I can't tell you. I've already told you too much."

"National security?"

"I can't tell you."

"Won't tell me? Or can't?"

He looked around the churchyard, and at the small house. He checked his watch, wondering how it had gotten to be past noon already. "Time flies when you're having fun," he grumbled.

"Tell me about it," Hope grumbled back. "Why won't you do anything about Santiago?" she insisted.

"Because I can't. Okay, if he shot at me, I'd be happy to shoot back," he conceded. "But if I need to use him to make a deal with Cardenas, then I use him. I can't let personal feelings get in the way of my job."

"Why not?" she shot back. "If you won't—can't—do anything, maybe I'll—"

"Do what?"

"Tell Cardenas that his loyal henchman betrayed him." She nodded emphatically. "We already know Santiago's scared that Cardenas will find out. That's why he sent someone to kill you."

"We don't know that. The gunman might have been acting on his own."

"What difference does that make?" she shouted at Tiger.

Tiger forced himself not to argue with her. He conceded that she had a point in wanting revenge for her family's murders. He was also well aware that there was no way she could do anything about Santiago on her own. She couldn't get to Cardenas—hell, he wasn't sure that he could if he didn't do something to make contact soon. "Woman," he said. "I am trying to rescue you. Stop trying to complicate the process."

Why should she be saved? Hope wondered. For what? What did she have to go back to? Her family was gone. The man she'd thought she'd loved had betrayed her. She didn't think there was anyone in the world who would actually miss her. In fact, the only person who showed any interest in whether she lived or died was the man standing belligerently in front of her. And why he protected her she wasn't at all sure. A part of her wanted—longed—for it to be because he cared for her.

She pushed that longing away, and labeled it weakness. She didn't ask for his help again, either. "Don't you have to be going?" she asked pointedly.

"We have to be going." He looked around the churchyard and back at the little house. "I can't leave you here by yourself, and they didn't know when Felipe would be back on Isla Sebastian at the shelter."

"I'd rather stay here," she declared. She figured that once she was out of Tiger's presence she'd finally be able to think clearly again. "Wait for the priest to come home. Maybe I could help out at this shelter."

Tiger's impulse was to make her come with him. He told himself that it was for her own good, but made himself examine his motives after the knee-jerk reaction passed. The truth was he didn't want to leave her alone because he didn't want to leave her. He couldn't afford this kind of selfish reaction. It wasn't good for her to be around him, and not just because it posed a threat to her physical safety.

He didn't like it, but he forced himself to grudgingly concede, "You've got a point, Harrison."

She was amazed that he actually agreed with her on something. A sudden ache also stabbed her heart as she realized that they really were saying goodbye. She swallowed the pain and gave an emphatic nod. "Well. That's that, then." What were they supposed to do now, she wondered. Shake hands? Should she offer to kiss him goodbye? No more memories, she sternly told herself. She had to forget about him and move on. "Thank you," she said. "For all your help."

Tiger wondered if she was about to offer him a tip. She looked, all of a sudden, so formal, so distant, so very out of his league. Her bland expression and tone might have been what she used when picking up her Mercedes automobile from valet parking. Well, why not? he thought with rueful bitterness. She didn't need him anymore, so she didn't have to be nice. Easier for him to say goodbye to the spoiled rich girl anyway.

"You're welcome," he answered. He gestured toward the path on the side of the church. "Come on. I'll take you to the shelter."

One last short journey with Tiger. She fought off joy at knowing they'd have a few more minutes together. She steadfastly fought off showing the pleasure she knew she shouldn't be feeling. Instead, she gave him a nod, and walked ahead of him back toward the dangerous streets of Isla Sebastian.

Chapter 7

When his cellular phone rang, Tiger wasn't surprised. In fact, he answered with a growled, "What took you so long?"

"Hungover," Rick responded. "Big-time. You and the girlfriend have fun?"

"What do you hear from Cardenas?"

"Guess not," Rick responded nonchalantly to Tiger's curt tone. "Back to business, right, man?"

"Right," Tiger responded. He stopped walking, and leaned against the wall of the nearest building. It was still damp from the rain. Water ran in swift streams down the streets. Muddy puddles had formed in potholes, almost steaming in the fierce midday heat. There was some traffic in the narrow street, mostly wheezing old trucks with barely room enough to pass each other. The drivers didn't show much regard for the few pedestrians using the same road.

He used the hint of danger as an excuse to hook an arm around her waist and draw Hope closely to his side. She didn't protest, fitted perfectly there, hip to hip, and waited in silence while he continued his conversation.

"Cardenas?" he asked.

"He called the boat. Said he understood that a storm had interfered with the pickup."

"So that was Santiago's story to his boss." Hope stiffened against him at the sound of the name. "I'll stick with it if he will."

"Cardenas said he understood how these things can happen."

"And? Does he still want to deal?"

"Face-to-face, man. Be impressed."

"Why?"

"Because you've got an invite to his private hideaway, from the man himself. You going?" Rick sounded eager. "It could be a trap, maybe he wants to kill you in person. Want me to come along?"

"You've heard too much about the parties at his place," Tiger answered. He glanced sideways at Hope. She had her head tilted toward him, almost touching his shoulder. She was obviously trying to listen in on the telephone conversation. He was elated at the prospect of finally making face-to-face contact with the one man who was a certain lead to the naval weapons thieves. Tiger was thankful that no matter what went down at Cardenas's place, Hope would be well out of it before then. She would be in no danger, and unable to offer any threat, no matter how inadvertent.

He concentrated on his assignment, and on his cover. "When's Cardenas expecting me?"

"Not us?"

"No," he told Rick. "I want someone I can trust guarding the shipment. In case Cardenas—or Santiago—decide they'd rather grab the goods without paying the bill."

"Good point," Rick agreed reluctantly. "Hate missing any fun."

Cardenas wouldn't try anything, Tiger knew. In fact, the man was famous for having an excess of what passed for integrity among his kind. He took pride in being gentlemanly, in betraying his business associates only if and when he had to. Cardenas himself was more of a middleman who brokered deals between criminals such as a small-time arms dealer with product to move, such as Tiger purported to be. Cardenas was capable of putting the arms dealer together with people who needed guns, such as drug dealers, revolutionaries and terrorist groups. Tiger's assignment was to get close to Cardenas, close enough to find out the name of the weapons thief. He'd spent a lot of time establishing his cover strongly enough so that Cardenas would be willing to trust him with picking up a consignment directly from the naval arms thieves. Then he could take it from there.

He'd thought he'd feel a sense of triumph when this moment came. What he felt was the solid weight and warmth of Hope by his side. He felt her curiosity, and her scorn as she came to her own conclusion about what she overheard.

"Let's just get it over with," he said—to Rick, himself, to Hope. Then he deliberately put his emotions away, pulled himself together and focused. He forced himself to forget about the woman, and all the warmth she brought into his life. Their interlude—for whatever it had been worth—was truly over. His voice was dead cold when he spoke. "I better get back to the *Rani* and get cleaned up. When does Cardenas want to see me?"

Rick named a time, and Tiger nodded. "Fine. I'll be there." He cut the connection and put the phone back in his pocket. He gestured to Hope and they set off down the street again, walking single file with him behind her. He sensed that she wanted to talk, and that his stony exterior kept her quiet. They had one more plaza to cross to reach the shelter, then she'd be out of danger and out of his life forever.

"Just point me toward the right one," she told him as she looked around the buildings that faced the plaza on all four sides. "And I'm out of your hair."

He pointed toward the least-damaged-looking building in the area. The ache in his chest at losing her—Lord, he'd never had her!—made it too painful for him to speak. He wanted to take her in his arms and kiss her goodbye, to have at least the memory of one more kiss. What he wanted was insane and impossible.

When she turned to face him, a brittle smile on her face, he kissed her anyway.

The plaza went up in flames around her as their lips met. The intensity was like nothing she'd ever known before. All the tension that had spun and coiled between them was suddenly unloosed. It left her trembling, needy. They'd kissed before, and each encounter had been intense, but this was nothing like the passion they'd leashed and fought with since the moment of meeting. This came from the soul, from spirit as much as flesh. This time they *meant* it. This was serious passion. She found herself wanting to cry out "Don't leave me!"

She wanted to push him to the ground and take him then and there, to do serious damage to his psyche to make sure he never forgot her. To come away from this insane encounter carrying a part of him inside her. She was wild and angry and desperate. This was for the last time, their last chance. Impossible as this was, as he was, she couldn't bear to part from him without—

This was no way to make love. Never mind that it wasn't the right time or place, but anger, desperation, loneliness—

what kind of emotions were those to bring to lovemaking? Honest ones, she thought, as much as she could think. Her hands roved over his back and shoulders. Her mouth pressed hungrily against his. She felt his heat and growing hardness against her belly and ground her hips against him.

Tiger guided Hope into a deserted alley, behind the shelter of an abandoned cart blown there by one of the recent storms. He couldn't take his hands off of her, but she was the one driving him crazy. Every touch sent waves of fire through him. He had meant to steal one last kiss, now she was stealing his soul. No, he was willingly giving it to her, what little there was left of it.

"This is crazy," he panted when he could find some breath to speak.

"You have a problem with crazy?" She panted back.

"Yes. No." His mouth found the peak of one breast straining beneath the fabric of her T-shirt. She gasped and arched her back as he teased and suckled through the thin barrier of cloth. Her moan of pleasure drove him on. He cupped her other breast in his hand, then his fingers slid down inside the waistband of her shorts. She was there before him, sliding down the zipper for him.

He definitely had no problems behaving in this insane fashion. It wasn't as if she didn't want it as much as he did. Neither of them were thinking. So what?

"Damn it!" he snarled furiously, and spun away. The speed and momentum of his action brought him up hard against the wall on the other side of the alley. The bruising force helped clear his mind. He stayed there, face pressed into rough boards, fist pounding against the wall in utter, agonized frustration. Fury boiled away desire, but not fast enough to snuff out pain that was as emotional as it was physical. He needed, damn it! He wanted. Why the devil did he always have to deny himself? He was a man, she was a woman! A woman who set him on fire and drove him crazy. So crazy that here he was half out of his mind, with her half out of her clothes in a stinking back alley!

This was no way to behave. No way to make love to a woman. He had no right to allow either of their emotions to get out of control. *She* was not responsible for her responses in this situation—she'd been traumatized, terrified, become dependent on him. The last time he'd kissed her she'd slapped him, but here he was assaulting her again. Her response this time was to take the lead. He couldn't blame her for trying to control the situation for once. He could blame himself for letting the situation happen. Again.

''What was I thinking?'' he snarled. ''What kind of a—'' He whirled back around, anxious to find out if Hope was all right.

''Woman am I?'' Hope asked, lifting her head proudly at his furious glare.

''Did I say that?'' he snapped.

''You look like you're thinking it.''

He crossed the alley in two steps. He reached for her shoulders, then dropped his hands to his sides before touching her. They balled into fists, the muscles of his arms corded with tension. ''Woman, what is the matter with you?''

''Nothing. Nada.'' Desire still thrummed through her. Looking at him made her hungry, sent aching need deep into the center of her being. ''Everything's the matter,'' she continued. ''But it wasn't my fault!''

''Did I blame you?''

''Don't men always?''

She didn't know what he had to be angry at her about, but she wasn't going to apologize for what they'd been doing, not going to take blame or express any guilt. Not this time. She wasn't going to let him make her feel responsible for both of their actions. She'd had quite enough of being manipulated like that. Enough to last a lifetime. She didn't regret anything but his having rejected her, no matter how unwise what they'd been doing had been. She wished she was better at being reckless. Or at least more successful.

Tiger forced himself to calm down, to drop any argument with Hope. She was upset, and justifiably so. Venting the emotions roaring through them as a verbal argument might do them both good. He knew that if he let the argument continue it was likely their verbal sparring would change into lovemaking. He couldn't trust himself to even talk to her at this point.

"Come on," he said, gesturing back toward the plaza.

She nodded, made a show of rearranging her clothing, then walked proudly ahead of him out of the alley.

Several cars had pulled into the plaza while they'd been gone. Some of the men who'd gotten out of the cars had spread out to cover the area. A group of three men waited by the largest of the cars, a white Jeep Cherokee automobile. One of the men held a cellular phone to his ear. All the men were holding guns.

Hope noticed all this in the moment before Tiger grabbed her and shoved her behind him. He started to back them into the alley, but a shout went up before they got more than a step. Guns came up, men closed in on them.

Tiger sighed, swore, and straightened his shoulders. He didn't make a move to draw his weapon. Instead he put his arm around Hope's waist. "Let me do the talking," he told her, and they stepped into the plaza. "Ibarra," he said, falsely cheerful as the trio of men came up. "Good to see you again. Quarrels," he added, with a nod toward a broad-shouldered man with sharp-as-lasers chocolate-brown eyes.

Hope's stomach curdled and sank at the mention of

Ibarra's name. Fear shot through her as she looked at Ibarra. He was small and wiry, with a scarred face and very evil eyes. Fanatic's eyes. Which he turned on her briefly before he concentrated on Tiger, flicking over her with contempt and arrogance before his gaze met hers and moved back to Tiger.

Ibarra terrified her, but she still moved unconsciously closer to Tiger, willing to share whatever fate being with him might bring. She even managed to lift her head proudly, not that any of the men were paying her any mind by this time.

"Thought you were out of town," Tiger said to Ibarra.

Hope found his cool, casual tone shocking. She couldn't tell if he was disturbed by the presence of Ibarra and all his henchmen or not. He was playing for time, of course, playing a macho game with an enemy. Why was Ibarra his enemy, anyway, she wondered?

"You murdered my brother," Ibarra snarled, effectively answering Hope's question. "Cold blood." He spat on the ground at Tiger's feet. "Business I understand, but not what you did."

Hope turned her shocked gaze on Tiger. Had he? How? Why? No! Even if he wasn't who he claimed to be, Hope did not believe he was a murderer. Yesterday she'd believed him capable of anything, but that was yesterday. People shot at him, he shot back. It was barbaric, but understandable. Today, at least at this moment, it was understandable to her. She licked suddenly dry lips, and waited breathlessly for Tiger's response to Ibarra's accusation.

"You know what happened," Tiger replied.

But I don't! Hope thought. She was tempted to stomp on Tiger's foot and demand a full explanation here and now.

Temptation she fought down as she looked around the plaza. She was hoping for help of some sort, even for Tiger's crew to come racing to the rescue, guns blazing. The only people she saw in the plaza were the ones Ibarra had brought with him. If people in the shelter or other buildings were watching, she doubted anyone was in the process of calling the police or intervening themselves. Isla Sebastian was an island overrun with criminals. Hadn't Tiger mentioned that Ibarra controlled the airports? How much power did he have on the island? Enough to get away with whatever he chose to do, she guessed.

"I flew in through the storm," Ibarra proudly informed Tiger. "Got a tip the *Rani* was in, so I had to come home, didn't I?"

"I don't see why," Tiger coolly replied. "You and I don't have any business together."

"Oh, yes we do," Ibarra replied darkly. "We monitored your cell phone frequency," Ibarra said, beaming and showing broken teeth. "That's how I found you. Isn't technology wonderful? Heard about you and Cardenas. Too bad you won't be able to make the meeting."

By this time Tiger had taken a subtle step away from Hope, was shielding her with his body. This forced her to look over his shoulder to follow his conversation with Ibarra.

"You jealous because Cardenas doesn't invite you to his place?" Tiger asked.

Ibarra laughed, not a pleasant sound. "I'm going to torture you for a long time," he said cheerfully. "Make sure you live long enough to regret what you did."

The man named Quarrels looked from Tiger to Ibarra. A scowl of disgust twisted his handsome features. "Do we have to do this, boss?" He made a show of looking at his watch. "Personal revenge is a waste of valuable time."

"My time!" Ibarra shouted angrily back. "My brother!"

"I didn't kill your brother!" It was Tiger's turn to shout.

"I was there. I saw what happened, but I didn't do it. You know damn well he killed himself, you just don't want to believe it."

"Jaime was strung out that day," Quarrels cut in. "Paranoid, talking crazy. It could have happened the way Rafferty claims."

Ibarra made a sharp gesture of denial. "Suicide is a sin. Jaime would never do such a thing."

"The drugs did it," Quarrels responded. "Maybe," he added at his boss's dark glare.

"You were there," Ibarra snarled at Tiger. "You were seen holding the gun."

"There were a dozen people in Remy's that day," Tiger responded. "Nine or ten of them have told you what really happened, how I tried to stop Jaime when he put the gun to his head."

"Carlos said you did it."

Tiger shrugged. "He's lying."

There were nods and exchanged looks from his men behind Ibarra's back. Several glanced expectantly at Quarrels. He licked his lips, and said, carefully and patiently, "Carlos lied to you. He was there as Jaime's bodyguard, but he screwed up. You already dealt with Carlos. Let that be enough blood. Let's get back to business. You need to get your focus back."

Hope realized from the mad look in Ibarra's eyes that Quarrels was taking a big risk in defending Tiger. She found herself being grateful to this no-doubt very bad man for his defense. She didn't want Tiger to die. Her emotions were crystal clear and focused on that fact. Whatever he was, whatever there was between them, the thought of Tiger Rafferty's death was devastating to her. It simply could not be allowed to happen. Too many people she cared for had already died. She wasn't going to watch it happen again!

"Don't do this," she heard herself saying to Ibarra.

Tiger gave her a swift look. "Please stay out of this, Hope," he said softly.

She knew he'd told her to let him do the talking, but couldn't keep quiet to save her life. She smiled ironically as the old saying crossed her mind. She doubted keeping quiet and hidden behind Tiger was going to do her any good, anyway. She had nothing to lose—except Tiger. She couldn't let that happen.

She moved from standing behind Tiger to speak to the sneering Ibarra. Tiger put his hand on her arm. "I'm sorry about your brother," she said, looking into Ibarra's eyes. Tiger drew her backward, and put his arm around her shoulders. She felt protected within the circle of his arm, despite being aware of their danger. "Isn't there some way you can settle this without more killing?" she asked him.

She knew what Ibarra was going to say as soon as she spoke, and blushed hot with shame as an ugly grin spread across his face. Quarrels looked disgusted. She glanced quickly up to see possessive anger flash across Tiger's features. Oh, dear.

Tiger swore inventively as he pressed her closer to his side. "Leave the woman out of this. It's between you and me."

Ibarra took a step back, the broad grin never leaving his features. "We'll fight for the woman," he announced. This was greeted with laughter and grins from his men.

Macho nonsense, Hope thought, but kept from sneering or making any disparaging comment.

"No!" Tiger protested. "This is between us, Ibarra."

"Do you want to buy us time or not?" Hope whispered fiercely to Tiger. "You can take him, right?" He glared.

She spoke quickly to Ibarra. "If Tiger wins, you let us go, right?" She had no idea where her words were coming from, what reckless angel was egging her on. She did not recognize herself, did not know where cautious, staid and unadventurous Hope had gotten to or when she'd be back. All she did know was that there was nothing to lose, so why not take the risk?

She looked expectantly at Tiger. "Why not go for it?"

He spun her around and grabbed her by the shoulders. "Do you know what he'll do to you?"

Of course she knew what Ibarra intended. The same thing he intended to do to her if he simply outright tortured and murdered Tiger. She didn't remind Tiger of that; instead, she tossed her head and said boldly, "Not if you win."

Tiger didn't know what had gotten into the woman, but he couldn't help but smile at her. The confidence and trust in the look she gave him struck him down to the bone. It made him want to fight for her—and win. And claim her as his prize. This feeling was insane, pure warrior male fantasy, so politically incorrect he thought it might actually be illegal. Then again, nothing was illegal on Isla Sebastian.

"Sure," he said to Ibarra, stepping away from Hope. "You want my woman, you're definitely going to have to fight for her."

Well aware of all the guns trained on him, he carefully shrugged off his jacket. Quarrels stepped forward and plucked Tiger's pistol out of its shoulder holster. Quarrels didn't prevent him from passing his knife to Hope. In fact, Quarrels covered her action as Hope carefully and quickly slipped the blade into her shorts pocket. Tiger was grateful for even this small bit of help from Ibarra's very business-minded second in command. Ibarra in the meantime had shed his own armament and backed into the center of the plaza. Tiger strode forward, and Ibarra's men formed an excited ring of spectators around them.

Hope didn't want to watch what happened next, but found herself staring in rapt fascination as two experienced street fighters got down, and very dirty. A lot of the dirt came from the puddles in the plaza, and a patch of slippery mud they got into as they kicked and punched and chopped their way back and forth across the wide circle formed by the gathered crowd. There was a great deal of shouting and jeering and jostling for views among Ibarra's men. Tiger had the advantage in height and reach, and martial arts training, Hope realized as she watched him spin, kick and dodge. His movements were accomplished with deadly grace, and seeming ease that had to come from long practice. What looked to be less formal moves were even more dangerous. He had no compunction about gouging, biting, trodding, stomping and punching any part of Ibarra's anatomy that came within reach. Both men were soon covered in blood and bruises as well as soaked and muddy clothing. Ibarra was vicious, small, wiry and as fast as a striking snake. He fought in an angry frenzy. He was reckless besides, not caring that he took punishment to land a blow.

The fight seemed to go on forever, and was painful to watch. Hope could only justify egging this on because every second Tiger spent fighting Ibarra was one more second he lived. She hoped and prayed that Ibarra was getting enough satisfaction out of hurting Tiger. That the fight would be enough, that it would satisfy his honor or guilt or rage or whatever was eating him up over his brother's death. That he blamed himself for his brother's suicide but was putting that blame on Tiger was obvious to her. Somehow she doubted Ibarra was the sort who would seek counseling for this problem. She certainly didn't intend to suggest it to him, assuming the chance ever came to bring it up.

She almost smiled at this thought, but winced instead at the sound of Ibarra's fist connecting with Tiger's midsection. Tiger used the move to grab Ibarra's arm and swing the man around. Ibarra staggered forward, followed swiftly by Tiger. The combat moved closer to where she and Quarrels stood. Ibarra fell to his knees, and Tiger was on him, looming, with his arm around Ibarra's throat. Hope realized their ragged breathing was the only sound in the plaza. Everyone else had gone stone-still. They were all staring, tension crackled around the silent circle of men. Even she was aware that the fight was over. That Tiger could easily break Ibarra's neck if he chose.

She saw a look pass between Tiger and Quarrels. She half expected Quarrels to respond by giving a thumbs-up or down sign, indicating life or death just as a Roman emperor would do to decide the outcome of a gladiatorial contest. Quarrels made no move, not even a blink, staying totally neutral in whatever happened next between his boss and Tiger.

Tiger's gaze then flicked to her. The coldness she saw in his eyes froze her, terrified her, but she didn't look away. The man was capable of doing whatever he had to do. She accepted this as his strength; it was who he had to be able to survive in this violent world. What he was, was not beyond her understanding, merely beyond her scope of experience. At least until now. She didn't know what she really thought, how she could deal with the naked knowledge of the man's soul in the long-term, but for now she gazed back at him with steady support. This was no time to wimp out on him.

The instant passed. His eyes shifted away from hers to

look around the gathering of armed men. Ibarra's men. He took a chance, and released his hold on Ibarra.

Tiger took a step back as Ibarra fell forward onto his hands and knees. "We're going now," he said and held his hand out to Hope.

She rushed forward. This time she was the one who kissed him, but swiftly and briefly. This was no time for a victory celebration. She heard someone let out a low, dirty laugh as she pulled away from Tiger. He put his arm around her as Ibarra struggled to his feet.

Ibarra turned on them, and snarled, "You're not going anywhere. Kill them," he ordered with a look over his shoulder at Quarrels.

Hope forgot to breathe as fear gripped her. Tiger's grasp on her tightened. She felt his tension, but he stood as still as stone. She was glad he was holding her, because she didn't think she would be able to stand on her own. No one moved.

"Kill him!" Ibarra shouted. He turned slowly around, glaring furiously at his men. "Did you hear me?"

"He won," Quarrels spoke up. "You made a deal."

Ibarra rounded on his second in command, and swore at him. "Do what I tell you!"

Everyone was suddenly looking at Quarrels. "Oh, hell," he snarled. He looked disgusted, and thoroughly annoyed as he stepped forward and punched Ibarra in the jaw. Ibarra went down, out cold. Quarrels gave a hard-eyed look around the circle of Ibarra's men. No one objected. He nodded, and pointed to two men. "Lock him up back at the house. I'll work it out with him later."

"You sure, boss?" one of the men asked.

Quarrels accepted the title easily. "I'm sure." The men didn't argue anymore, but moved to do as they'd been told. Quarrels approached Tiger.

Tiger was not surprised at this change of leadership of the Ibarra crime family. It had been coming for a long time. He was surprised to be alive. He wondered what Quarrels wanted from him, to have made his move to take over by saving his life. Ibarra had certainly played this situation wrong, not by losing, but by reneging on his implied agreement to let them go if he lost. He'd left himself wide-open to what had just happened. The men of Isla Sebastian did have a code of honor and conduct, macho and brutal though it was.

"You should have killed him for me," Quarrels said to Tiger. "Would have made both our lives easier."

"Sorry about that," Tiger answered coolly.

"I'll deal." Quarrels gestured toward the white Jeep. "I'll give you a lift to Cardenas's place."

So that was what the man wanted, an introduction to the most powerful man on the island. Now that he'd become the second most powerful man on Isla Sebastian. This was interesting, but none of Tiger's business. He needed one name from Cardenas, that was all.

He also owed Quarrels his life. "Sure," he said, with a nonchalant shrug. He tugged on his filthy shirt. "Need to clean up for the party first, though."

"No need. Cardenas runs a full-service resort for his guests."

That was true. What Tiger really wanted was to drop Hope off at the shelter. It was only across the plaza. One of those so close but so far away problems, and he couldn't see any way out of it. Ibarra was still alive, still vengeful. Quarrels's reign over the family empire could be a short one. There might be some way Ibarra could get to Hope if she was left here alone where Ibarra's men could find her. Besides, it was now firmly established that she was Tiger's woman. There would be suspicion if Tiger left the woman he'd just fought for behind.

There was nothing he could do but take Hope along. Somehow, he was going to have to warn her, threaten her, convince her, to keep her mouth shut and simply play the bad guy's girlfriend for as long as it took him to get the job done and get out.

Damn! If he had any sense, he'd find a way out of this situation. Maybe he should even forget about the assignment in order to keep her safe.

That wasn't an option, though, was it? Not with Quarrels walking beside them toward the Jeep. Quarrels handed his gun back, Hope returned his knife. He was armed again, but Tiger knew this was no time to cross the man.

"Fasten your seat belts," he found himself inanely quoting from an old movie as he and Hope settled into the vehicle. "It's going to be a bumpy night."

"Hey, I'm a great driver," Quarrels laughed as he started the engines. "You two lovebirds can sit back and let me take care of everything."

Chapter 8

Luxury did not begin to describe Cardenas's compound. Officially it was the Isla Sebastian Resort Complex, a place where the ultrarich came for romantic, very secluded getaways. It was also the very secure nerve center of Cardenas's international empire. Tiger took in as many details as he could after the Jeep was waved through the guarded gate and Quarrels drove up the winding road to Cardenas's private mansion. The buildings were painted in bright colors and roofed in red tiles, the second- and third-floor balconies were surrounded by decorative, white-painted wrought-iron banisters. The wheels of the Jeep crunched on a thick bed of crushed white stone, the rocks flecked with shining veins that spark like diamonds in the bright light. Drapes of vivid flowering vines hung from trees and shaded pergolas. Blooming hibiscus trees shaded the lawns and guest houses. Glimpses of the beach and surf below the cliffside paradise could be seen in the distance as Quarrels steered around the sweeping curves leading to Cardenas's secluded mansion. Tiger took it all in, and was reminded of ads for honeymoon resorts and romantic getaways—and found it all quite…charming. There were couples strolling hand and hand on the lawns, playing in a swimming pool the Jeep passed, sharing delicacies from fancy hampers at the picnic tables. These couples had eyes only for each other despite being far from alone. They were happy, content in each other's company, in love. Laughter filled the air, and the air of romantic bliss made Tiger want to take Hope's hand and join in the fun.

Oh, Lord! What was getting into him? When did the dangerous world become such a rosy, hopeful place for him? Why? The sky overhead was the same painfully pure blue he'd been living a dangerous charade under for months, the vegetation as wild and riotous and as green. There were probably armed guards patrolling in the bushes. Yet, everything around him seemed more vibrant today, more alive. More…real. Maybe it was having survived the fight, or being so close to his goal at last. The truth was, his acute reaction wasn't to the day, or to any other stimulus other than the presence of the woman seated so closely beside him. He needed to focus on the assignment, to plan and prepare. But Hope was warm and soft resting against him. Her hand rested lightly on his thigh, her hair softly tickled his cheek. His arm was around her shoulders, a protective, possessive, utterly natural position. He had no idea if his closeness offered her any comfort or reassurance—or any pleasure. He wanted to get her in private, and not just because they needed desperately to talk. No, what he desperately ached and needed to do with Hope Harrison didn't really have anything to do with talking. He could easily forget, like those people beyond the windows of the Jeep, that there was anyone in the world but the woman beside him.

Tiger found himself closing his eyes. Seeing himself and Hope hand in hand on the beach. Then he was holding her close, his mouth on her, her hands in his hair. He could taste her skin in his memory of things that had yet to happen, see the look of passion in her lovely, large eyes, hear the soft moans of her pleasure. Pleasure he gave her with long, lingering touches, with thrusts that took her to heaven, and him with her.

But… They weren't alone.

Tiger swallowed hard, fought off the tightness growing in his body, made his muscles relax, forced down the raw male need that wanted to control him. Adrenaline left over from the fight with Ibarra, he told himself. That's all this was.

"You asleep?" Quarrels called.

Tiger's head snapped up, his eyes flew open, and he realized that he had actually dozed off for a few seconds. When he blinked and looked around his gaze met the worried eyes of Hope.

"You all right?" she asked. "Ibarra didn't hurt you, did he?"

Her concern touched him, and memory of his brief dreaming sent hot embarrassment through him. Her gaze trapped his, the anxiety gradually turning to some intense emotion he wasn't prepared to try to define. He had his own confused state of mind and heart to deal with. He couldn't dare ask her what she was thinking, and not just because Quarrels was so near by. Eventually a fine, pink color suffused Hope's lightly tanned cheeks, the heat of her reaction warming the air between them, warming his skin where it touched hers. She stirred slightly in his embrace, then turned her head away to gaze out the window. He could hear her breathing, practically feel the swift flutter of her heartbeat.

Sometime ago, she'd asked him a question. "I'm fine," he said, though he had to clear his throat twice, and force himself to look away and stare through the front window of the car before he could speak.

"You look great," Quarrels joked. "I haven't seen such sartorial splendor in—ever. Where do you two shop?"

"Very funny," Tiger snarled back. He noticed his ragged clothing, and that Hope looked pretty tattered herself. "We were caught in the storm, you know. You do recall the storm?"

"Oh, yeah, that. Well, here we are," Quarrels announced, bringing the Jeep to a halt before the entrance of Cardenas's private residence.

Hope had been lost in a dream for the last hour, maybe longer. She might have dozed off, and really had no idea how long the drive had been. In the Jeep's air-conditioning, her position next to Tiger had been comfortably warm. His hard-muscled, sinewy frame somehow made a comfortable resting place. She was surprised that emotion and exhaustion had combined to put her out, or at least numb her awareness of everything but the safe, warm feeling of Tiger's arm around her. Safety. There had been nothing safe about the look in his eyes just now. Nothing safe in the racing response of her heart, the thrill it sent through her blood. No man named Tiger could possibly be "safe."

She sighed, reluctantly renouncing the lovely illusion that all was well when she was with him. It was exhaustion that had put her out, she told herself. She hadn't surrendered to it because Tiger was on guard, but because she was simply tired, in body and soul and nerves. Surely she wasn't foolish enough to really let herself relax for any other reason in this man's presence. What about sleeping in his arms last night? Oh, and the night before? You're making a habit of trusting this man. Watch out, her inner voice warned. "But get out of the car first," she murmured.

"What?" Tiger asked.

"Nothing," was her cross response. She peered out the window, seeing shallow marble steps, a wide veranda, and huge double doors of dark, carved wood.

Quarrels said, "Wonder why there's no welcoming party."

"Guards at the door wouldn't be civilized," Tiger answered the driver.

"Might make the honeymooners nervous," Quarrels agreed. "Plenty of electronic surveillance, I bet."

"And people on the inside," Tiger added.

"No doubt. We'll have to mind our manners."

"I always mind my manners."

"I'm the soul of discretion."

"I've noticed that about you."

"Noticed a few things about you, too, Rafferty. Think we should leave our guns in the car?"

"It'd be the polite thing to do."

"Guess so."

Quarrels opened the Jeep door and got out. Hope noticed that neither he nor Tiger left their weapons behind. The two men seemed quite comfortable discussing another bad guy's security arrangements, but a jolt of fear went through her at their matter-of-fact conversation.

"Let's go," Tiger said, nudging her to get her moving. His cheek brushed hers as he moved, the brief contact electric, the heat of his skin and the stubble on his chin a potent reminder to her of his masculinity. Hope's knees were actually weak from reaction as she slid from the Jeep to stand on the bright-white gravel of the driveway.

"What's the matter?" he asked. She couldn't find her voice to answer, so shook her head in reply.

Just tired, she told herself as Tiger stepped away from her. That's all it is. Stressed out. Then why was it that looking at him made her blood sing? That his touch sent fireworks through her? She remembered the alley, and being all over him. There was an ache in her to start that madness again. This wasn't the time or the place. He wasn't the right man, but wanting him was very real—a thing almost separate from herself. Could passion have a life of its own?

Hope forced the strange thoughts and erotic longings away. Not the time or place, she reminded herself sternly. Then when would be? a forlorn little voice cried in her mind. Never, she answered it sternly. Never and a day. Where am I? she wondered again, blinking in the bright light that bounced mercilessly off the white stones beneath her feet and the white marble of the stairs and the white paint of the house's walls. Only the intricately carved double doors showed any darkness in this white landscape. Looking around, she became aware of the rich greens and riotous colors of the landscape, but the white building still left her cold, the dark doors filled her with dread.

Then the true meaning of what waited at Cardenas's house hit her with the force of a blow. She found herself clinging tightly to Tiger's arm.

"Santiago!" The word was only a rasped whisper, but sounded like a shout to her. She looked around wildly, half expecting the murderer to step out of shadows that weren't there.

"Let's go," Quarrels urged as Tiger turned back to her. "We're being watched," he added.

"Right," Tiger acknowledged. "Excuse us a moment." He put his arm around Hope's waist and led her a few feet back down the driveway. He took her into a tight embrace as soon as they were out of earshot of Quarrels. Hope would have tried to break away, to run in panic, but his hold was too tight. And his presence too surrounding and protective. She knew, on some logical plane, that this was an illusion. On every other level, those levels she couldn't trust, his embrace was pure comfort and she never wanted to leave the circle of his arms.

"Let me go," she said, and made herself want him to. She stood stiffly, unyielding, as he pulled her closer instead.

"Listen to me," he whispered, putting his lips close to her ear. "We don't have time to talk this through." His voice was stern, adamant. His grip was like steel bands around her. Hope couldn't have fought out of his hold no matter how hard she tried. "Quarrels is right," he continued. "We're being watched. We're going to be watched every minute while we're here. If we're going to get out of here alive, you have to do exactly as I tell you."

"I've heard that before." Her tone was bitter, but her whisper was as soft as Tiger's. She was so sick of being told what to do. What about what she wanted? Needed. "What about Santiago? What about justice?"

"Cardenas is interested in profit. Justice doesn't come into it. I'll deal with Santiago."

"How? When?"

"I don't know."

"You don't care about justice, do you? You won't help me."

"Santiago isn't—"

"Important? Is your cover the only thing that's important?"

"*Don't* mention that. Ever. Don't say anything that anyone can question. Better yet, don't say anything at all. You're a woman in a man's world," he continued. "Stay quiet and in the background and no one will pay any attention to you. Act the part and no one will notice you."

Her gaze flashed angrily to his. "What part?"

His kiss was swift, rough and possessive. His eyes were predatory and bright when he lifted his mouth from hers. "You know what part," he told her. They were both panting from this quick, hard kiss.

Hope's eyes filled with tears of outrage, fury and shame. "Damn you!"

"While we're here," he stressed, "you're my woman."

"Don't use me," she snarled.

"I will," was his cold answer. "Go along with this, or get us both killed," he added.

His words struck painfully into the deepest, weakest core of her, pounded away at every insecurity she tried so hard to defend herself against. A swift wave of hatred for this man consumed her, burning all the longing to smoldering ash. She blinked hard to keep back the tears, and gave him a look made of stone and ice.

"Come on you two lovebirds," Quarrels called before either could say anything more. "Can't keep our host waiting."

Tiger gave her one more hard, demanding look. Hope lifted her chin proudly and didn't give in to the urge to look away. "Lovebirds," he said as he tried to stare her down. His lips lifted in a cold, false smile. "That's what we are. Isn't that right, Hope?"

"When pigs fly," she whispered back. He patted her cheek. The gesture might have been reassuring, if she hadn't felt the threat behind it. For once his touch left her cold. It had more to do with the look in his eyes than his actual touch. Those were the eyes of the man she'd first met on the deck of a yacht. The eyes of a man determined to keep his cover safe. He wasn't asking for her help, but demanding it. Reminding her that she didn't have to like him, but that she did owe him her life. Several times. He was demanding that she pay up, shut up and play along.

That she was his woman in truth, in this place and time. For as long as the charade was played out. Now, wasn't she?

She swallowed hard, and nodded her head in acquiescence. She was being manipulated, used. Again. Somehow, her heart had almost come to trust him. She knew she couldn't trust any man and was thankful for this harsh reminder. She might hate Tiger Rafferty with all her heart, but she was his woman. For now.

"Good," he said. She felt as though he was reading her every thought and emotion, could anticipate anything she might say or do. At least she felt helpless against him. "Smile," he added as he turned, took her by the hand and led her back to where Quarrels waited by the Jeep. To the other man's curious look, Tiger commented, "Girl's had a rough couple of days."

"Your concern's touching."

"That's me," Tiger responded with an edgy laugh. "All heart."

The "girl" felt like she'd just been run over by a truck. Her spirit was at its absolute lowest ebb as she accompanied the men up the shallow steps and across the wide, sunny veranda. The door opened before Quarrels could press the doorbell. A smiling woman in a gray maid's uniform and equally gray hair ushered them into a wide entryway. She took them from there into one of the largest, most luxurious rooms Hope had ever seen. Despite her own wealthy background she was more than impressed. *Overwhelmed* might be a better term for the sensation she experienced finding herself amid so much opulence. Especially after the past several days spent in the storm-ravaged slums of the town on the other side of the island. She was dressed in grubby rags, and hadn't had a shower in days. Being rainwashed didn't count, since no soap had been involved. She must smell, her hair must be a fright. Since she wasn't being faced with overt threats of death at the moment, she had the time to feel filthy and inadequate, and be bothered by it. Tiger certainly didn't look any better. In fact he looked like a derelict, albeit a very dangerous one.

"It's a wonder they didn't send us around to the servants' entrance," she heard herself murmur.

Tiger fought down a smile at Hope's quiet comment. He kept his expression neutral as he took careful note of the three guards standing in strategic positions in various parts of the big room. He also took in the priceless art objects—the paintings and statues and a case full of beautifully lit art glass, and found himself wondering just what he was going to do to win Cardenas's trust now that he was finally going to meet him face-to-face. He'd worked hard for this moment, though he hadn't expected to arrive at this much sought for meeting with the extra baggage of Quarrels, who had his own agenda. The last thing Tiger had expected would be that he'd have to face Cardenas with the woman who stood at his side. The point when he'd started this was to get in, get the name, get out.

That was still the point. He simply couldn't let Hope distract him. He'd protect her as much as he could, but if she got in the way of his assignment… He knew that he'd do everything in his power to get her out. Damn it. Damn her. Damn him, most of all. He should have left her to fend for herself back on the yacht. That would have been the smart course. Now, here he was—but here she was, in danger he'd put her in. Even worse, she was a loose cannon, an unknown element. She could ruin the whole operation for the sake of revenge, get herself killed, and all with only a word. The thought of something happening to her ate at him. He cursed her for that, cursed himself even more. Focus! he ordered himself. Keep your mind on your work and your hands off Hope and you'll get her out alive.

His attention focused instantly when a man entered the room. The guards came alert, their protective attention trained on the newcomer. Tiger noticed Quarrels's slight nod as he perceived the change as well.

Hope saw the distinguished middle-aged man dressed in linen trousers and a dark-blue silk shirt and realized how well he fit in the magnificent surroundings. There was an aura of self-assurance and understated power about him that was magnetic. Her uncle had had that leader of men, lord of all he sees sort of presence. Cardenas's keen black eyes and eagle nose might have belonged to an Incan prince. His smile as he approached them held a genuine warmth it was impossible not to respond to. She knew that this was the evil head of some sort of criminal empire, but he had the sort of bearing she found familiar, an aura of assured power.

She sighed and fought off the impression that here was a man she could trust. Hadn't she already learned the hard way that no man could be trusted? She sent a quick, hostile look toward Tiger as the thought crossed her mind. Then the newcomer spoke, and all her attention was caught by his smooth, deep voice.

"Welcome, welcome. You look tired." He gestured toward a grouping of furniture set on a priceless Persian carpet. "Let's sit and get to know each other. Drinks for my guests, please, Maria," he said to the maid who had lingered by the hall doorway. "Coffee, I think. You look as if you're barely awake," he added, turning his smile and discerning gaze on Hope. She was unable not to respond, and gave a weary smile and nod.

"I am Dante Cardenas," their host introduced himself,

and shook Tiger's and Quarrels's hands before leading them across the room.

Cardenas settled into a deep, brown leather chair, Quarrels took an identical chair opposite him. Tiger and Hope sat on a couch. Tiger took his arm from around her shoulder, but sat close to her. She was tempted to sidle over to the farthest end of the long leather couch, but didn't. Moving would draw attention to herself, and she had to reluctantly agree with Tiger Rafferty that her keeping a low profile for the moment would be for the best.

"You've heard of me, I think," Cardenas added after they were seated. "And I've heard a great deal about you." He shifted his gaze from Tiger to Quarrels. "But we have yet to get to know each other. Santiago—"

Hope stiffened at the name. Tiger's hand covered hers, fingers squeezing gently. A warning? Or reassurance? She found herself looking at his hand, aware of the strength in the fingers holding hers as Cardenas continued to speak.

"—told me how the patrol boat, and then the storm interrupted your meeting at the contact point."

Tiger fought the urge to share a quick glance with Hope. He kept his cool gaze on Cardenas. "Pity about the storm, or we would have rendezvoused. Glad Santiago made it back to the island in one piece. Sorry your shipment was delayed."

"Act of God," Cardenas waved away the inconvenience. "I am glad that so few were lost despite the storm sweeping two of my men overboard. I hope your crew is intact, Mr. Rafferty."

Hope let out a breath she hadn't realized she'd been holding. So that was how Santiago had covered the fact that his attempt at stealing the arms shipment had failed. Hope fought down the urge to blurt out the truth. If Santiago had been in the room she didn't think she'd be able

to hold her peace, but he wasn't here. She had no idea how
Cardenas would react, and Quarrels was an unknown factor. The new head of Ibarra's gang might not be at all
reliable, despite having saved them from his former boss.
She didn't want either man to see Tiger as weak, or to take
advantage of him. She didn't want to put Tiger in any more
danger. So she kept her knowledge to herself. For now.
Even though it meant that she was letting Tiger manipulate
her into doing things his way. At least she was aware she
was being manipulated. As long as she was wary of Tiger
Rafferty, her emotions would be safe from him. Wouldn't
they?

"Where is Santiago?" It was Quarrels who asked the
question. He leaned back in his chair and crossed his legs.
He looked relaxed and comfortable, as if he were an invited
guest at this little tea party. "Haven't seen him for a week
or so," he added. He ducked his head and smiled at the
sharp look he received from Cardenas. "Santiago's a friend
of—my former employer," he replied to the look. He
paused to give a charming smile to the maid as she brought
in a tray laden with cups, saucers and a tall china coffeepot.

"Santiago is currently running an errand off the island,"
he told Quarrels. "Thank you, Maria," Cardenas said politely to the maid.

Hope didn't know whether to be furious at having to wait
for a confrontation with Santiago, or relieved that one had
been put off. She was tempted to speak her mind now, but
a swift look from Tiger got an unthinking nod of agreement
in reply from her. He flashed her a smile that sent her heart
fluttering, before returning his attention to their host.

She watched Cardenas's very intense attention focus on
Quarrels. "And how is it that Ibarra is now your former
employer?"

The slight emphasis on *former* was enough to make terror sing up Hope's nerve endings. She noticed how very still and poised Tiger was. The intensity of his watchfulness gave her another clue to why he went by the nickname "Tiger."

Quarrels, however, didn't seem to notice any tension in the room. He took the time to calmly take out and light a cigarette before he answered Cardenas's question. "That's quite an interesting story." He glanced significantly toward Tiger and Hope before going on. "I suppose you've heard about Ibarra's brother's death?"

"It's old news," Tiger interrupted.

"But interesting," Quarrels insisted. "Romantic—in several senses of the word."

"Really?" Cardenas's smile lit the room. He leaned forward, showing intense interest. "I'm something of a romantic." He turned that intense smile on Hope. "In several senses of the word. You look very tired, my dear," he added. "I feel I'm being a terrible host in letting such a lovely young woman remain in such a disheveled state in my home."

Hope almost spilled what was left in her coffee cup as Tiger's arm came protectively around her shoulder. "She's fine." His voice was a rough, possessive growl.

Mindful of the sudden slight chill in Cardenas's eyes, and of the bodyguards, Hope made herself smile gratefully at their host. "He thinks I look fine no matter what," she excused Tiger's tone. "But I know I look terrible. In fact," she confided, "I think it's a gentlemanly act of true courage to let us in your house at all."

"You've been out in the weather, I take it?"

Hope couldn't help but respond to the genuine concern Cardenas showed. "For days."

"Being chased by Ibarra's men," Quarrels added.

"They're tired, and hungry. And Tiger here had to fight for his woman's honor only a couple hours ago."

Tiger glared at Quarrels, obviously annoyed at the man's effusiveness. "I don't think Mr. Cardenas is interested in—"

"Rafferty's being modest," Quarrels said, cutting him off. "He beat Ibarra hand-to-hand in a public fight."

"I was the prize," Hope added. Tiger turned his glare on her, but she turned a sweet smile on him. This was a small act of revenge, but a satisfying one. She lovingly touched his cheek, acting the part of "his woman" that he'd demanded of her. She even managed to flutter her eyelashes a bit. "His prize."

"You impress me, Rafferty," Cardenas said, with a sage nod to Tiger. "A man should protect his woman. I commend your chivalry."

"So do I," Quarrels said heartily. "Man ought to be rewarded for taking care of the woman he loves."

"You are absolutely right, Mr. Quarrels," Cardenas said, and rose elegantly to his feet. "I am being a very rude host to you two. Mr. Quarrels and I have the business of running the island to discuss."

Tiger stood. "You and I have business as well, Mr. Cardenas."

Cardenas waved his words away. "It can wait. The two of you need some rest first. Any fool can see that you are weary to the bone. And wish to be alone together," he added with a smirk.

"Lovebirds can't keep their hands off each other," Quarrels contributed. "Man can't think straight when he needs his woman, Rafferty," he added as Tiger gave him a poisonous look. "You'll thank me for reminding you of it in the morning. This place is a honeymoon resort," Quarrels

Turn the page & find out if you have the LUCKY KEY!

1. Wi
   wh
2. Se
   Th
   bu
3. Th

Y
A
v
it
y
j
I

©
tr

FREE GIFTS!

NO COST! NO OBLIGATION TO BUY!
NO PURCHASE NECESSARY!

PLAY THE
Lucky Key Game

Scratch gold area with a coin.
Then check below to see the gifts you get!

YES! I have scratched off the gold area. Please send me the 2 Free books and gift for which I qualify. I understand I am under no obligation to purchase any books, as explained on the back and on the opposite page.

345 SDL CYAK   **245 SDL CYAC**

Name
_____
(PLEASE PRINT CLEARLY)

Address _____ Apt.#_____

                                                       Postal
City _____ State/Prov._____ Zip/Code_____

🔑🔑🔑🔑 2 free books plus a mystery gift	🔑🔑🗝🗝 1 free book
🔑🔑🔑🗝 2 free books	🔑🗝🗝🗝 Try Again!

DETACH AND MAIL CARD TODAY!

The Silhouette Reader Service™ — Here's how it works:

Accepting your 2 free books and gift places you under no obligation to buy anything. You may keep the books and gift and return the shipping statement marked "cancel." If you do not cancel, about a month later we'll send you 6 additional novels and bill you just $3.57 each in the U.S., or $3.96 each in Canada, plus 25¢ delivery per book and applicable taxes if any.* That's the complete price and — compared to cover prices of $4.25 each in the U.S. and $4.75 each in Canada — it's quite a bargain! You may cancel at any time, but if you choose to continue, every month we'll send you 6 more books, which you may either purchase at the discount price or return to us and cancel your subscription.

*Terms and prices subject to change without notice. Sales tax applicable in N.Y. Canadian residents will be charged applicable provincial taxes and GST.

If offer card is missing write to: Silhouette Reader Service, 3010 Walden Ave., P.O. Box 1867, Buffalo, NY 14240-1867

BUSINESS REPLY MAIL
FIRST-CLASS MAIL   PERMIT NO. 717   BUFFALO, NY

POSTAGE WILL BE PAID BY ADDRESSEE

SILHOUETTE READER SERVICE
3010 WALDEN AVE
PO BOX 1867
BUFFALO NY 14240-9952

NO POSTAGE
NECESSARY
IF MAILED
IN THE
UNITED STATES

reminded Cardenas. "Why don't you give them the use of one of the guest houses?"

"I think that's a very good idea," Cardenas agreed with a wide, warm smile. "You will accept my hospitality," he spoke to Tiger. "The shops, the restaurants—everything you and your young lady's hearts desire. We'll talk after you've had your 'honeymoon.' There's no hurry, I assure you. I think you and I will have a long association, Mr. Rafferty. Consider my hospitality a perk of the job, if you wish."

"I'm a man who likes getting the job done," Tiger responded.

Cardenas waved his words away. "In a day or two. My interest in doing business with you won't dissipate. Consider this a reward for ridding Isla Sebastian of Ibarra's unstable influence."

Tiger's impatience was palpable to Hope. She stood and put her hand in Tiger's, squeezing meaningfully. "Please Tiger, can we?"

His eyes were furious when he looked at her, but his expression was indulgent. "I'd love to, sweetheart, but you know how I am about business."

She felt the tension in him, muscles corded and strung with it. His frustration sang to her, but turning down Cardenas's offer would not be good strategy. Cardenas was engaging in high-level corporate recruiting tactics. She recognized that, had the background to see it, but Tiger didn't. She repeated, "Please, Tiger. Think about how much more efficient you'll be after you've rested for a while. How much more focused. Mr. Cardenas understands that."

He had the sense not to protest further. "Sure," he said, and kissed her on the cheek. He put his arm around her as he addressed Cardenas. "I appreciate your thoughtfulness, sir."

"Think nothing of it." Cardenas waved Tiger and Hope toward the door. "You'll be shown to the guest accommodations. My only requirement is that you enjoy yourselves for the next couple of days." With that dismissal he turned his attention back to the uninvited, but obviously welcome, Estaban Quarrels.

Couple of days. The words echoed dismally in Tiger' ears. He understood that this was some sort of test Cardena had set him. Something to do with patience, maybe. Something to do with character? His personal relationships? Wa the man behaving more like a corporate recruiter than crime lord? All he could do was go along with it. Any more show of stubbornness would not get him into the man' confidence.

A couple of days. Alone. With Hope Harrison. Lor knew what would become of the fragile threads of duty an responsibility that kept him from making passionate love to her. He feared they'd get frayed past the breaking point He also knew he was trapped in a situation any other ma would consider paradise. There was nothing he could do but fight his own erotic urges while seeming to be a devote lover. He called that hell. For a couple of days.

Chapter 9

"This is ridiculous."

Hope held the vividly yellow silk dress up in front of her as she stood in front of the three-way mirror, and said, "You're right. Not my color." Even though she knew very well that Tiger was talking to himself.

She could see Tiger's reflection in the mirror. He stood a few feet behind her, arms crossed, gaze shifting restlessly all over the brightly decorated store. He looked about as out of place as a tiger at the opera. She doubted the manager would have let them in the door of the shop if they hadn't been accompanied by Mr. Morris.

Maria followed Cardenas's orders by calling Mr. Morris, who had driven up to Cardenas's private residence a few minutes later in an aqua Land Rover automobile. He introduced himself as the general manager of the resort complex. He was polite, and enthusiastic about making their stay perfect, and as romantic as possible. He had beamed with the beatitude of a guardian angel in Bermuda shorts,

and brought them to the resort's shopping complex while
chatting amiably about all the magnificent activities he
could arrange for them. They were Mr. Cardenas's guests,
and nothing was too good for them, nothing too much trouble! But first, of course, they had to refresh their wardrobes,
and what a pity all their luggage had been lost during the
storms!

Hope had no idea how Mr. Morris came to the conclusion that they were victims of the lost luggage demons, but
neither she nor Tiger tried to correct this assumption.
Who'd believe the truth, even if Tiger let her tell it, anyway? The truth, of course, would not set one free in this
instance, but get one killed.

That was why she'd let Tiger keep his arm around her
on the drive here, why she'd snuggled close, and practically
purred when he'd dropped a kiss on her cheek or temple
every few moments. Why she'd put her hand on his thigh,
and on his throat and smiled up into his icy cold, hard eyes.
While his hands were busy playing the lover's game, his
heart wasn't in it, and his mind was certainly elsewhere.
She reacted to all those false kisses, caresses and hugs as
though they were real. What her mind knew her body did
not. Which made her body very foolish indeed, and she
wasn't going to listen to it when she had far more interesting things with which to pass her time.

Shopping in a very exclusive boutique, for example. One
where everything on the racks carried a designer label, and
a price tag she would have laughed hysterically at back
home in Baltimore—and she wasn't exactly a poor woman.

"Though I would be soon if I paid full price for things
like this," she murmured as she glanced at the tag on the
dress in her hands. She hung the short, sleeveless bit of silk
back on the clothes rack and chose a similar style, in ice
blue. "What do you think of this one, Tiger? Better?"

"What are you talking about?" He stopped his surreptitious perusal of the other customers in the shop long enough to frown at her. "What are you doing?"

"Shopping," she responded. "I don't exactly have my American Express card with me, but if Mr. Cardenas is going to pick up the tab, I'm happy to spruce up my wardrobe. Such as it is," she added, with a tug on her T-shirt. "This thing needs to be burned, before it walks out of here on its own." She pointed toward the other side of the large shop. "Men's wear is over there."

She seemed to be having a good time, which annoyed him no end. Didn't she know they were in danger? His nerves were frayed, and his patience exhausted, and the little show of affection they'd put on in the Land Rover had done nothing but irritate the need he couldn't satisfy. It was bad enough he couldn't get the woman off his mind, but this forced affection was killing him!

It had been a show, right? "Can we get out of here?" he complained to her. "Dear?"

"Soon," she replied. "Darling." She spoke the endearment in a tone so sweet it made his teeth ache. "I need to try a few things on first. So do you." She pointed again. "I see some club shirts that you'd look sexy in." She gave him a perky little smirking smile. "I want you to go try them on for me right now. Baby."

He wanted to strangle her. It was so tempting to put his hands around her long, slender neck... Okay, maybe he wanted to do something with his hands around her besides strangle her, but the glint in her eyes was *so* irritating. Why was she having such a good time? When had the captive, frightened and rebellious by turns young woman developed a wicked sense of humor? Maybe it was the setting, he surmised. She had to be more comfortable and sure of herself in a setting that was seemingly more civilized and safe.

He could only hope that she remembered that there was more danger here in the lap of luxury than there had been in the slums on the other side of the island. Right now there was no overt way he could reinforce the need for discretion.

All he could do was smile stiffly back and say, "Sure. Honey. Anything for you." He turned toward the men's section of the shop, figuring that the sooner they both picked up a change of clothes, the sooner they'd be out of here. He desperately needed to get Hope alone.

To talk to her. Only to talk to her.

Right. And what the devil was a club shirt?

Hope watched Tiger move across the room with a lithe speed that should have been impossible among the rows of crowded racks and shelves—but, then, he was a tiger, after all. She smiled slightly at the thought, and reminded herself to stop having fond thoughts of the man. She had to make a deliberate effort to turn her attention back to making her own selections rather than surreptitiously watching her counterfeit lover. Every now and then she found herself glancing Tiger's way, but that was all. She firmly fought down the urge to march across the room and pick out his wardrobe for him.

However, once, she did let herself call out, "Black is not the only color in the world. Darling." In response to his vicious glare, she added, "It's not even technically a color—no matter how sexy you look in it." He grumbled, but put the black shirt down and picked up a white one. He gave her an irritated, questioning look. Hope gave him an approving nod, and went back to what she'd been doing before interrupting Tiger's shopping.

He got his revenge a few minutes later by presenting her with a negligee so filmy it might as well have been invisible. "You'd look great wearing this. Briefly. Sweetheart."

Hope went hot all over with embarrassment, but responded easily to the teasing look in Tiger's eyes. "That is not an item of clothing," she informed him coolly. "It is plastic wrap."

"It's blue. Plastic wrap doesn't come in blue."

"You don't spend a lot of time in kitchens do you?"

"You shouldn't, either. Baby." He held the nightgown up to her shoulders. "I can hardly wait to see you in bed in this."

"Does the term *when hell freezes over* have meaning for you?" she whispered, viciously, but very quietly, back. Actually, for a piece of fluff and lace that weighed less than a handkerchief but was less useful, the nightie was a pretty thing. Tiger was certainly right about its only being meant to be worn briefly.

"We're honeymooning," he answered, in a tone meant to reach the ears of anyone nearby. "You don't want to sleep in that old T-shirt on our honeymoon, do you?"

"Darling," she added for him.

"Darling." Tiger didn't know what devil of mischief had suddenly taken possession of him, but he didn't suppose it hurt for him to get into the spirit of the charade. Besides, the look on Hope's face was priceless. And she really would look good—briefly—in the blue nightgown.

Having selected some clothing for himself he'd followed Hope into the unknown territory of the women's underwear section of the store. He hadn't been able to resist teasing her by picking up the first item that came to hand. That it turned out to be a sexy little nightgown that he really would like to see on her disturbed his sense of duty only a little. He was a man, and he wanted this woman very much. He wasn't going to act on the longing, but it was a little late to try to hide from the desire that sang between them now. Maybe accepting it would help control it, since efforts to deny it in the past several days had only ended up in episodes of very nearly giving in to it.

It. What a euphemistic, neutral word for the emotion that raged through him. Was desire even an emotion? *Desire* was a pretty tame, civilized word too, when what he really was thinking was that she made him so horny it was driving him crazy. Maybe that's what the mood that had overtaken him was. He was crazy from suffering from all sorts of frustrations—the job, the woman.

"Stress," he muttered. "You're driving me crazy," he added. He saw by the sharp look of annoyance and hurt in her eyes that Hope didn't take this as a compliment. "I meant," he waved the nightgown at her. "You would. In this."

"Fine," she said, and snatched it out of his hands, eyes blazing with challenge. "I will."

"Oh, no you won't!" He declared, panicking at what he knew would happen if he did see her wearing that sexy little thing. He stepped forward, intending to take it from her, but Mr. Morris came up to them before he could.

The resort manager smiled obsequiously at them. "Made your selections, I see. Good." With brisk, professional cheerfulness, he deftly took what they carried from them. "Of course you picked out bathing suits? And you have a cocktail dress. Good. I'll have these sent to your residence. Now," he said, focusing his smile on Hope. "Time for your spa treatment. I know you don't want to be away from each other for long." He cast a coy glance at Tiger, then looked back at Hope. "So I've arranged for you to spend the rest of the afternoon having a massage and facial. And getting your hair and makeup done for a romantic dinner, together, of course. Alisa," he called, and a young woman hurried over from behind the counter in the front of the shop.

"Yes, Mr. Morris?"

He gestured toward Hope. "Please take this young lady to the Island Spa. We'll make sure there's something nice for you to wear when you're all finished," he confided sotto voce to Hope.

"Thank you," she responded.

"Spa?" Tiger asked. He moved to Hope's side and put his hand on her shoulder. "I don't think so. We'd rather go to our room, and rest," Tiger said, attempting to draw Hope toward the door. "We don't want to be any more trouble than we've already been."

"You," Morris declared firmly, "are our guests." He looked hurt that anyone would decline the delights and pampering the place had to offer.

Hope slipped out from Tiger's grasp on her shoulder. "But, sweetheart, I'd love to try the spa," she said, looking up at him with a show of teasing devotion. She ran her fingers along his jaw, made her voice throaty with promise. "You won't be disappointed." She didn't know what devil had gotten into her, but if it helped keep the grief and fear at bay to act on her resentment of being used by Tiger Rafferty in this way, she saw no reason not to go with it. Teasing him like this was harmless revenge for the way he was manipulating her and ordering her around. Maybe if he'd asked her nicely to go along with the charade that they were lovers before they'd entered Cardenas's house she'd have complied without this aching knot of anger influencing her every move. Maybe if he hadn't tried to make their being in danger out as somehow being her fault... Well, he'd done what he'd done. She hurt because of it. He could live with her response to the pain. This wasn't lashing out, or acting out; it was doing what she had to, to retain some self-respect, to emotionally survive.

"I'm going for that facial. And the massage."

"I can always give you a massage," he answered. His tone was sultry, his eyes were furious.

"But can you do my hair? How about a manicure?"

"Your claws could definitely use trimming," he conceded.

"I'm not the one called Tiger," she answered back.

Tiger noticed Mr. Morris watching this byplay with a friendly, but fixed smile. He supposed his and Hope's bickering *might* look suspicious, might not sound genuinely romantic, might be reported back to Cardenas. The last thing Tiger wanted was for Cardenas to suspect him in any way. Hope's reckless behavior was making him equally reckless. He had to stop responding and start thinking, not let her get to him. Somehow. He stepped back and looked her over. She was scruffy, and wearing dirty rags, but those rags showed off firm, lovely skin, sexy curves and long, elegant legs. Her very existence was a walking, talking, tempting provocation. The fiery look in her eyes drew him like a suicidal moth. And angered him as well. He shouldn't blame her because he desired her, but he did.

He could blame her, and did, for her sudden turn of uninhibited teasing wildness. This was no time for rebellion. He didn't know what she was capable of doing in this mood. She hadn't yet mentioned Santiago's name, but it could slip out as easily by accident as by design. She hadn't yet done anything to dispel the illusion that they were simply a pair of devoted lovers. He couldn't risk letting her spend any time at this spa. He did not want to let her out of his sight for a moment. He didn't want to trust her.

"Why don't we go to our room and share the shower, sweetheart?" he coaxed. "We can get cleaned up there, then come back to the dining room for a candlelight dinner." He edged close to her and rested his hands on her hips. His touch sent a heated shiver through her. "It'll be romantic. I promise."

Hope smiled as she looked into Tiger's hard eyes. His touch was gentle, but uncompromisingly firm, stirring unwanted arousal that she had to use her resentment to fight off. Her smile was for Morris's sake. The wicked edge to it was for herself. She knew exactly what Tiger was thinking. That he couldn't trust her to do or say something stupid. That he didn't dare let her out of his sight—for her own good, but mostly for his. She might do something foolish that would break his cover, put his life and assignment at risk. How dare he assume she didn't have the brains God gave a gimlet!

That had been one of her aunt's pithy sayings. She wasn't quite sure what it meant. She was only sure that she'd never see her aunt alive again. She knew she shouldn't blame Tiger for that, but she did.

Not enough to get him killed, though. Surely he had to understand that. And that she was no fool. But he didn't, and she'd make him pay in a way they'd both survive for misjudging her so badly.

She put her hands on his broad shoulders and gently pushed Tiger away. "Don't be so possessive. I won't be gone that long. Think how beautiful I'll be for you when I come back from the spa. Can you remember the last time you saw me beautiful?" she added.

It occurred to her that Tiger had never seen her looking even vaguely attractive, in a dress and makeup, wearing jewelry and with her hair done. For a brief moment the notion of appearing beautiful to him took on immense importance to her. She wondered what she'd see in his eyes when she walked into a room looking like a woman rather than a drowned and dirty rat. Would the warmth of his smile catch fire between them? Would he take her in his arms with tenderness and respect rather than the exciting rough neediness she'd experienced from him so far? Foolish as it was, she ached to know if taking care to look beautiful for him would make a difference in how he treated her, reacted to her.

She'd been told that she had poise and style, that she was attractive. Of course those compliments had been paid to her by her cheating, manipulating ex-boyfriend. She mentally pushed thoughts of Mark out of her mind, but they left a dark feeling nonetheless. What difference did it make what Tiger thought, how he reacted? This wasn't about being pretty for him. This was about taking care of herself—and getting a little harmless revenge.

And getting clean. She very much wanted to get clean. So much so that she almost gave in to his suggestion that they share a long, hot, private shower. Lord, but that was tempting! She could almost feel the heat of the water rushing over them, his hands caressing her soap-sleek body, her hands working the scented lather across his chest and down the hard muscles of his stomach. She'd never made love in the shower, but she could easily imagine how it would be, with her back against the smooth, wet, heated tiles, her legs wrapped around Tiger's lean hips as the water steamed over and around them....

Good, Lord! Where did that fantasy come from? From the feel of him touching her, she supposed. The point was that she had no intention of making love to this man, wasn't it? They were simply playing pretend lovers. Working undercover. So to speak. And there was nothing simple about it. He was too big, too close, too much *there* for her to think straight, get herself under control. She had to get away from him! Not escape. She wasn't so foolish as to try that again. Despite being guests at a fabulous luxury resort, she was well aware that they were also prisoners in a guarded compound. Nothing was as it seemed, hadn't been for a long time. She desperately wanted her life to be simple again, but right now she would settle for a few minutes alone to think about the situation logically, to get her head on straight. And her hair washed.

Hope pushed Tiger's hands away. Tiger Rafferty could not have everything his way. Time for him to learn that. She turned determinedly to the waiting resort manager. "He'll go with you now, Mr. Morris. Go," she commanded firmly, and shook her head when Tiger would have argued further. He finally responded to the adamant look in her eyes and shuffled after Morris. After giving her one more stern warning look.

Hope smiled at the image she presented when she entered the glass-walled entrance of the very ritzy spa. Rather like a beggar at a banquet, or a crow suddenly appearing amid a flock of snowy doves. Needless to say, people looked at her a little strangely when she stepped out of the warmth of the tropical day to the pristine, air-conditioned perfection within. The place was all cool white marble, gold trim and extravagantly bright tropical flowers in crystal vases. The staff members who came forward as soon as she opened the door were dressed in short white smocks over aqua shirts and khaki shorts. The guests waiting in the wide lobby were mostly thin women who showed off their well-toned bodies in designer bikinis. The sight of them was enough to make her feel not only grubby, but inadequately endowed, and flabby besides.

She sighed, and said to a young woman in the white smock, "Do what you can with me."

"I'm Joanie."

"Hi," Hope responded, sounding forlorn. "I'm hopeless...Hope.'' Blast! She hadn't used that lame joke in years! "Hope Harrison."

"Let me be the judge of that, if you please, Ms. Harrison," was Joanie's answer.

Joanie looked Hope over from bruised toes to storm-combed hair, took in the stained, torn clothes, and finally met Hope's anxious gaze. She shook her head and tsked. Several other spa employees had gathered around Hope by this time.

After what was only a few seconds, but seemed like hours, Joanie looked at the other white-smocked staffers clustered around Hope and said with a wide grin, "Somebody get this woman a piña colada and a crab sandwich! This is going to take a while," she said, and took Hope by the arm. "Fortunately," she confided to Hope as she led her out of the lobby, "we *love* a challenge around here. I'm taking you on myself, Ms. Harrison. Get me a piña colada while you're at it," she directed the young woman who jumped smartly to obey. "You do like crab sandwiches, I hope, Hope?"

Hope's stomach rumbled happily at the mention of food. She inquired cautiously anyway, "Are they bland?"

Joanie laughed. "Nothing stronger than a little cracked black pepper."

"Thank goodness! I'll have a dozen, please."

"You look like you've been living on island food for a few days, and I know what that can do to you."

"How can you tell?" Hope answered as they reached a pink-curtained changing room. The curtains were made of heavy brocade. Hope wanted to stroke the rich material, and was half-ashamed to even touch it in her current state.

"You've got that kind of feisty look women get from eating all that spice," Joanie told her, and patted her on the arm. "There's an aphrodisiac in it, I think. Either that, or you're in love," she added with a wicked laugh.

"Must be the spice," Hope told her quickly. Denial rushed through her, and a hot flush rose on her skin at the very notion of being in love. Tiger Rafferty's image filled her mind—handsome, arrogant, sensual. The memory of his demanding kisses, the taste of them, filled her mouth. It was as if she could feel the touch of his hands all over her, and the heat of reaction simmered deep inside her. "Lust," she murmured. "Definitely in lust." She would have happily denied even that, but it was the wicked truth. Besides, she remembered, coming to her senses, she was *supposed* to be feigning that she was deeply, rapturously in love with the gunrunning outlaw. Which made her his moll, she supposed. "Love seems like such a weak word for what Tiger and I have," she added, for the curious Joanie's sake. Her words *were* meant for the sake of the masquerade, weren't they? "Make me beautiful for Tiger," she added with what she hoped sounded like fervent adoration, in case, somehow, someone was listening in on her conversation with the other woman.

Joanie patted her shoulder, handed her a robe of soft turquoise satin, and pointed her toward the curtained changing room. "I'm going to make you so beautiful your Tiger's eyes are going to pop out," she promised. "First, though, trash the refugee look and let's work on getting you beautiful for you."

Hope closed her eyes for a moment, sighing as images of the pampering to come danced in her head. She wanted to forget everything for a while—death, terror, revenge, even Tiger Rafferty—and simply let herself relax. "Oh, I like the sound of that."

Hope deliberately put the heartache of grief and guilt that threatened to rise up and overwhelm her aside. She'd had her private space to grieve the night before…had it only been the night before? No matter what else she might think of Tiger Rafferty, she'd always be grateful to the man who'd held her in nonjudgmental silence while she cried her heart out—right now she had the roll of gangster's adoring girlfriend to play with as much enthusiasm as she could muster. Plus, she wanted to get her hair washed, and a manicure, and shave her legs, and that massage she'd been promised, and the sandwiches and icy drink to sustain her through it all. So, no crying for her! Not until she somehow got home to Baltimore, and the quiet, uneventful, empty life she told herself her truly dull soul craved.

She went into the changing room, stripped off her soiled clothes and wrapped herself in body-caressing satin. Her reflection in the changing room mirror looked anything but dull. There was a wildness about the woman who looked back at her that made the gangster's girlfriend image seem like the real Hope, and not the woman she had been a few days ago. This woman didn't look like she was wearing a reckless adventuress's mask, but was the genuine article. Hope laughed at the notion, told herself it was her overheated imagination, and threw back the curtain.

"I'm all yours," she announced happily to Joanie. "Do your worst!"

It was early evening by the time Joanie's staff declared laughingly that there was nothing more they could do with her. "That's it!" Joanie announced as Hope studied her transformed reflection one last time in the gold-tinted mirror behind the desk in the spa's reception room. "Get out of here," Joanie ordered, gesturing toward the glass doors with a flick of her hand. She laughed wickedly. "Our job is finished here. You're on your own with your Tiger now."

Her Tiger.

The world spun around her, reality shifting in and out, then in again. Hope gripped the edge of the desk hard, forgetting to breathe for a moment as images, heady and dangerous flooded through her mind. Hot, needy reaction raced through her blood and bones and senses in instant response to those images. Once she walked out those tall glass doors she was indeed on her own with a tiger. In a private honeymoon suite. Just the two of them. Alone.

They'd been alone before, and in bed together. And every time had been a more dangerous encounter. She could feel his hands on her now, his mouth, and hers on his. They'd come closer with each kiss to falling over the edge of desire that drew them inexorably to each other. All the anger and mistrust between them didn't stop the desire. You didn't have to *like* someone to be attracted to them. He was a using, manipulating, arrogant, denizen of a world where she didn't belong. She hated him. But she wanted him. This place had been a sanctuary where she'd put that wanting on hold for a while. Now she'd have to go out those doors and play a lover's game with Tiger Rafferty as her costar, and fight giving in to the wanting in circumstances that were just going to make the temptation worse.

She looked down at the peach silk top that outlined her breasts and trim waist, and at the ankle-length broomstick skirt that swirled mysteriously around her long legs. She recalled that she'd picked the warm color because it showed off her tan. She glanced at her perfectly made-up face in the mirror behind Joanie, noted how it skillfully emphasized her cheekbones and large eyes, and somehow made her mouth sultry and seductive. She caught an enticing whiff of the spicy perfume that had been dabbed on her wrists and throat and behind her ears.

What had she been thinking of! Was she crazy?

Didn't matter. It was too late to demand her mud-stained

shorts and T-shirt back now. Too late to ask if she could hide out here for a few days. She'd started this game of playing devoted lovers.

What she had to do now was go out and act her part and not let herself fall into believing that it was real. She most definitely was not going to let herself fall into bed with Tiger Rafferty. He'd used her. He was not to be trusted. She might look the part, but she was not his sort of woman at all—didn't have an adventurous bone in her body. He led a glamorous life, but one she had no business being entangled in. Temptation was one thing. Give in to it? Surely she was stronger than that.

She made herself smile at Joanie while her mind continued to race with thoughts of another night with Tiger despite all her logical arguments against it. "I'm off," she announced, and waved airily with more enthusiasm than she felt. She went, past the staff of the open-twenty-four-hours-a-day luxury spa, and a waiting room full of a new group of customers in designer bikinis. No one paid her much mind on the way out.

No one, that is, except the broad-shouldered man by the door. She noticed him not just because he was a male in a haven of femininity, but because of the sunglasses he wore indoors, at night. And because of the sport jacket worn over a brightly flowered shirt. And because his head turned to follow her as she walked past him. Chances were the man was the husband of a customer waiting for his wife to finish her treatment, and the jacket he wore was because he was dressed to go to dinner in one of the resort's more formal dining rooms. Maybe he looked at her because she was a not unattractive female dressed in an outfit that was meant to show her off at her best.

Or maybe there was a gun concealed by his jacket. Maybe he was one of Cardenas's goons set to watch her and Tiger's movements. She told herself she was being too paranoid, that if Cardenas was going to have her and Tiger watched, it would be done in a indirect way. This man was probably perfectly innocent, but his presence was a shocking reminder to her of the true danger in this place. Hope still didn't allow herself more than one swift glance at the man as she walked out the door.

All she wanted to do now was rush back to the dangerous safety offered to her in the arms of Tiger Rafferty.

Chapter 10

There were orchids everywhere. Great swathes of living, exotic blossoms in a hundred shades of purple and waxy-white, pinks and greens and scarlet hung from the high ceiling, climbed up gold-and-marble pillars, and framed the arched windows that looked out onto the water. The tiled floors were done in an orchid mosaic pattern. The walls were painted in frescos of giant orchids, the table linens were all in delicate shades of orchid purple. Fresh orchids in crystal vases adorned the center of each table. The watery, ephemeral scent of orchids perfumed the air. If the overall effect hadn't been so unique and beautiful it might have been quite overwhelming.

There's nothing subtle about orchids, Hope decided as she gazed around the flower-bedecked dining room. Orchids were the most frankly sexual flower creation had ever come up with, the folds and layers of their shapes nothing short of gloriously erotic and quite happy to blatantly point out to any passing pollinator that their function was strictly of the reproductive variety.

"It's enough to make a human blush," she murmured. She took a sip from a long-stemmed glass of wine a waitress dressed in pale purple had brought her. Then again, she reminded herself, it was humans who saw sexual symbolism wherever they looked. Orchids didn't pay humans any mind, it was the humans who made the value judgments. Humans had sex on the brain. All the time. "Well, some of us do," she added with a sigh, and confessed to herself that she certainly did.

It was the setting, she explained her mood, as she found herself glancing toward the entrance once more. There was an intimate feel to this room, despite the size of the place. A deliberately sensual suggestiveness. All the tables were meant only for two occupants to sit close together, placed so that pillars, trellises and the draping sprays of flowers provided each couple with a measure of privacy. Candlelight and soft, indirect lighting added to the intimate feel. The view outside the windows was utterly romantic. At the moment the sky was orchid pink and purple in the west, shading to indigo overhead. The sea was calm and slate-gray, with hints of sunset-copper thrown up in the spray as waves washed gently onto the shore.

At another time, Hope knew, she could have been content merely to watch the wash of the waves for hours. Right now, though, she could barely spare a glance for the beauty outside the windows. All she wanted was to see Tiger Rafferty walking through the door. A few hours ago all she'd wanted was to escape from his overwhelmingly commanding, thoroughly male presence. Maybe forever. She thought she'd be able to think straight away from him, to get him out of her head. Now, even though she resented him, she still found that she missed him.

Why? She asked herself the question with a certain de-
gree of sarcasm. Why? Because she'd had a little fright on
her way out of the spa a few minutes ago? The staff here
in the dining room had been nothing but solicitous, effi-
ciently getting her seated at this secluded little table, telling
her that Mr. Rafferty would be joining her soon. The waitress had provided the wineglass with a warm smile. While
the wait staff was attentive, the other couples at their secluded tables paid no attention to Hope. There was nothing
ominous or sinister about the Orchid Room. In fact, the
atmosphere was even more relaxing than in the Island Spa.

Or maybe it was the wine that was so relaxing, Hope
conceded as she took another tiny sip. Why was she so
anxious to lay eyes on Tiger? She couldn't stop her ironic
smile at the question. Memory and anticipation joined inside her, forming an almost physical ache to be with him,
forcing out irony and all sense of emotional distance from
the subject of Tiger Rafferty. It was that overwhelmingly
male thing he had going, she supposed. Her reaction to him
was totally female, as blatantly sexual as the appearance of
the orchids all around her. Her smile turned into an angry
frown at the thought. She didn't know whether to be more
annoyed with him or herself because of her visceral response to Tiger's animal allure.

"Tiger indeed," she whispered, and took another sip of
wine. She narrowed her eyes as she glared at the doorway.

The entrance to the Orchid Room was guarded by a vigilant, attentive maître'd, who turned and looked up as a
very tall man appeared by his side. For an instant Hope
didn't recognize the long-limbed, broad-shouldered man
dressed in a tab-collared shirt of crisp white cotton and dark
slacks, face smoothly shaved and thick brown hair combed
back off his forehead.

Her suddenly racing heart recognized him, as did the

sudden singeing heat in her blood. Hope stared, started to rise as he walked toward her. She had trouble taking a breath as she watched him move lithely forward, yet she heard herself whisper, almost worshipfully, "Tiger!"

Hearing the tone of her voice made her furious, at herself because of her reaction to him, at being caught unaware by it. At him for daring to clean up better-looking than a man like him had any right to! The one thing she did not want Tiger Rafferty to be was even handsomer than she thought he was.

It was even more disconcerting to notice that he didn't look out of place in this exotic setting. He simply looked more male.

While she didn't have her racing pulse quieted by the time he reached her, she managed to get under enough control to keep from jumping up and throwing her arms around his wide shoulders. Then she recalled that they were *supposed* to be lovers, and thought better of controlling her impulses.

At least when she stood up and moved eagerly into his embrace, she did it knowing it was necessary for this undercover lover's game they played. That didn't change the fact that she *wanted* to do it. Didn't change the prick of pain in her soul and the bruise to her pride at knowing how very professional he was at playing games.

The last thing she expected Tiger to say was, "You smell *so* good!" Or for those words to sound so genuinely full of pleasure and surprise.

The ripple of delight that spread through Hope was also a surprise. She very nearly preened with happiness. She did draw him into a tighter embrace as one hand moved up to brush fingers through the thick, soft hair that brushed against the back of his neck. "You're gorgeous," she said, and meant it. And he smelled good, too!

Gorgeous? He was gorgeous? Tiger didn't know about that, but the word more than applied to Hope Harrison at the moment. He hadn't needed the maître'd to show him which table she was at to find her in this dim and overdec- orated room. Her presence glowed like a beacon to him, would have drawn him to her even if the place had been pitch-black. He didn't know why this was so, but he didn't question, at least for this moment, that his heart had found her.

He simply held her close and reveled in the feel of the perfect fit of her body pressed to his. He luxuriated in the way her hair softly tickled his cheek, in the warmth of her skin, in the way the fresh scent of her skin mixed with the sensual allure of her perfume. His hand slid over the smooth silk of her clothing, molding the long, elegant con- tours of her back. She was perfect and beautiful and…

"I missed you," he told her, and it was the absolute truth. He forgot to be angry with her, forgot his resentment. For the moment, in this time and place, at the sight of her, he let Tiger Rafferty go.

Besides, if they had to play this lover's game, he might as well let himself enjoy it, even if only for a few hours. Santiago was a danger, but he wasn't on the island right now. Cardenas's attention was on his business with Quar- rels. That they were being watched he had no doubt, that any out-of-character behavior would be reported was a given, but as long they did nothing unexpected they were safe enough. Or so Michael tried to make Tiger believe. Michael wanted to relax, to be himself, and he had the upper hand right now.

I will take care of you, he silently promised as he made himself let Hope go. She smiled up at him as he stepped back. Her ardent expression melted his heart. His breath caught at the sight of her, and he decided to pretend for a little while that everything they said and did wasn't undercover acting.

She had wonderful, big, expressive eyes, he noticed as he took the other chair and she sat down very close to him. He took her hands across the narrow width of the table and got lost looking into those wide blue eyes.

"Hi," he heard himself say at last, with no idea how much time had passed.

"Hi," she answered, and somehow these monosyllables were adequate enough communication for a while longer. He was aware of her hands in his, of running his thumbs slowly, repetitively across the backs of them, of her practically purring in response to this slight, insistent touch. This small, intimate contact was enough for a while as well. Great emotion communicated by the merest contact, the smallest movement of sensitive skin sliding across receptive skin.

For the longest time Hope found herself utterly fascinated by the smallest details of Tiger's face, memorizing the perfect width and tilt of his cheekbones, the exact warm-brown shade of his tanned complexion. She appreciated how the bright-white shirt contrasted with the brown of his skin, and the way the color of his skin enhanced the blue of his eyes. When he smiled his eyes narrowed, and the skin around his eyes crinkled in laugh lines. He smiled now, adding the beguiling charm of dimples to his handsome features. There was nothing boyish in his smile, nothing safe. It was a rakish kind of charm that beckoned her in, promised and teased, and definitely pleased. He looked as good in candlelight as he did in the bright island sun. Shadows suited the sharp angles and length of his face.

He touched her gently, the slow sensual movement seductive and comforting at once. Arousing, in a slowly building way as time slowed down and her awareness grad-

ually focused in on nothing but the growing arousal in his
eyes the way he way he was touching her.

Who knew what might have happened next if the waitress hadn't stopped in front of the table and said, "May I
bring you a glass of house wine, sir?"

Tiger felt intoxicated enough, but he managed, after the
first wrenching shock of returning to the real world to turn
his head and look at the young woman who had dared to
interrupt them. "Yes," he told the smiling waitress. He
somehow politely returned her smile. "Thank you."

"I'll be back with your wine. Here are your menus,"
she added, and handed one to each of them.

They had to stop holding hands to take the large lami-
nated sheets. Hope was devastated when his hands parted
from hers, the sudden loneliness bringing almost physical
pain. After an instant, she smiled, and shook her head. "Get
a grip, girl," she murmured, then peeked over the top of
the long menu to meet Tiger's gaze once more. She
laughed, and so did he, and Hope had no doubt that they'd
shared the same bracing reaction to it.

"Lobster," she said after making herself read the menu
rather than continue to stare at Tiger.

"'The claws that grip, the something that bites…'" Tiger misquoted.

"There's no Jabberwock on the menu," she replied to
his reference to the Lewis Carroll poem. "Or were you
talking about something else? Handholding, perhaps?"

"Lobster," he answered. "Lobster claws always remind
me of that poem."

He read poetry. Well, well. Interesting. She wondered if
she should tease him about that. "I love *Alice in Wonder-
land*," she told him.

Tiger gave a one-shouldered shrug. "Never actually read
it," he admitted.

"Oh."

"But I read the poem in high school." He sounded defensive. He ducked his head behind the menu again. "You read a lot don't you?" he said from behind its shelter.

She hated for him to think she was an intellectual when she was far from being one. "Not as much as I should," she answered. "I like fantasy novels, and high-tech thrillers—saving the world from terrorists sorts of things."

"Tom Clancy?" he asked, still from behind the menu.

She peeked over the top of hers. "Love his older stuff."

"Me, too."

Hope was both amazed and pleased by their suddenly sharing a little bit about themselves with each other. Finding common ground with him as a person was *important* to her, though she told herself it shouldn't be. "What are you going to have?" she asked him.

"Steak," he answered promptly.

"Of course. How about the baked brie appetizer?"

He made a face at her suggestion. "French onion soup."

She lowered the menu and raised a sardonic eyebrow at him as the waitress approached. "Onions? Darling?"

Tiger laughed, and put the menu down on the table. "Onions," he insisted. "Sweet pea."

"You'll regret this," she told him, putting every bit of seductiveness she could in her voice.

Tiger leaned forward, a wicked grin on his face. "Bat your eyelashes like that at me anymore and I'm going to kiss you silly."

"I don't do silly," she answered. This teasing threat sent her head spinning, affecting her far more than the wine she'd been drinking.

"You will when I'm done with you."

"Oh, yeah?"

His hand touched her shoulder, then slid up to trace his fingers around her ear and down her jawline. "Yeah."

The gesture and the promising glint in his eyes sent a warm shiver all through her. Heat settled and pulsed deep inside her. Hope sighed. She capitulated. "Okay, have the soup. But I still don't do silly."

The waitress did not comment on Hope's comment as she returned to the table, but Hope saw her smile. "Decided?" she asked them instead. Hope made no objection when Tiger assumed the traditional male prerogative of ordering for them both, though she was amazed at how many dishes he did order.

"We'll never be able to eat all that!" she protested when the waitress was gone.

"We?" he asked innocently. "Oh, did you want to eat, too?"

It wasn't a particularly funny or original joke, but Hope giggled anyway. Giggled. She did not normally giggle. Maybe the man was capable of making her act silly, after all. She tried to resent such light-headed behavior, but instead found it a welcome relief after all the pain, terror and tension of the last several days. Instead of being annoyed, she found herself looking at him with astounded gratitude for something so simple as making her laugh. There was a wary tiredness still deep in the man's eyes that told her that he could use a few laughs himself.

Over the next two hours she found herself trying to return the favor. They laughed, and talked as dinner came and wineglasses were refilled and soft music played in the background. Their low-voiced conversation ranged over safe topics, neither of them ever completely forgetting that this seeming privacy was really being played out in a public place. They kept the subjects light and neutral, getting to know each other in a surface sort of way. They spoke of movies and music and sports. For some reason he was surprised to discover she was an enthusiastic basketball fan. She tried in vain to understand why baseball, especially as played by Detroit's team, held a major fascination for him. They discussed the weather, and he told her the history of the island as he'd learned it from Father Felipe.

And he touched her, in the casual, familiar, possessive, intimate way of a lover. Light caresses on her hand, her arm, her cheek; a finger drawn lingeringly along her collarbone; a touch on the lips as he emphasized a point; a tap on the tip of her nose as he laughed at something she said. Hope didn't know if Tiger was aware of what he did, but she was deeply aware of the electric jolts of need that flashed through her with each brief contact. They took her breath away and comforted her fears at the same time. Made her feel cherished, wanted. Made this whole mad situation feel real.

That she was touching him in the same way was something she didn't notice until near the end of the meal, as the waitress set dessert plates on the table, and Tiger had to move his hand from under hers to make room for the plates.

Hope moved her own hand into her lap, and stared at it, as though it was not part of her. How long had she been...doing that? And did he like it, or even notice? Tiger, she reminded herself sternly, was a man who lived undercover, he was used to playing a role. Whatever he did or said, it wasn't real. It was hard to remember that, but she had to. *Don't get caught up in this romantic nonsense!* she warned herself as sternly as she could. Too much has happened in such a short time, and she knew she was off balance. Reality was not something she could really be all that sure of right now. Tiger Rafferty was the least real thing in this mad world she'd ended up in. *His whole life is a lie, you fool! It's nothing but an act, and you learned the hard way from Mark that no man can be trusted!*

Then he looked in her eyes with that teasing smile on his face, and offered her a forkful of key lime cheesecake, and all Hope's stern intentions ran off and jumped through the window. She said, "Mmm..." around a mouthful of cheesecake and found herself picking up her fork and feeding him the same way. It was all perfectly ridiculous, and a part of her knew it. But it was so easy, so natural and so much fun....

Taking his gaze off Hope was harder than it should be. Keeping his hands off her was proving very nearly impossible, but as the time approached for them to leave the Orchid Room he made himself peer surreptitiously at other semi-secluded tables where lovers sat lost in each other. They didn't look any different from any other couple in the place, Tiger decided as he and Hope shared the last few bites of dessert. Good. That he hadn't felt any differently than any of the normal men seated near women they loved for hours bothered him now. He tried to pull his emotions back, to find objective distance. He almost made it, then Hope smiled at him, put her hand on his wrist to push away a last forkful of dessert, and made some sexy little sound and everything about her drove him crazy. Delightfully crazy. He had never felt this giddy rush of delight at being with a woman before. Never had this pleasurable sizzle of desire buzz between him and a woman before.

He loved the way she looked mysterious, sultry and enticing in the candlelight, loved the warm, rich sound of her laughter, loved the way the colorful, clinging silk of her blouse outlined her round, firm breasts. He loved the sound of her voice and...

Love is not *the operative word here,* he reminded himself sternly. He shook his head, trying to clear it, and anger began to burn inside him. At himself, and at her for making him forget himself so easily. The woman drove him crazy all right. Crazy that could get them both killed. He shouldn't be having a good time. *Distance yourself, you idiot!* She would never know who he really was. They would never see each other again. *Why not?* an insidious voice in his head questioned. The voice belonged to a man named Michael, a man who had a life beyond a cover identity and an assignment. The assignment had to come first. He had to forget that other self if he was going to stay focused. He couldn't let a woman distract him.

He put down his fork and got to his feet, ducking his head to avoid a hanging spray of flowers. He held his hand out to Hope. "Time to go."

Hope was shocked by the harsh tone of his voice. Harsh enough to throw cold water over the remainder of her dreamy mood. The tenseness she was used to from him, the barely concealed anger was back. There was a well-known hardness around his mouth and eyes now. Whoever she'd been having dinner with, whether he'd meant any of the sweet things he'd said and done didn't matter. Tiger was back.

Good, she told herself, and nodded emphatically. She steeled her own emotions, stood without taking his hand. The interval among the orchids was over. She didn't need or want his help.

"Fine," she said, deliberately keeping her distance from him. "Let's go." She didn't look back as she proceeded him toward the door.

Chapter 11

Hope hadn't realized how tired she was until she settled her head against the leather headrest of the passenger seat of the Land Rover. "What time is it?" she heard herself ask wearily, even though she hadn't planned to say anything to Tiger for the rest of the evening. She'd decided to have nothing more to do with him when he'd slithered up beside her as they approached the dining room's doorway and slid his arm around her waist. He'd pulled her close, hip to hip, and kissed her on the temple.

As reaction to this kiss shivered through her, he whispered, lips close to her ear, "Watch yourself. Remember you're supposed to love me. Worship me. Be my baby."

"Drop dead," she whispered back, suddenly infuriated by his possessive touch and flippant words. "I'm nobody's baby."

He cocked an eyebrow at her. His smile was broad and suggestive. "No?"

She'd been too annoyed to say a word. In fact, she decided that talking to the man did no good anyway, so why bother? So they walked out arm in arm into the warm island night to where a parking valet already had one of the resort's luxury sport utility vehicles waiting for them, engine decorously purring.

"Late," Tiger answered as he put the vehicle in gear and let it glide slowly from beneath the awning that covered the drive on this side of the resort's main building. "Very late," he added after glancing at his watch. "This day's gone on so long I don't remember how it started."

With me waking up in your arms, Hope thought, with an ache that was wistful, bitter and sweet. *Hush!* she angrily shouted down that gentler inner voice. "It was raining," she told him, rather than dwell on her emotions. "I remember that."

Tiger yawned loudly, then grunted in a way that told Hope he was surprised at this sudden evidence that he was tired. She smiled slightly, and gazed through half-shut eyelids at the slowly passing scenery. The moon wasn't yet full, but it waxed large enough to give filmy silver illumination to the elegantly landscaped grounds. The walks and roadway were lit at regular intervals by tall light poles with frosted glass shades. These shone gold, contrasting handsomely to the moon's silver. Stars arced overhead, added jewels on velvet to the rich impression of the night. In the distance she could hear the restful murmur of the sea. The air was scented with the salt spray and night-blooming jasmine.

She closed her eyes and breathed it in, let the gentle breeze coming in from the open window soothe her. Paradise, she thought. As prisons went, that is. Hope sighed as she remembered once more that everything around her was an illusion no matter how pretty and peaceful it seemed. The man beside her was the biggest illusion of all.

Don't forget! she warned herself. Without opening he
eyes, she asked him, "You do know where we're going
right?"

"Don't I always?" His bravado sounded forced, and h
yawned again.

"No."

"Thanks."

She yawned as she kept her gaze on the white grave
roadway before them. The Land Rover was climbing uphil
in a long, curving ascent. Her sense of direction was prett
good. "We aren't headed for Cardenas's mansion, ar
we?"

He heard the nerves in her voice, and didn't blame he
for being worried. "We have a place near there. A smal
house. Secluded. Private. With one very big bedroom."

"Oh."

She sounded even more nervous when he told her that
and he couldn't help but smile. Anticipation speare
through him.

"Watch out!" Hope shouted as his adrenaline rush o
reaction caused him to nearly swerve the Land Rover of
the road.

"Sorry." He mumbled the word, and cast a brief loo
her way, catching a glimpse of big, worried eyes in th
darkness. He put a hand out, not sure whether he meant i
as comfort, or covetousness or simple yearning, but sh
slapped it away before he could touch her.

Which was just as well, since touching her was too mucl
of a temptation. Soon they would be alone together in
place where they were expected to make love, where th
whole atmosphere was set up to make people want to mak
love. He remembered the king-size bed, and ached wit
longing to use it. "It's going to be a long night," he mut
tered, and turned into the last long curve that led up to thei

private hideaway. He felt Hope's curious look, but said nothing more. Within another minute he brought the Land Rover to a halt before the elegant little house.

Hope stared at the front door of the building as Tiger switched off the car engine. She heard his door open, then close, and made herself sit up and bravely square her shoulders. She wanted to show a bit of maidenly modesty and state that she'd be happy to sleep in the back seat of the Land Rover, but that was downright silly. She was not, as she believed she'd pointed out earlier, a silly person. She was a serious, deadly dull, ploddingly unadventurous woman who was caught in strange and unusual circumstances.

Besides, she was tired. She got out of the Land Rover and followed Tiger to the door, telling herself as she did so that Tiger was as aware of the charade aspect of their alleged romance as she was. Nothing was going to happen behind that door once they were alone together. Was it? That trepidation *and* anticipation rushed through her annoyed her no end. Or maybe what she was feeling was no more than exhaustion, and the letdown of coming off an hours-long adrenaline jag. When Tiger unlocked the door and gallantly ushered her in before him, she marched through the door—and ended up staring, openmouthed as he switched on the recessed living room lighting.

"Wow," was all Hope could manage to gasp after a few moments of trying to take in the decor of the beautifully appointed room.

"That about sums it up," Tiger agreed. He put his hand under her elbow. "Come on, let me show you the garden."

"But, I want—"

"We'll go to bed in a minute, sweetheart," he told her. He slipped an arm around her and pulled her close. "Let's make out under the stars first.'' He added in a faint whisper in her ear, ''Talk. Outside.''

She understood. A shiver of nerves went through her as she accompanied him through the other darkened room, out to a terrace, and a little ways down a steep moonlit path.

He kept his arms around her when they came to a halt, holding her, swaying with her in the center of the path as though they were dancing to a silent song. It felt good being held like this, the slow rhythm perfectly suited to the way their bodies fit together. She found herself wanting to hum as a favorite, slow, romantic song began to play in her head. Her arms went around his waist, holding him, closing her eyes and imagining slow, seductive music. It was almost enough to make Hope forget the reason they were out here.

He kept his lips very close to her ear when he spoke. ''Don't think the house is bugged,'' he whispered. She stiffened in his embrace. He took a deep breath. ''Damn, that perfume's nice. But I don't *know*,'' he added. ''So we have to pretend we care for each other a little while longer. Say you understand, Hope.''

She couldn't respond for a moment because of the merciless fist that tightened around her heart. Of course there was nothing real about what they did. He was right to be blunt about it. It was just that— She sighed, and whispered back, ''Of course. I'm not a fool,'' she added, though she felt like one for the ridiculous way her heart and soul reacted to this man no matter what her head knew to be true about him.

''I know,'' he answered. His voice and warm embrace offered a reassurance she knew was utterly false.

She stepped away from that embrace. ''I have to get some sleep,'' she announced, her eyes and throat burning with unshed tears. She really was exhausted, that was probably why she was reacting so badly to truths she already knew. He moved toward her in the moonlight, but she waved him back. She walked back uphill through the night-blooming flowers, with Tiger moving silently behind her.

She didn't bother trying to find light switches when she entered the bedroom from the terrace. Darkness was fine with her. She somehow doubted there were infrared cameras in the bedroom, and was too tired and dispirited to care if there were. Moonlight poured in from the terrace doorway, and provided enough light for her to find the bathroom. She had to go through a dressing room to get there, and found her new clothes neatly arranged on shelves and hangers. The bright-red T-shirt she put on to sleep in was from a neat stack on Tiger's side of the closet, but there was no way she was putting on the filmy negligee he'd picked out for her earlier in the day.

Tiger was already in bed when she walked rather defiantly out of the dressing room in his shirt. She didn't look at the bed, or at him, she simply slipped hastily in beside him. The darkness helped. That he rolled over and put a hard muscled arm around her didn't. Nor did the fact that she came to rest against a solid wall of hot, hard muscles, but she didn't protest at his holding her. Didn't try to push him away.

In fact, within moments, she relaxed completely within the false security of his embrace, and fell blissfully asleep.

He dreamed they were dancing at his sister's wedding. He was in his dress whites, and Hope wore a little black lace dress that clung to her curves like a second skin. It didn't matter what the band was playing, they still danced slowly together, bodies fitting together in perfect harmony. There was an admiral in the crowd somewhere, and his commanding officer, both frowning at him. Michael paid them no mind, though he knew they didn't want him dancing with a civilian.

In the dream it was easy to ignore those disapproving faces, to forget about duty while lost in his lover's arms. It wasn't quite so easy when he came awake suddenly, fully aware that Hope was no longer in the big bed with him. He should have woken when she moved, he was a light sleeper. Had to be in his business. But he'd been lost in a pleasant dream and...

Tiger swore as he sat up and looked around. Where the devil was she? He had no sense of danger—but then, he couldn't trust his senses where Hope Harrison was concerned, now could he? Instead of calling her name, he got up and padded silently across the bedroom, bare feet buried nearly up to the ankles in the deep-piled carpeting. He'd slept with a gun under his pillow, and his knife tucked under the mattress, within easy reach. He took the knife with him as he crossed the room to the terrace doorway. Tiger relaxed only marginally when he saw Hope sitting outside at the glass-topped table set under an overhanging canopy of flowering vines. She was dressed in red shorts and a flower print halter top. He saw her face in profile, looking both pensive and rested, and the sight of her took his breath away. She was looking out to sea, with one long leg curled under her, a china coffee cup cradled in her hands. The morning sun tinted her ash-blond hair gold, and she seemed very much a creature of the light. He watched her as she closed her eyes and lifted her face to the warmth of the sun. He forgot everything else in that long moment other than the yearning. She was a creature of the light, and he belonged to the night. The bitter thought brought him back to earth, back to reality. He left the knife on a side table and went out onto the terrace. "What are you doing out here?"

Hope flinched at the harsh demand in Tiger's voice, but she didn't let any trepidation show as she glanced over her shoulder at him. "You are such a grouch in the morning." She gestured toward the pot on the table. "Have a cup of coffee. World always looks better after coffee." She looked back at the view. "Though how anything could look better than this, I don't know." That wasn't exactly true. She thought the sight of Tiger Rafferty, unshaven, hair disheveled, wearing only a pair of white briefs, and looking like he was ready to take a nasty bite out of the world was about the most gorgeous sight she'd ever seen.

There was definitely something wrong with her sensibilities this morning. Her sense of aesthetics was way off. Or maybe that broad-shouldered, bare-chested long drink of water standing in the doorway did look good enough to eat. "Toast?" she said, gesturing at the table once more, and all the covered dishes sitting on it. "Muffin? Omelette? Orange juice?" She put her cup down as he stalked up to the table.

"Where'd this stuff come from?"

"Room service." She couldn't keep the teasing smile off her face as she added, "I suppose it came from a kitchen, cause I doubt there's a replicator someplace programmed to beam it out of thin air."

Tiger came forward, and dropped a quick kiss on her cheek. For form's sake, she supposed, in case they were being spied on somehow. He was so very good at remembering to play his role. Then he took a seat on the other side of the little table. Hope politely poured a cup of coffee and passed it to him. She attempted to look lovesick as she did so—for form's sake. Trouble was, she knew it wasn't difficult to look at him that way at all. Fortunately, he didn't seem to notice her acting this morning.

After he took a sip, he eyed her suspiciously. "Replicator? You're a *Star Trek* fan, aren't you?"

"Don't sound so suspicious. It's not like I go to conventions and dress like a Klingon, you know. At least not recently," she added in a whisper as she poured herself yet another cup of coffee. She'd done that sort of thing in college, back before she became a staid, normal, absolutely dull person. She looked at the untamed male seated across from her, and felt a moment of hopeless pain, knowing she had no business wanting such a magnificent creature. What the devil would she do with him back in the real world? She forced away these foolish thoughts and explained. "I called room service when I woke up. A nice young man delivered all this about fifteen minutes ago."

This served to only deepen Tiger's frown. "And I slept through all this?" She realized it was himself he was annoyed with, and not her.

"You did. Why not? I called from the living room, and he brought it around to the terrace without even coming inside. You were sleeping like the dead," she added. And smiling in your sleep, she recalled, wondering what he'd been dreaming about.

She didn't tell him that she'd watched him sleeping for a while after she woke. It sounded too sentimental, too...romantic. She knew she had no reason to feel romantic toward this man. But sharing a bed with him, sharing danger with him, made it hard not to feel something other than the resentment she should be nursing if she wanted to keep her heart whole for the day she and Tiger parted company for good. Heart whole? Hope laughed at herself. Yeah, right.

"What's so funny?" Tiger asked, and hoped she wasn't laughing at him. Unlike her, he wasn't exactly the most beautiful sight in the world the first thing in the morning.

She shrugged and turned her attention back out to sea. He took the cover off a plate and dug into a fluffy omelette. "Thanks for ordering for both of us," he added after Hope failed to answer his question. "This is delicious."

"Can't imagine anything here not being perfect," she answered. "Wonderful food, wonderful accommodations, magnificent view." She lifted her cup in salute, slanting a sideways glance at him. "We're in paradise, Tiger."

"It is beautiful here," he agreed, in between bites.

"Enjoying yourself?" Then she laughed again. This time he was pretty sure it was at his expense. "Shall we discuss the weather next?"

He knew instantly what she meant, that their conversation was quickly slipping into banal generalities, and that she hated the fact that they were unable to speak and act freely. He couldn't have agreed more. He glanced down the terraced hillside to the wide swathe of beach below, to the aqua surf and the jade sea beyond. It was a crystal-bright morning, the sky overhead free of any clouds. The unseasonable storms seemed to have blown themselves out at last. The beach was empty, no people in sight, and it looked to go on for miles. They could be alone there. The yearning to be alone with Hope tugged hard on all his senses. To walk on that beach with his arm around her, to make love on the sand...

Tiger tried to blink that thought away, but once it had surfaced, it wasn't going to go away. Didn't matter. He'd cope. And freedom still called.

He finished the last of his breakfast and got to his feet. "Let's go swimming," he said, grinning. He looked down at what little he wore as she looked him over with one eyebrow raised. "I'll even put on a bathing suit," he promised.

He did more than put on a bathing suit; he shaved and

showered and brushed his teeth. He wanted to look good. In fact, he behaved exactly as though he were getting ready for a date, even though the black Speedo swimsuit he ended up wearing actually covered less of his anatomy than the briefs he'd slept in. And that was just fine with him, he decided as he walked hand in hand with Hope down the switchback garden path toward the beach. She kept glancing at him, flushing prettily, and looking away—only to take another quick peek. He wasn't vain, but knowing that he looked good to her pleased him immensely. Maybe it shouldn't have, maybe he should be all business, but at least he had the excuse that their acting attracted to each other was business as well as being the truth.

She certainly looked good to him, and he didn't bother trying to conceal his appreciation of her in the pale-pink bikini she'd put on. Oh, she had a sheer pink…thing…on over her bathing suit, but the cover-up didn't cover much of anything. *Enhance* is a better word, he thought, with a smile that was more of an open leer than it was a sign of amusement.

This time when she looked at him she blushed, as expected, and shoved his arm. "Stop that!"

He couldn't help his wicked laugh. "You really want me to?"

She took a sharp breath. Looked away, then boldly back at him. "No."

Hope stopped in the middle of the path, shocked at her response, and the wave of need that rushed through her as their gazes fixed on each other. She dropped the tote bag full of beach supplies she carried to the ground. Sunglasses, water bottles, towels and sunblock spilled out at her feet, but she hardly paid them any mind, other than to kick them aside as she took a step away from Tiger. She wasn't trying to escape, she backed off a short distance in order to get a better look, as there was so very much of his tall, rangy form to look at. Her attention was riveted on the big, sun-browned man before her, on his long, solidly muscled limbs, the width of his chest, and his hard, flat stomach. On his big, long-fingered hands, so full of deadly strength and gentle grace. Even the memory of his touch sent shivers of anticipation through her. She focused on his throat, and wanted to kiss it. She wanted to kiss the tip of ear that peaked out from his casually brushed back hair. She wanted to run her hands through that hair; it was such a warm, rich shade of brown, so thick and soft.

She couldn't keep her attention off him, hadn't been able to since the moment they met. She could barely keep her hands off him most of the time, no matter how angry he made her, or how frightened, or how confused. She didn't trust him, knew she was a pawn in his undercover game. Not just a pawn, but a liability. She couldn't let herself care for him, but she did. She shouldn't want him, but she did. It was stupid, really.

Ridiculous. Impossible.

What was?

What she wanted. From him. With him. She wanted to sleep with a tiger, and that was the honest truth. She wanted to make love to him, right here and now. Looking at him ignited the spark; his touch would send her up in flames. She desperately wanted him to touch her.

Oh, God, she thought. Here we go again!

She had thought—how?—that they could manage a day without this sizzle of desire arcing between them. How typically naive of her. Why? Because they'd gotten through one more night sharing the same bed without giving in to any carnal urges? She knew very well that if they both hadn't been so tired by the time they crawled in the night before, something would have happened. Something was going to happen now. Or, if not now, soon.

"No," she said aloud, and found the strength to hold her hand up to ward him off as he took a step toward her. She backed farther down the hill, while all the time wanting to rush into his arms. "We're going swimming," she told him. "There's an ocean full of cold water down there," she added primly. "I think we should take full advantage of its therapeutic properties, don't you?"

Tiger threw back his head and laughed. "You are absolutely right. Cold salt water is very—bracing."

"Calming."

"Restorative."

"Clears the head."

"Invigorating."

"We don't need to be invigorated."

"You're right," he agreed. "Race you!"

He shouted the words as he ran past her. Hope snatched up the stuff that had fallen out of her bag, then took off after him. She dumped her wrap, sandals and the bag where the jungle met the beach and ran across the sun-warmed sand to follow Tiger into the water.

He swam out to a rock that jutted above the rolling surf a short distance from the shore. He was sitting on an overhanging ledge, feet dangling in the water when she reached him. "Tigers like to swim, you know," she told him as she treaded water. She was a little winded from the short swim, and had to almost shout to be heard over the slap of water against the rock. Tiger wasn't even breathing hard.

He looked down at her, stretched and scratched his wet chest. "Do they?" He turned his face up to the sky. "I think I'd rather stay here and take a nap."

"You'll burn."

He raised an eyebrow. "In hell?"

"That's not for me to judge."

"Take a shot."

"Okay," she said as she bobbed in the rolling surf. "I figure you've got at least a fifty-fifty chance, but I was talking about sunburn."

"I'm fine." He waved her concern away, then reached down to give her a hand as she clambered up the slippery surface of the wet stone. "It's nice here," he said when she'd joined him on his perch over the water. "Private."

Hope sighed with relief, and not just to be out of the water. "Private is nice."

"As long as we're relatively quiet," he cautioned. "Sound carries a long distance over water, you know."

"I know," she answered. The memory that came immediately to mind was of gunshots ringing out over the empty ocean. She looked down at the water, possessed by sudden anger for everything to do with the warm tropical sea. "I don't like the ocean. I don't like the heat. I don't like boats. I don't like adventures. What the devil am I doing here?"

"I've wondered that myself, Hope Harrison," Tiger said. His arm came around her waist. It offered comfort, support, and, she thought, deterrence in case she was thinking of throwing herself into the water in a paroxysm of grief.

She wasn't about to do anything of the sort, but she appreciated his concern. Assuming it was concern. Hope frowned at her own suspicions, and relaxed against Tiger's side. She could only manage to be so paranoid, and right now she just wasn't up to it. She decided to take the man at face value and enjoy the day. She certainly enjoyed sitting next to him, drinking in the heat and the sunlight as it sparkled on the water, and the sheltering, comforting, exciting feel of being beside him.

Hope tried to concentrate on the less erotic aspects of

being so close to him. The comforting aspect, for example, was especially tempting. She put her head on his shoulder, and sighed. The words came out before she could stop them. "Feels good." Nor could she regret them once they were said, no matter how vulnerable they made her sound.

She couldn't mean being with him felt good, Tiger decided, though a part of him wanted very much to believe that was what she meant. It was such a beautiful day, the mood they shared so peaceful all of a sudden. Tiger had no choice but to let the cynical part of himself, the one that worked so hard at keeping him emotionally distant from everyone he encountered, have the day off. He wouldn't let himself have regrets; for now he let himself pretend it was the truth. He simply couldn't work up the necessary paranoia right now.

"I'm going to regret this tomorrow," he said.

"You should have worn sunblock," Hope responded, her face turned up to the sky.

"That's not what I'm going to regret," he answered. If he got burned it wasn't going to be by the sun. She looked at him curiously, mouth open to ask a question. He didn't give her time. He wanted to kiss her, so he did.

Her response was everything he dreamed of, her mouth hot and willing on his. Their tongues met and twined as he drew Hope closer. His hands roamed and explored, teasing and caressing her sun-warmed flesh. Her lips tasted of sea salt; her mouth was honey and heaven.

"You know," she said, after they'd kissed for a long time and finally come up for air, "I never know if we should stop doing this—or take this thing to its logical conclusion."

Tiger leaned back on his elbows and stared at passing seagulls while fighting down nearly overpowering urges. After a few seconds he turned his head to look at her.

"Nothing logical about it."

"I suppose not." She should have been angry with him, slapped him for taking liberties. She laughed breathlessly instead as she readjusted the top of her bikini. "There are some parts of my anatomy I'm not prepared to expose to sunlight," she told him. "Besides, there's a sailboat out there, and I'm not flashing these—" she said, cupping her bikini-clad breasts "—at total strangers."

He recalled the sight of the soft pale flesh of her breasts, the nipples pink-tipped and rosy, and gulped. His hands ached to touch them again, to hold their solid weight in his hands. He said, "Yeah, I can see their—your—point."

She laughed again, the bright sound filling the morning air as he had the grace to blush at the pun.

"Uh-huh."

"Did I tell you how good you looked last night?" Tiger rushed on. He rolled onto his side, his legs dangling out over the water. "How beautiful you were?"

"You mean fully clothed for the first time in our acquaintance?"

He recalled that she'd been dressed in a bikini when they'd met, much like the one she wore now. He couldn't recall the color. Who cared? She'd looked great in it. Like she did now. "You look good fully dressed," he conceded. "But...half-naked is better."

"Men," she complained, and shoved against his shoulder.

This almost sent him tumbling into the water. "Hey!"

"Sorry!"

She grabbed his arm and helped him to sit up. Tiger promptly settled his head into her lap. "Feels nice," he murmured as he claimed a shapely thigh as a headrest. She smelled of the sea, and coconut-scented sunblock. "Men are pigs," he agreed, looking up at her. "You're beautiful upside down."

Hope didn't know whether Tiger was role-playing, or if he meant the words. She did know that they took her breath away, sending her into a delirious spin. She shook her head to clear it, but it didn't help. She was reacting to kissing him, being with him right now, far more strongly than she had to any of the fine wine she drank at last night's dinner. His touch had left her on fire, but his words set off fireworks.

She briefly closed her eyes and balled her hands into fists, trying without success to calm down. She was crazy, she knew it. It felt quite nice, actually.

Hope ran her fingers through Tiger's damp hair and looked back toward the nearby beach. Jungle reared up the steep hillside just beyond the long strip of golden sand, lush with a hundred shades of green, bright with vibrant tropical blossoms. It was landscaped jungle, she knew, but she found she preferred it that way. Safe, she thought, a place with the illusion of wildness. It would have made so much more sense if she'd talked her aunt and uncle into spending their vacation at a resort like this. Renting the yacht had been such a horrible, fatal mistake. But how could she have known? She sighed sadly. It was all her—

"What were you doing on that yacht?" Tiger asked.

He'd either read her thoughts, or perhaps she'd spoken out loud. She glanced down quickly, to find him looking up at her, his gaze steady and serious. There was something trusting, and trustworthy, in his eyes as well. Something that tugged on her heart as never before, melted her defenses and made her feel—whole. When he sat up and put his hands on her shoulders she wanted to cry, but not with grief. His gaze never left hers, and she knew what she was feeling, deep and unnameable though it was, shone in her face. For once the raw vulnerability didn't bother her.

When he said, "Tell me," she could do nothing but comply.

"I work in a bank," she said. "My family's bank. My uncle ran the bank. He worked too hard, needed some time off. I needed time off," she admitted. "I wanted to go someplace where nobody knew me."

"Why?"

She'd known he would ask. She wanted to evade the question, but looking into his eyes she couldn't. "There was a man involved."

"A jerk."

She shrugged beneath his hands. "Well, I certainly thought so."

"Someone you'd been with for years, that you expected to marry, that you trusted. Who cheated on you, humiliated you."

She narrowed her eyes as she looked at him. "Have I been talking in my sleep?"

He shrugged. "Lucky guess. You don't trust me," he added. "Some jerk gave you good reason not to trust men."

She cocked her head to one side. "And you're different?"

"You know I am."

She didn't want to discuss any issues of trust, not on this beautiful, perfect day. Yet she found herself explaining, "Mark wanted something more exciting than I could give him. Someone more exciting, but he wanted me as well. I was everything proper and respectable. He thought we should have an 'understanding'—as in he could sleep with whomever he wanted and take me to social functions and business dinners. His friends—our friends—knew all about his affair. He was quite open about sharing his bewilderment at my rejecting the arrangement he wanted.''

"Jerk."

Hope swallowed hard, and realized the strong emotion she was experiencing wasn't the usual pain of public humiliation, but a cold, righteous anger. It mirrored the fury in Tiger's eyes. This clean anger was something new, and it felt good. "Jerk," she agreed.

"He went looking for sympathy, didn't he? Made out to all your friends that the breakup was all your fault."

She nodded. "He said I was being unreasonable. I should have understood how these things are done."

"And you listened, didn't you?" he asked, drawing her closer. "Let him blame you for his cheating?"

Hope flinched at what he said, and his harsh, mocking tone. She didn't disagree, though. "I know it was stupid, okay? I have issues—"

"I hate that."

"What?"

"That 'I have issues' crap. It's such a stupid catchphrase."

"Oh?" she asked sarcastically. "You don't have 'issues' with anything?"

"Plenty," he responded with a quick half smile. "I just don't call it that. So, you have issues with guilt?"

"Taking blame. I have spent my entire life thinking I'm to blame for everything, and fighting feeling that way. Everything is not my fault!" Except for the really big, ugly, horrible things that are, she thought.

He looked thoughtful, ran his tongue over his lips, then nodded. "Which is why you got so furious at me yesterday...when I said it would be your fault if Cardenas found out I was working undercover."

"You were out of line and infuriating," she acknowledged.

He tilted his head, and gave her the most sincere, little-boy puppy-dog contrite expression it was possible for a male to turn on a female. She couldn't help but respond with a dazzled smile to such a look. "Would it help if I apologized for being a jerk now?"

She tilted her head to match the angle of his. "It might. Are you going to apologize?"

He tsked, and looked thoughtful. "Don't know. I'll think about it. But in the meantime my knees are killing me."

Hope laughed, and nodded in agreement. They shifted their positions so that they were seated side by side. He put his arm around her shoulders and they dangled their feet in the warm sloshing water. Sailboats dotted the bay, all of them a good distance from the shallow water near them.

"This feels good, doesn't it, Hope?" he asked after they'd sat in silence for a while. She made some soft agreeing sound, happy to let the warmth of the sun and Tiger's nearness lull her into peaceful contentment. She could have stayed like this for hours. It was too bad he added, "So, why do you think you're to blame for everything?"

Her initial reaction was to want to tartly demand to see his credentials as a psychologist. She wanted to tell him it was none of his business. She said, "Because people I love have this tendency to die."

"People die."

That was a good answer, a true one, certainly. Everyone was mortal. He would be fatalistic, of course, considering his very dangerous business as an undercover agent. She wondered at his chances of survival, but quickly put the thought out of her head, but not before the insidious words *not good at* all floated through her mind.

And maybe she would be to blame if he—

"When I was ten," she told him, "my parents died in a plane crash."

His arm tightened sympathetically around her shoulder. "I'm sorry."

"I walked away with only a few bruises."

He sat up in surprise. "You were in the plane crash?"

"Yes," she answered, the old familiar pain tightening around her heart. She kept her voice dead level as she went on. "In high school, my best friend died in a car crash. I suffered a couple of broken ribs."

"I—uh—"

"You saw what happened to my aunt and uncle."

"Good Lord!" Whether the man was swearing or saying a prayer was impossible to tell.

She'd done a lot of both over the years; sometimes it helped. She fought hard to keep her emotions as neutral as her voice. "As you might think, I don't consider myself to be particularly lucky. In fact, you might not want to stand too close to me if we get the news that giant meteors are heading toward earth."

Tiger saw how the woman could have developed a sense of being jinxed. Knowing Hope's history made him want to protect her, comfort her, promise to never let any harm come to her. He wanted to promise to shelter her from the world for the rest of their lives. He caught his breath as this realization struck him. He looked out to sea, gaze unfocused, afraid to look at Hope, knowing that if he did he would tell her how much she meant to him.

And how much is that? The cynical side of his nature forced the question on him. *You've known her only a few days, and half the things you've said to each other have been lies.* He told himself that what he felt for her couldn't be trusted. The physical attraction was undeniably real, but he could not allow himself to become emotionally involved. As if he wasn't already. Since when? he wondered, trying to pinpoint the exact moment when she'd truly become important to him. No! Such speculation was maudlin and dangerous. Better to keep his feelings out of this, keep them unexamined and tucked away. He couldn't follow his own advice, but he refused to put a name to what he was feeling.

Tiger was still tempted to offer her comfort, to reassure her that, despite his stupid comments yesterday, nothing that had happened was Hope's fault. The one thing he couldn't do was promise her that nothing was going to happen to him. All he could do was say, "We'll both get out of this." He smiled, and tenderly touched the tip of her nose. "Have to. My sister will kill me if I don't show up to give her away at her wedding."

This sudden look behind the mask into Tiger Rafferty's real identity fascinated Hope. The intriguing notion of his being a "normal" person, someone with a family, with places to go and things to do drove away her melancholy. She fixed him with curious attention that would not be denied.

"Sister? Wedding? When? Where?"

"Oops." He looked around as though expecting the media to show up with cameras and helicopters at any moment. "Hope—I can't, shouldn't—tell you anything about myself. 'Need to Know,'" he added.

She refused to be offended. "Don't give me that bull. I told you my life story. If we're going to be—friends—you have to talk to me, too."

He waved her words away. "I'm boring. Dull."

"You threw a knife at me when we met."

"That was business. Reality—" He shrugged. "Dull. You wouldn't want to know."

"I do. I'm not asking for the details of your—business."

She tugged on his hair. "Spill. Tell me about your sister's wedding at least."

"What is it with women and weddings?" he wanted to know. "Why do you find them so interesting? Guys would rather talk about sports."

"Which you did last night. Endlessly."

"Oh?" He cocked his eyebrow—a gesture she wished she didn't find endlessly endearing—and drawled, "Weren't you the one going on about the NBA?"

"And didn't Dennis Rodman, one of the best rebounders the game of basketball has ever had, once wear a wedding dress to a book signing when his autobiography was published?" she countered. "See, it's all connected. Female logic," she added.

"Gotta love it."

"Tell me about your sister. Why are you giving the bride away?"

"Dad's dead. I'm the oldest of four. Only one sister, Julie. Works in Washington. Marrying some civilian named Franklin."

"And?" she urged.

Tiger took a deep breath, and rattled off a staccato stream of facts. "Church wedding. St. Margaret's. Four bridesmaids. In blue. White dress. Lots of flowers. Hotel reception. Honeymoon in Michigan."

"Michigan?"

"I have no idea."

She hadn't had to ask 'Why Michigan?' He had understood her question, just as she understood his answer. In fact, she could picture exactly what he meant about all the wedding arrangements with only those few terse words of description. The communication between them was easy, open and invigorating. In this moment she felt as if she'd known him all her life, and would know him for all eternity.

It felt wonderful! The joy that bubbled in her was like nothing she'd ever felt before.

Hope threw back her head and laughed. Tiger took the opportunity to kiss her throat, turning the joy into sizzling heat within her. Then his lips moved farther down, kissing first one, then the other of her mostly exposed breasts. Desire stirred even more powerfully in her. She gazed up at the nearly cloudless arc of azure sky and knew there was no one in the world but the two of them, nothing more important than the passion that sang between them.

"It's beautiful here," she murmured as his fingers moved to stimulate her already puckered nipples. His response was a wordless hum. She ran her fingers through his hair, massaged the taut muscles of his back. It was indeed beautiful out here on this rock dangling just above the warm turquoise waters of the small bay. The breeze was fresh and fragrant, the sun was a gold ball high overhead. The beauty was unreal to her, the situation that brought them to this moment had the quality of a strange dream. In fact, only Tiger and the way he made her feel held any reality. She had never felt more alive, more free, more—

She took a hard, sharp breath as his hands moved over her. Hope licked her lips and moaned.

"Let's get out of here."

Her words surprised them both. Tiger's head came up. His gaze burned hotly into hers. His voice was rough when he spoke. "If we go back to our room…"

The deep ache of wanting him pulsed through her. She nodded slowly to the question, the craving and the need in his eyes. She shared everything but the uncertainty. "I know," Hope told him. "Let's go back to the house."

"Do you know what you're saying?"

She nodded. "That I want to spend the rest of the day

making love to you. Alone. In bed. Soft mattress. Air-conditioning.''

He laughed, but before Tiger could say another word, she took his hand in hers and they slid into the shallow water. It was a short, quick swim to the shore.

Chapter 12

Hope gathered up the abandoned tote bag and they walked up the path from the beach arm in arm. Nothing needed to be said, their closeness, the way they touched said everything. The air around them sizzled with anticipation. Hope didn't feel the heat of the sun or the ground beneath her feet; the heat came from within and she moved through the world in a delicious, sensuous haze.

About halfway up the steep path Tiger stopped. He took her in his arms and held her close. "I don't want to make love to a stranger—don't want you making love to a stranger," he told her.

That he used that word for what they were about to do stunned her. She was even more stunned at his other words. Something inside her melted and ached and glowed with fierce warmth. She thought it was her heart. She couldn't find any words, but held him tightly to her in response.

"You don't know my real name," he continued. "Not all of it, anyway. I can't tell you, because there are more lives at stake than just mine. If I could—'' He rubbed his hand slowly up and down her bare back while she continued to wait in silence.

It hurt that he didn't trust her. She'd done her best not to trust him, but it hurt to have him do the same to her. Hurt, but… She lifted her head and met his gaze. ''I understand.'' She wasn't sure she did, but she tried. ''Security. I still want to.'' She couldn't say the rest. She couldn't let herself think about loving a man who didn't trust her, even if she comprehended his reasons. ''I want you.''

''I had a friend,'' he rushed on. ''My best friend since high school. He died in the line of duty while on this same case. There was a woman involved,'' he added. ''She betrayed him.'' She took a sharp, angry breath, but he put a hand over her mouth before she could voice a protest. ''She didn't mean to—he talked too much and blew his cover. You wouldn't mean to, either. I know that. But the less you know about me, the better it is for both of us. I'm going to finish this case.'' He knew that he'd only compromised himself further with every word he'd spoken this afternoon, but what he wanted with Hope went beyond base physical need.

''It's all right,'' she said after a while, and her voice rang hollowly in the sultry air. She stepped away from him, and took his hand. There were faint spots of color in her cheeks, and her eyes were too bright. She took him by the hand and led him up the path.

It really is all right, she told herself with every step that brought them closer to the house. Trust didn't matter. The future didn't matter. It would be all right. At least that's what she told herself until they were within a few feet of the terrace. When Hope saw the squat, powerfully built man who stood waiting for them, cold-eyed and statue still, reality rushed back in on her with the force of a tidal wave.

The stranger didn't wear the casual uniform of the resort, but his obvious air of danger advertised that he worked for Mr. Cardenas's other business.

Tiger swore under his breath, and resisted the urge to protectively push Hope behind him. The fog of desire that had filled his brain cleared instantly, as all his senses became alert to danger. He silently cursed Hope for making him forget his duty even for a minute, and he cursed himself because he knew she was no more to blame than he was. Less.

This was no time for recriminations. He focused on Cardenas's errand boy with an expression just as ruthless as the other man's, but he didn't say anything. The stranger broke eye contact first.

"Honeymoon's over," he said. "Get dressed. I'll wait in the car. Bring the woman," he added, before sauntering off the terrace and taking the path toward the front of the little house.

Tiger swore again, but neither he nor Hope said a word to each other. Not while they dressed, certainly not on the drive from the secluded hideaway to the grand mansion that dominated the top of the cliff. They held hands, and the white-knuckled pressure Hope exerted with her fingers twined against his told Tiger how frightened she was to be thrown suddenly back into the ugly reality of his world. It made him realize that making love to her would have been a big, big mistake. Because once he started making love to her he wouldn't want to stop. He would start thinking about a future with her. Being together wasn't an option. Especially after what she'd told him about her loved ones' deaths. He couldn't ask her to love a man who risked death as part of his profession. Who knew when he'd have to take another field assignment, leave her worrying while he was out of contact with her for months? Maybe get killed in the line of duty?

She'd been through too much already. What he had to do was get her safely off Isla Sebastian, then try to forget her. Fat chance, he thought, then forced himself to put the job first and concentrate on one thing at a time.

Dante Cardenas was as urbane and affable as Hope remembered. He welcomed them in his living room once more, and beamed with pleasure as Tiger politely and profusely thanked him for the wonderful private interlude he'd given them.

"You look rested and relaxed," Cardenas replied. He looked Hope over with a satisfied nod. "You are quite lovely, my dear. Those clothes suit you so much better than your former half-drowned refugee ensemble."

Hope couldn't help but return his smile. She'd changed into a short denim wrap-skirt and sleeveless blue knit top. More of a honeymooning tourist than a gangster's moll look she supposed, and wondered if she should have made more of an effort to look like a bimbo. At least she had the fact that she was blond going for her. Then again, did being naturally blond count? She figured she must be extremely nervous to have her thoughts running off in such odd directions, and quickly gathered herself together as much as she could. "Thank you," she told Cardenas politely. "You are a very kind and generous man."

"My pleasure. Excuse us, my dear." Cardenas turned to Tiger, and gestured toward a doorway. "Let's talk in private, shall we, Mr. Rafferty?" Tiger nodded, and the two men walked through the door. One of the room's security men silently shut the door behind them, then stood in front of it. He looked about as broad and immovable as a wall. Hope looked away from him, and took a seat on the couch.

She remained well aware of the men who were discreetly placed near the room's exits. She went cold at the realization that she couldn't leave if she wanted to, but tried not to show any of her fear. She had forgotten for a few wonderful hours that she was a prisoner. She doubted she'd forget again. She couldn't help but wonder what Cardenas wanted to see Tiger about; what business the menfolk conducted in private while the little lady waited. It was so much fun being an accessory item here in the world of gun-toting macho criminal types. Fortunately for her shredding nerves and temper, the men weren't gone for very long.

When they came back Tiger was stiff with tension and suppressed fury. Hope rose to her feet as he approached. She half wanted to comfort him, and half of her wanted to run. The swirling anger in the man's eyes reminded her of the storm that had torn across the other side of the island a few days ago.

"What?" she asked with hushed anxiety as he took her by the arm.

"Outside." He gave her no time for more questions, but led her past the guard at the veranda door and out into the garden that overlooked the ocean.

"What?" she asked again when they reached the wall at the edge of the cliff. They were as far away from the house as it was possible to be but Hope still whispered the question. She faced him and put her hands on his rigidly tense shoulders. She saw desperation when she looked deep into his eyes, and a lot of trouble.

"I'm sorry."

Her stomach curdled, and a fist tightened around her heart. Terror shot through her. "You're—sorry?" She couldn't bring herself to ask about what, but searched his face for some sign of softness; she found none. Something awful was about to happen, she knew, and it was going to happen to her.

"I have the name. That was my assignment, to find out a name. A naval officer's name."

She saw that he was angry with himself for telling her this much. She wondered why he was so disturbed when he should have been elated. "That means your assignment's over, right? That we can leave?"

His response was to pull her into a fierce hard kiss. It was so desperate and needy that she had no choice but to respond in the same ferocious way. The sensation that passed between them was utterly passionate, and yet she came away from it terrified.

Hope looked at Tiger with frightened eyes when she asked, "What's going on?"

Tiger turned from her and leaned against the wall, his hands flat on the stone surface, his back and shoulders tense as he gazed out to sea. "I have to go."

She put her hand on his arm; the muscles were as taut as steel. "Let's get out of here, then."

"I have to go." He repeated the words without looking at her. After a few seconds of tense silence he finally added. "You're staying here."

The hot Caribbean sun beat down, washing the world with heat and light and false security. The day went dark around her and Hope's blood ran cold. Her heart filled with pain. She heard Tiger's words, their meaning struck terror deep inside her, but the only thing she could say was, "What?"

"You heard me."

His harsh tone grated against her senses. Tears stung her eyes and the back of her throat. "But…"

"Cardenas was impressed." Tiger laughed. The sound had no amusement in it, and hung ominously in the space between them. "Impressed by my determination to get the first shipment to him. Impressed because I faced down Ibarra for the sake of the woman I love. Impressed at what he's seen of our deep, abiding love. He'd kill us without a blink, but other than that he's an honorable, old-fashioned, romantic guy."

"And he thinks you are, too."

He didn't react to the acid sarcasm in her voice. He went on tonelessly. "Cardenas has decided to give me a job. He's trusting me to pick up and deliver a shipment from his very high-tech American supplier. Valuable cargo." He gave another soft, bitter laugh. "Dangerous work. So of course I'll want my lady to remain safely out of the way. He's extending you his hospitality. Insists that you be his guest while I'm gone, that it's his pleasure to have your company. I'm going. You're staying. Cardenas has spoken."

"You can't do this to me."

Tiger didn't answer. His jaw worked, but no words came out. He continued to stare out at the sparkling water, his face an expressionless mask.

Hope knew one thing: he had promised to get her out, now he was walking away. Rescuing her had never been part of his mission. He'd given it a shot, but her life wasn't all that important in his scheme of things. Duty had to come first. Tiger Rafferty now had the information he wanted. His assignment was over. Duty accomplished. He could go home now. Could and would.

As seconds went by in silence, hysterical anger began to invade her being. With strength she didn't know she had, Hope grabbed Tiger's shoulders and forced him around to face her. "At least look at me when you betray me, you bastard!"

"Betray you?" His hands came up to cup her face. "Are you crazy?"

"Yeah. Crazy to trust you even a little."

"An hour ago you wanted to make love to me, but you don't trust me now?"

"You didn't trust me then!"

"I couldn't."

"How dare you use the word *love* when we were going to have sex!" she snapped as her heart cracked open and bled.

"Because—"

"No." She shook off his far too tender touch. She would have backed away, but he caught her by the shoulders. "Don't bring sex into this, Rafferty," she snarled in a savage whisper. "Do you think I was stupid enough to believe you cared about me just because you wanted to go to bed with me?"

Tiger didn't believe he was hearing this! He had expected her to be frightened; he hadn't expected this venomous anger. He'd been so stunned himself that he'd had a hard struggle conveying the news to her. Keeping his emotions under control was costing him dearly. He wanted to howl and rage and shout, but not at her. He couldn't do what he wanted. He couldn't fight Cardenas on this. And he couldn't afford to fight with Hope now. At least she wasn't screaming her hurtful accusations at him for the whole world to hear. He certainly couldn't answer them. Explanations might lead to both of them shouting loud enough to draw a crowd, and they were anything but alone.

"There are armed men not a hundred feet away," he reminded her. He backed her against the waist-high wall and put his hands flat on top of it on either side of her. "Listen to me very carefully," he said, his face close to hers. Fury pulsed off her like heat haze. He trapped her gaze with his and wouldn't let it go. "And don't say a word."

"Don't," she answered, her diction very precise, "give me orders."

He couldn't afford to react. "I don't want to do this, Hope. I have no choice. I will be back."

"I don't believe you."

"You have to. Trust me. I promised to get you to safety and I will. Believe in me, Hope Harrison. If you never believe in anything else before or after, believe in me now. Trust me," he repeated. "Just hold on, and trust me to come back for you."

"I don't get a choice, do I?" was her cold response.

Because he was standing so very close to her he was aware that Hope was trembling, but her voice betrayed none of her fear. He knew she'd reject any effort he made to comfort her.

"No choice," he agreed. "None at all."

"Then why bother trying to convince me to trust you?" She shrank away from him as much as she could in the space he'd confined her in. She turned her head to look out to sea. "Just go."

"Because I—"

He made himself stop. He made himself step back. She was absolutely right. Explanations weren't necessary, neither were words of comfort and reassurance. She didn't want them. She didn't want anything to do with him. She didn't believe in his sense of honor or duty. She'd never trusted him and probably never would, and he couldn't let it matter. Only it did, and her response hurt like hell. He'd keep his promise to her whether she trusted him or not.

He bent forward and kissed her cheek while she continued to look out at the water far below. For form's sake, because he knew they were being watched. "Be very careful," he whispered. "I'll be back in a few days."

"Sure you will," he heard her murmur as he walked away. He didn't know which was more bitter, the sound of her words, or the ache in his soul when he heard them. Didn't matter. He would be back.

He isn't coming back.

Hope looked out at the calm, beautiful water as the words roiled and crashed over and over in her head. It had been two days and despite a wholly unreasonable, desperate belief otherwise, she hadn't been able to get these words, and words like them, out of her head for more than a few minutes at a time since Tiger had left her in the garden. She stood on the veranda of the mansion now, with an iced drink in one hand that had been brought to her a few moments ago by the ever attentive Maria. There was a lunch tray waiting for her on a nearby table, and a guard wearing sunglasses and a white linen suit standing by the living room door. Hope ignored him, and looked out at the same spectacular view she'd looked at yesterday, thought the same thoughts, and hated every moment she spent in this illusion of paradise.

He could be dead. What if he's dead? He could be dead and I'd never know.

Her heart ached at the thought that clawed through her brain, and it chilled her with fear for him that was far stronger than any she felt for herself. The fear she had for her own life was almost an afterthought, a shadow, compared with the terror of thinking something had happened to Tiger. She kept reminding herself that he'd abandoned her, that trusting any man was foolish, but...so what? That didn't mean she wanted anything to happen to him.

While she was a prisoner, a hostage against Tiger's return, it was a luxurious prison, her jailer charming, urbane and polite. The level of comfort in which she was living only served to add fuel to the lurid scenarios of Tiger's fate spun by her imagination. She remembered the rough men of Tiger's crew all too well. She hoped the plan was to arrest them as well as the smuggler he was after. They could have turned on him the way Santiago had tried to desert Cardenas. Whatever scheme had been acted out to capture the arms smuggler might have gone badly.

"He could have been eaten by sharks," she murmured, and took a sip from the icy glass.

Joking about it didn't help lighten her mood any, but she knew wallowing in helplessness was a waste of time. It took an effort, but she turned from watching the sea and sat down to stare at her lunch plate. She had little appetite, but pretended otherwise. She pretended to confidence Tiger would return when his job for Cardenas was finished, to being relaxed and happy to be staying in such sumptuous surroundings. She'd held long conversations with her host in the past two days; she supposed he found her interesting because he always seemed reluctant to leave her. Problem was, she concentrated so hard on playing the role of Tiger Rafferty's devoted lover that she barely remembered any of what they talked about.

I don't know why I bother, she thought now as she speared a wedge of pineapple with her fork and brought it to her mouth. Tiger wasn't coming back. She was certain the urbane, civilized-seeming Cardenas would eventually have her killed. All she was doing was prolonging the inevitable. And why?

Because some idiot part of her wanted to believe that Tiger would keep his promise. No, not wanted—that sloppily sentimental part of her did believe in him, did trust him. The same way you trusted Mark, she bitterly reminded her softer side. Look what happened with him. That wasn't life and death, the soft side responded. And Tiger isn't at all like Mark. All men are like Mark, she argued back.

Then again, she thought desperately, maybe her jinx had gotten Tiger killed.

She told herself to give the paranoia a rest, but her worry over Tiger's safety was too strong. She couldn't stop thinking about him, and not just about the things that could go wrong, or the fear that he had abandoned her. She missed him. She'd gotten used to sleeping in his arms. She was used to his touch. She missed it, even the times he grabbed her and yelled. She missed his voice, the rare smiles and laughter. She missed the way he smelled, the feel of his skin, the warmth of his body. She vividly remembered the shape of his hands, the outline of his lips, the grooves of his dimples, the exact shade the sun had browned the flesh on his chest and back. She remembered his hands on her, and hers on him; how they set each other on fire. She remembered the way he kissed, and it drove her mad with grief to think she might never know the taste of his mouth again.

She knew she was a fool, but her greatest regret in life was that she had never made love to Tiger Rafferty. It was enough to make her cry, and it did, when she was alone in her bed every night. She'd been crying herself to sleep for many reasons, but mostly because she so desperately missed the man she feared had betrayed her.

Was she nuts, or what?

Before she could answer this question a rich, polite voice at her side said, "May we join you?"

Hope jumped, and would have knocked over her drink, if Cardenas hadn't quickly reached out to steady the glass. She took a swift breath, then made herself smile up at her host. "Please," she answered, and then noticed the man with him.

The man was handsome in a brutal, chiseled way. There was no emotion in his face, nothing in the dark gaze he flicked over her. It left her with a chill running up her spine, making her grateful when his attention fixed on Cardenas and stayed there. When Cardenas sat on the other side of the table, his companion took a chair near him. It seemed to Hope that the ambient temperature in the area went down a few degrees because of this stranger's presence. It was a ridiculous notion, of course, but there was something so sinister yet familiar—

Her gaze flew to him as every muscle tensed. Her hands bunched into fists in her lap as her heart tried to hammer out of her chest. She wanted to scream, but had had too much practice lately in keeping her emotions bottled up to let a sound to give her away now. She couldn't stop from nervously licking her dry lips, but gave no other sign of what she was suddenly sure of in her bones. She certainly didn't speak.

It was Cardenas who said, "Santiago."

He said something else along with the name, made a polite introduction, she supposed. The only word she heard was *Santiago*. The name reverberated in her head for long moments, drowning out any other words that were spoken, submerging thought. Eventually, though only seconds actually passed. Hope's survival instinct pushed the hated name aside; she refused to let her throw herself blindly at her enemy or run away in terror. Instead of remaining frozen in place she made herself smile at something Cardenas said.

She made herself say, "Yes, some more ice tea would be lovely."

Oddly enough, she had no recollection of being asked

about iced tea. It must have been the right answer because Cardenas beamed at her while Maria came forward with a pitcher and poured tea all around. Santiago, she noted, looked disgusted at being given such a mild drink, but aside from giving the attentive housekeeper a dirty look, made no protest. Maria ignored him in a stiffly disapproving way that told Hope the woman was used to the man's bad moods, and wasn't in the least intimidated by them.

As her senses began to settle down Hope tried to keep her attention on Cardenas, or even on her lunch plate; to look anywhere but at the man responsible for so many deaths, but he drew her gaze no matter how hard she tried to ignore him.

So, he's back at last, she thought, and made herself take a long, hard look at him. Though she'd gotten a glimpse of this man as he'd escaped from the yacht, she had to admit she'd forgotten what he looked like. Did that make her a traitor to her family and the crew's memories, she wondered, not remembering what their murderer looked like. In fact, she couldn't clearly remember how many days it had been since Santiago had violently invaded her world and Tiger had changed it. It seemed like forever. Hadn't she vowed to bring Santiago to justice somehow? Hadn't Tiger stood in the way of her doing so? Well, here he was, and Tiger had left her to face him alone. What was she waiting for?

Cardenas claimed her attention by saying, "I have an appointment with Father Felipe to discuss a cellular telephone account for the church in a few minutes, so I can't stay long. I wanted to see how you're doing, my dear." His smile was graciously understanding. "You seem so lonely."

"Father Felipe?" she blurted out. "You know Father Felipe?"

He chuckled. "Everyone on the island does. We're old friends." Cardenas gestured expansively. "In a way, Father Felipe is responsible for all this." He looked disapproving at Santiago's snort of amusement. "He influenced my decision to build the resort, my efforts to bring tourism to the island. It's a way for me to employ dozens of people. Isla Sebastian is a beautiful but very poor place, sharing its beauty with the rest of the world helps the economy."

And a good way for you to bury some of your illegal transactions in the legitimate bookkeeping, Hope thought. She was a banker, and understood how such things could be done. She didn't mention this observation to her host, however. She was nothing if not circumspect around him. She was furious with herself for having reacted to mention of the priest.

"You know Father Felipe?" Cardenas asked her now.

"No," she answered honestly. "I've heard a great deal about him, though."

Santiago stood abruptly. He was restless, his annoyance with his employer barely kept in check. "If you have to waste your time with the priest we better go," he announced. He gave Hope a brief glance that told her he thought her no more than a bug, and another drain on time better spent on business. She didn't know if he knew she was involved with Tiger, and hesitated to ask. To mention Tiger would remind Santiago that he had betrayed his boss. She didn't know if Santiago had yet learned that Tiger had met with Cardenas. She didn't know anything, really!

She did know that Santiago frightened her, and that she was more afraid for Tiger than she was for herself. She wanted justice, maybe even a little sweet revenge. She had nothing to lose—except Tiger Rafferty.

She knew why she didn't denounce Santiago to Cardenas, because she couldn't. Not yet. She had to be sure

Tiger was safe first. She couldn't speak until she was certain that her actions could in no way harm the man who had saved her from Santiago. She didn't know what Santiago could do to Tiger, but she wasn't going to take any chances that might hurt the man who had protected her. The man who had promised to come back for her.

He's not coming back, she told herself as she watched Cardenas and his traitorous henchman disappear back into the house. *No man is to be trusted!* Intellectually, Hope knew Rafferty would not return, but her heart believed.

She was such a fool.

"I'm going back, sir."

"The devil you are, Lieutenant." Commander Corrigan eyed Tiger sternly up and down. "You did a fine job finally stopping the arms flow, now your duty is to make a final report before letting the assignment go. You've been working undercover too long," he added. "Forgotten that you don't have to work alone. No cowboy stunts, do you hear me? You're getting debriefed, taking some leave, and then moving back to your desk job at the Pentagon. I did you one favor in letting you take over the undercover operation when your friend was killed. That's the limit of my generosity, young man. You have your orders. Accept them and go."

"I have my orders, sir," Tiger responded, standing stiffly at attention before Corrigan's desk. "But I can't leave Hope on Isla Sebastian. It was my actions that put this woman in danger. I owe her—"

"You're far too emotionally involved with this woman," Commander Corrigan announced. "Your friend learned the hard way where that leads. I'm not losing another man." He steepled his fingers on the top of his desk. His steel-gray eyes swept over Tiger once more. "Look at you, dressed like a pirate, and ready to start yelling at me if you don't get your way. That's right, isn't it, Lieutenant?''

Tiger didn't think jeans and a T-shirt constituted pirate attire, but Commander Corrigan was correct in his assessment of Tiger's mood. He was furious, desperately worried, restless to be gone. The four walls of this spare office on a Florida navy base barely contained his frantic energy. ''I promised her I'd be back, sir.''

''I don't think you had the right to make this woman any promises.''

''But I did make them. I keep my promises, Commander.''

''How very commendable. Your integrity aside, that doesn't make you the best man for the job of retrieving her, now does it?''

''I know where she is. Cardenas is expecting me to return. My going back for her is the easiest course of action.''

''Also the most dangerous for you. Your cover is flimsy at best, even more so now that the men who crewed the *Rani* are in custody. Those men and the vessel added credibility that is no longer available to you. Your appearance on the island would be highly suspicious. Cardenas is bound to find out about our shutting down the smuggling operation soon. He will instantly suspect your involvement. Your turning up to collect your ostensible girlfriend could easily result in both of you getting killed.''

Tiger tried desperately to make the man understand. ''She'll die if I don't go back. She's being held hostage to ensure my return. I'm responsible for her being in this situation!''

''Yes, you are,'' Corrigan agreed. ''But that still doesn't make you the best man for the job. The matter is in my hands now.''

''But sir—''

"Why are you arguing with me, Lieutenant? Dismissed." He then deliberately turned his attention to the computer on the left side of his desk.

Tiger waited for a moment in a dark silence that was only punctuated by the hum of air-conditioning and a muffled roar of a jet taking off in the distance. There was no arguing with the man's tone. Tiger saw that there was no getting past Corrigan's indifference to the fate of one lone woman when there was so much more at stake. Corrigan was a busy man; military security was all that mattered to him. And he thought that it was all that should matter to the men he commanded.

Tiger thought frantically as the silence built around him, but after a few seconds of watching the stern, unyielding profile of the man he normally respected, all he could do was turn on his heel and leave. He had his orders, he had a new assignment. He had his career, and even the life he'd missed so much back.

And what did any of that matter without Hope in his life? Her death would be his fault; her fate was tied to his. He had been told there was nothing he could do about it.

Tiger waited until the door to the office Corrigan was using was closed behind him before he murmured, "We'll see about that, now won't we?"

She had a plan. It wasn't much of a plan, but Hope didn't have much to work with. She paced back and forth across the plush grass-green carpeting in her guest room and considered her options one more time, even though she was supposed to be on her way downstairs to join her host for dinner. It was raining outside the glass door that opened on the balcony that faced the sea. It was a gentle sound, one that should be soothing but wasn't. The evening rain was nothing like the hideous storm she and Tiger had been trapped in on the other side of the island, but rain would always remind her of Tiger Rafferty.

Tiger.

Hope stopped her pacing as memories flooded through her. She stared at the vividly rendered detail of a parrot flying over a blooming jungle that covered one wall of the bedroom while her thoughts flew as free as the gorgeous bird. It took a long time to push memories and images back and return to thinking about her escape plan. The key was Father Felipe, of course. The priest had always been the focal point of her getting off Isla Sebastian. She'd never met the man, yet she had hopes that he'd help her. Okay, he associated with criminals like Cardenas and Ibarra—and Tiger; but maybe he was just doing the best he could to help the people in his parish with what he had to work with here on Isla Sebastian. It was the criminal element that ran the island, but that didn't make the priest one of them. Tiger had taken her to Felipe for help. If Father Felipe hadn't been off the island, she'd be safely back in America by now. She would never have gotten her life and emotions entangled with Tiger, either.

Problem was, Hope didn't know whether she was glad or miserable to have gotten involved with Tiger Rafferty.

"Both," she said to the painted parrot. She was alternately brokenhearted and elated from moment to moment because of Tiger. Damn the man! And, please, God let him be safe! What she knew she couldn't do any longer was allow her twisted-up feelings for him get in the way of taking a chance at self-preservation. Her will to live had been distinctly absent of late, clouded by grief, by a hunger for justice, by guilt, by maddening sexual attraction to Tiger. All these conflicting reactions had weakened her will, made her unwittingly dependent on other people to determine her fate. She feared Cardenas. She was terrified of

Santiago for Tiger's sake. She'd let it all become too much for her, and turned into a dithering fool.

"Forget that," she muttered now.

She'd decided that she wanted out alive, and knew that she was the only one who could arrange it. So what if Tiger had promised to rescue her? Maybe he'd lied to her. Maybe not. So what did lies or promises have to do with her taking her fate into her own hands? And why had it taken her so long to determine that she really wanted to live after all?

She'd considered confessing all to Cardenas and throwing herself on the seemingly kind man's mercy. He was so polite, so nice to her. It was tempting, but she wasn't actually suicidal. No, Cardenas was out. She was going to have to sneak past the guards and security system, past the vigilant housekeeper. She had come up with a flimsy plan, and worried over it as she paced, nervously anxious because she couldn't put the plan into effect until tomorrow morning.

Hope nearly jumped out of her skin when someone knocked on the door. She whirled around, heart hammering in her chest. She was thoroughly rattled, and stared around guiltily, fearing she'd been caught out. Then she realized that she was late for dinner and it had to be Maria come to remind her.

She was laughing at her fit of nerves when she crossed the room. But the laughter stopped as she opened the door. Every thought fled. All that was left was an intense, overpowering rush of emotion as she saw Tiger standing in the doorway.

Chapter 13

She came into his arms with a sob of both joy and relief. His embrace was as fierce as hers. The mouth that found hers was as hot and needy. The kiss they shared as desperate and welcoming. She pressed herself against his hard-muscled body and reveled in his unyielding strength as he pulled her even closer. They fit together so very perfectly it was as though they made one complete being when they were together like this. No—not quite perfect. Not yet. She felt his sudden hardness pressing against her thigh, and knew what was necessary for them to be complete.

"Yes," she whispered, but wasn't sure if she spoke aloud. "Make love to me." She was sure that, somehow, he heard her plea.

His hands moved over her, frantic, seeking, arousing. She pulled him inside the door, and heard him slam it shut with his foot. They moved to the bed, two hungry creatures intent on mating, coming together through loneliness and fear and undeniable need. Every touch brought growing arousal and swift reassurance that they were alive, surviving. Their mouths clung to each other, the taste sweet and triumphant.

Hope's heart pounded so hard she was sure he could hear it, or even feel it, her pulse pounding against his skin. Her breath came in sharp, needy gasps, and every breath brought his scent and heat deep inside her. She was filled with fire. Blinded with it. All she could do was close her eyes and feel. He kissed her throat, sending waves of longing through her. She caressed his back, and felt his shudder of desire. He kissed her shoulder, then his lips moved down to her breasts, mouthing the tips through the thin silk of her blouse. Her nipples hardened into tight pebbles and he suckled one then the other through the wet cloth.

Hope threw her head back, her spine arching against Tiger's supporting embrace. Her knees went weak, her insides melting and molten. "You came back," she murmured, voice hoarse with panting urgency and raw astonishment. The confession came out in a wild rush of words while his mouth and hands seduced all sense and caution from her. "All I wanted was to see you again. I missed you so much! I didn't think I'd see you...couldn't endure it!"

Her words were lost in a wordless cry of pleasure. She suddenly couldn't bear to keep her eyes closed, as the intense sensations were driving her mad. She intended to look her fill at his perfect, sun-browned, long-limbed body. She'd seen him wearing very little, now she wanted to see him in nothing at all.

They found the bed and tumbled onto it, limbs tangling briefly before they set about tearing off each other's clothing. Her hands moved of their own volition. She had his shirt off within seconds. He quite literally tore the silk tank top off her and she laughed with barbaric delight when he did it. She had never acted with such abandon, but with

Tiger this wildness came naturally. Mating with a tiger, she realized, was *supposed* to be an act of wild abandon.

At another time she might have been afraid of such uncontrolled passion, but not now. She was ready for the wildness of a tiger in her life.

The rest of their clothes came off with equal speed, and with breathless laughter as well as urgent moans. She helped him put on a condom, her fingers caressing his hard length. Every brush of his hands was heaven against her hypersensitive skin. She ran her hand across the neatly defined muscles of his arms, his furred chest, his flat belly and farther down.

Being away from her had been agony for Tiger. This was agony as well, sweet agony. He moaned in delicious pain as her hand closed over him. He hissed a low, urgent, "Yesss!"

He kissed her deeply, letting his tongue match the stroking rhythm of her hand on his hard shaft. He caressed her, too urgent to be gentle as his hands sought out every soft, yielding part of her. Her avid response told him she didn't mind, spurred him on. She cried out in pleasure when he found the swollen bud between her thighs. She opened to his touch and cried out eagerly against his lips. He stroked and teased for a long time while she panted and whimpered, arching against his hand.

"Like that, huh?" he asked, breathing the question into her ear as he made a slow circle with his questing fingers. She gasped, fingertips digging into his bare shoulder.

"Like that?" she asked, and imitated the circling gesture around the tip of his penis.

His answer was a growl of need, and to move swiftly up between her open legs. He buried himself inside her in one hard stroke.

She welcomed him with a wild cry of, "Yes!"

Hope didn't have a single coherent thought for a long time after that. She rode with the building pleasure, aware of nothing but how perfect they fit together, moved together, and the glory that perfection brought her. The heat and friction of skin sliding against skin filled her senses, fire raced through her and exploded with each stroke that joined them. The explosions built and built, pushing her higher, bringing them together, bringing them over the edge and down a long, wonderful roller coaster of a drop that left her limp and laughing and completely satiated for the first time in her life.

"Tiger," she said as some point that seemed hours later, "That was—!"

"Better than sex. It was making love." He breathed the word reverently, tiredly, and she stroked his sweat-damp hair and silently agreed. "It was stupid," he added after a while.

She wasn't offended. She knew exactly what he meant. Her answer was laggard and lazy in coming. "Yeah."

"We're idiots."

"Uh-huh." She yawned as satisfaction seeped through her, flowing sweet and slow as warm honey. She felt as soft and malleable as warm butter; even the tingling after-shocks of pleasure came in sultry, leisurely waves. She could go on feeling like this forever, if she didn't fall asleep first. She yawned again, and turned her head to rest it on Tiger's lovely naked shoulder. His arms came around her, holding her close against his heart. It felt to her that their hearts beat as one.

"Nice," she murmured, and napped.

Tiger wanted to stay here like this with Hope wrapped in his arms forever. He kissed her shoulder, and tasted the salty sweat of their lovemaking on her skin. Her skin held the glow of a rich golden pearl in the soft bedroom lighting.

He wanted to kiss her all over, taste the sweetness of her again, and would as soon as he could work up the strength. Tiger yawned.

No, he reminded himself. *I can't go to sleep.* It took him a long, reluctant moment to remember why. When he did, he sat up, swearing.

The inventiveness of Tiger's vocabulary both shocked and amused Hope, even as it brought her fully awake. "The man's definitely a sailor," she said with a chuckle. "Why'd you move?" she complained as Tiger rolled out of bed. "I was comfortable."

Tiger grabbed her hand and pulled her out of bed. When she was on her feet he said, "Get dressed. We're going."

Hope had to shake her head to clear it, to bring their insane reality back into focus. She glanced from the rumpled bed linen to Tiger, who was hurriedly throwing his clothes back on. "Go," she said hesitantly, afraid to hope. "Cardenas is letting us leave?"

He didn't answer her question. He said, "I came back for you."

Hope didn't let herself ponder the ambiguity of his reply; she did hurry to put on the darkest clothing she could find, midnight-blue shorts and matching top. It was an outfit she considered suitable for an escape attempt. She wondered what Tiger had planned, or if they were going to improvise as they went along. She tried not to let her nervousness show.

She was surprised to find Tiger standing very close to her when she turned from dressing. He put his hands on her shoulders and looked her over worriedly. "You are all right, aren't you? Everything went fine while I was gone?"

Her heart warmed at his concern. "Fine," she answered. "No problems." She kept all the stress and her fears about and for him to herself.

Or tried to. His expression clouded. "You said you didn't think I'd come back." His hands dropped to his sides and he backed away from her, radiating hurt. The bruised look in his eyes nearly killed her. He shook his head. "I don't believe you, Hope Harrison. How can you be so—"

"Untrusting?" she supplied, though it hurt like fire to say the word.

"You thought I lied to you, didn't you? You didn't believe me when I said I'd be back."

His bitterness tore at her soul. She blinked through sudden tears and looked away, unable to face his betrayed anger. Her own pain seethed in her, black and engulfing. She walked to the balcony door and rested her palms on the cool smoothness of the glass. Water ran gently down the outside of the window. She wished she were out there, free in the darkness, letting the rain soak her upturned face and mingling her tears with the clean water from the sky.

But she was here and far from free. It wasn't captivity in Cardenas's house that bound her, either, but ties to Tiger Rafferty that chained her soul. She was bound to this man, had been since the moment they'd met, even more so now that they'd made love. She didn't know if this was a good thing, or a bad one; but, she was thankful for the connection despite her pain, though she deeply regretted the pain she'd caused him.

"I believed you'd come back," she finally answered him. "Believed it in my heart and soul. But I was afraid you wouldn't."

"Couldn't?" he demanded. "Or wouldn't want to? Did you really believe that?"

"Yes," was her answer to all his questions. "I'm human, Tiger. Flawed and weak and mortal—and I've been left alone before."

"Not by me. I promised."

She rubbed her hands up and down the cool glass, then pressed her cheek against it. The memory of his touch, of touching him was so strong in her she could feel nothing else. Her breath came out in a sigh that frosted the glass. "I know."

"You should believe me."

The pain in his voice stabbed into her, mingled with her own, bled her from the inside. She could accept her own pain, but she couldn't bear knowing that she'd hurt Tiger. She turned back to him. "It's safer not to believe in anyone. Safer not to trust." She sighed, and wiped tears off her cheeks. "It's not safe for me to be with you."

It took Tiger a moment to understand what she meant. When he did, his heart filled with a joy he didn't want to believe in. Happiness he didn't want to trust. Happiness that eased the anger, hurt and resentment—eased but didn't completely dispel it.

"It's not safe for me to be with you, either," he answered. He'd put his career on the line for her, and his life, and knew that neither was as important as getting her to safety. Honor demanded it, so did duty. Most important of all, so did the deep, inexplicable way he felt about this difficult, defensive, altogether wonderful woman. Whatever she felt about him didn't matter as long as he made sure she was safely out of danger at last.

That he'd come back for her meant more to her than he could ever know—unless, of course, she told him. She was tempted, but then Hope considered where they were and decided that this was not the time for passionate declarations. The passionate thing they'd spent the last hour or so doing had been the most important act of her life, but it had, objectively speaking, been a waste of their precious time. What had they been thinking of! Explanations could

wait, they had to go. They weren't out of trouble just because Tiger was back. Were they?

She crossed her arms and made herself be all business.
"What now?"

"We, uh—" He scratched his jaw. "We go down to
dinner."

Somehow she'd expected something a little more dramatic. "Dinner?"

"We're late," he added. "But Cardenas said he'd understand if we were."

"I—see." She didn't. "Dinner. We're still guests." She
tried hard not to hesitate significantly before saying *guest,*
but didn't quite succeed. Tiger nodded in reply, and held
his arm out as though gallantly offering to escort her down
to dinner.

"That's okay, I have an escape plan," she whispered
when she joined him. "You can come in on it if you like,"
she added as he tilted a curious eyebrow at her. "We have
to get to Father Felipe."

"Shouldn't be hard," he whispered back. "Father Felipe
gave me a ride from the airport. He's waiting downstairs."

"Oh." Maybe Tiger did have a plan. That was good.
Then a jolt of anxiety went through her. "Santiago!" she
whispered. "He's here." She didn't know if Cardenas's
henchman would try to get in the way of their escape or
not, but she felt Tiger had to be warned. His expression
turned both curious and wary. Hope understood without his
having to say a word. She shook her head, then confessed,
"I didn't do anything. I thought it might put you in danger
if I did."

Tiger was flabbergasted. He knew how recklessly hopeless she'd been, how willing to risk her own life to get
revenge for Santiago's crimes. She didn't care for herself,
he knew, but had tried to protect him. Even though she'd

been afraid he wouldn't return. Like she'd said, she'd believed in him despite her fear of betrayal! Wow.

And that was all very well and fine, but what about Santiago's presence in the house? The man had not been at Cardenas's side when Tiger had had a brief interview with him in the living room. Maybe Santiago wasn't in this evening. Maybe they could get away without an encounter with the man. And a brief encounter might go off without a hitch—Santiago had a lot to lose if Tiger told Cardenas the truth about Santiago's trying to take the arms shipment for himself. Why had Santiago returned to Isla Sebastian when he'd had the opportunity to desert when Cardenas sent him on a business trip?

Didn't matter, Tiger concluded. Santiago was Cardenas's problem. He and Hope were out of here tonight. She was going home to a safe life in Baltimore, and he was through with undercover work. They just had to get out the door, and Father Felipe was here to ensure they managed that.

Tiger kissed Hope's temple reassuringly as he put his arm around her shoulder. "Let's go down to dinner, shall we?"

"It's a pity Father Felipe couldn't stay," Cardenas told Hope as they sat down to dinner. He gallantly held the chair next to his at the head of the table until she was seated. "It would be nice if you could meet him at last."

Hope managed to smile up at him. It was a wan, distracted stretching of her lips while her heart continued to sink and her thoughts ran riot. "I was looking forward to it."

"To arrange a wedding, perhaps?" Cardenas asked with a teasing smile. He took his seat and turned his glance to Tiger, who was sitting on the opposite side of the table from Hope. "Felipe would be happy to marry the two of you."

"As soon as the roof on St. Cecilia's is fixed," Tiger replied. "He and I talked about it on the way here. Too bad he had to hurry back to town."

"A pity," Cardenas agreed. "But when a message comes to give last rites to the dying, what can a priest do but go?"

Tiger couldn't help but wonder just who the priest had left to pray over, if it had some bearing on his and Hope's chances of leaving tonight. He did know he couldn't seem to let Felipe's absence spook him. They were supposed to be friends and allies here. He wanted to ask where Santiago was. No, all he really wanted was to take Hope and get out. There was a small plane waiting at the airport that Ibarra had once controlled, but the airport was on the other side of the island. The key element in his plan had been called away while he and Hope were making love. Tiger cursed himself for being a reckless fool. The hour he'd spent indulging his passion might have cost them their lives. All he could do now was hope that Cardenas didn't receive any faxes or phone calls disproving Tiger's assertion to him that the arms shipment had been delivered and that all was well with Cardenas's U.S. Navy contact.

Hope tried not to worry. At least she tried not to show it. She'd turned into quite a good actress over the past few days, even if she did say so herself. She managed to smile at Cardenas, give Tiger a warm look that had nothing to do with acting, then put a fork full of grilled sea bass in her mouth and swallow it. She didn't taste the fish. That would have been asking one thing too much of her heightened senses, but at least she looked like a person who wasn't in the least concerned about anything. "Delicious," she complimented her host.

"Maria will be happy to know you think so," Cardenas replied.

"I'll have to apologize to her for keeping the meal waiting. And to you, too, of course."

"Think nothing of it. You're young and in love."

Hope blushed. She searched in her memory banks for some kind of polite response, but was saved from finding words as Maria showed Estaban Quarrels into the dining room.

Quarrels paused briefly in the doorway, his dark glance passing over Cardenas and herself as his attention centered on Tiger. "Well, well," he said in his deep, rough voice. "Look who's back."

"You have a problem with that?" Tiger responded. His tone was mild as milk, Hope noted, but the cold look in his eyes was deadly.

Quarrels shrugged. "No problem. Good to see you again." He looked at Cardenas while he spoke. Quarrels was aware that Cardenas required polite behavior from anyone in his home, Hope supposed. Quarrels didn't wait to be invited to dinner, though. He pulled out a chair at the end of the table and took a seat. The handsome scoundrel grinned at Hope in a way that she might have responded to before she met Tiger Rafferty. "Did you miss me?" he asked.

"Were you gone?" she asked back.

Quarrels dropped his flirtatious act and looked at Cardenas. "You've heard about Ibarra, I suppose?"

"Father Felipe was here when you called him," Cardenas answered. "Good of you to send for the priest."

"Ibarra was a religious man."

Hope noted the past tense, and gulped nervously. She wanted so desperately to get away from these evil people and the mad world they inhabited. She shot an imploring glance at Tiger, who gave her a slight, but reassuring nod. They would go, that gesture promised. Soon.

She believed him implicitly. Despite the constant dread that seemed to have become her natural state, there was something wonderful, something life-affirming in allowing herself to trust another person. No, she hadn't *allowed* it; her feelings for Tiger had just *happened*. As she was a staid, methodical, logical person. Hope knew these feeling needed to be taken out and properly examined, but there was no time for that right now. No, there was no time to think, but she did offer Tiger a smile in response to his reassuring nod.

Tiger wasn't sure what was going on, but the atmosphere in the room definitely didn't feel right. You didn't survive undercover without being a pretty good judge of situations, and characters. Quarrels was up to something, but Tiger didn't figure it was any business of his. His annoyance came from Quarrels having decided to make his move now and complicate their escape from the island. Then again, maybe this could work out in their favor. He rose to his feet, and Hope followed his lead.

"We hate to miss the rest of dinner," Tiger told their host, "but we don't want to interrupt your business, either. Besides, I don't like to be away from the *Rani* any longer than necessary." He shot Quarrels a look. "Especially if there's some unrest in town. No reason for me or my men to be involved in anything more to do with Ibarra, is there?"

Quarrels looked him over carefully, then answered. "No reason at all. If you want to get your butt off Isla Sebastian, Rafferty, you have my blessing to go."

Too bad I don't have your car, too, Tiger thought. He silently cursed Quarrels for Father Felipe's unplanned absence. He hated the thought of asking for a loan of a car from Cardenas. There would be a driver involved, as well as the necessity of getting the driver out of the way. Planning escapes was so much easier on television, where hitting unnamed henchmen over the head or simply killing them was an easy task. Real life henchmen were people, and hitting them over the head wasn't always practical or easy; killing them was even more complicated, what with the moral and ethical overtones involved.

"It has been a lovely visit," Hope said sweetly to Cardenas, before Tiger could work out how to acquire the necessary transportation. She went on in a breathless gush while Cardenas beamed at her. "I've enjoyed the stay, but now that Tiger is home, I'm dying to get back to the boat. I hate to ask one more favor of you, Mr. Cardenas, after you've been such a perfect host, but could we get a ride back into town from one of the resort drivers? Father Felipe was going to take us back with him, but..." She looked at Quarrels. She turned a cajoling smile back on Cardenas. "It seems there's been an unforeseen complication to the evening, for all of us. And we'd hate to interrupt your business discussion, as Tiger said." She stepped away from the table. Tiger came to her side, and slipped an arm around her waist. She went on blithely to the other men, "Why don't you two go on with carving up empires or whatever, and we'll be on our way."

Tiger held his breath, waiting for disaster to strike. Quarrels stared, frowning at Hope's words. Cardenas, on the other hand, looked amused by her airy description of his and Quarrels's nefarious dealings. He chuckled indulgently. "She's been quite an amusing guest, Mr. Rafferty. It would have been very sad if something untoward became of her during your absence."

The mildly spoken words chilled Tiger's blood, but neither he nor Hope showed any signs of concern. She must be getting used to acting the role of Tiger Rafferty's woman, as she didn't so much as tense in his embrace. He nodded coolly, while Hope said brightly, "I wouldn't have missed this for the world." Her gaze was on Tiger when she spoke these words, and, for a moment, he thought she meant them. He thought the look of trust and caring in those big blue eyes could sustain him through any emergency.

It was Cardenas's turn to stand and push his chair back from the dinner table. "Why don't you make sure Maria has finished packing for you, Hope?" he suggested, though he was clearly dismissing her. "While Mr. Quarrels and I have a few more words with Mr. Rafferty."

Hope didn't argue. She went, trying not to give the appearance of running from the room. She didn't care why the little lady had been dismissed from their business conversation. That this was a man's world didn't bother her one little bit. She would fight her battles for equal rights and shattering glass ceilings back in Baltimore should she live long enough to get there.

She found a packed suitcase waiting for her in the guest room. She had no interest in taking it, but supposed it would look suspicious if she and Tiger simply walked out without the appearance of mundane normalcy. Mundane and normal was something she was good at, she reminded herself. Mundane and normal was who she really was. She still couldn't keep from taking a quick look around the room where she and Tiger had made love not so long ago. The room was all neat and orderly and held no trace of the heaven she'd experienced in it. She told herself she'd remember the heaven and not the terror as she grabbed the small red bag, and ran—though to all outward appearances she moved with decorous speed. The running was entirely in her head. So was the praying to please, please let this be over with in the next few minutes.

Luck, however, was not with her. Her prayers went unanswered. Santiago came into the dining room from a different doorway at the same time she entered from the hallway. She saw him, and stopped in her tracks.

He saw Tiger and drew a gun.

What happened next could best be described as all hell breaking lose, but it began with Santiago shouting, "I'm glad Rafferty told you! I should have killed you and taken over long ago!"

Every man in the room brought out a weapon, and suddenly there were more men in the room—Cardenas's guards, people on Santiago's side in a sudden takeover attempt, probably people working for Quarrels. Hope didn't see everything that happened, and wasn't able to piece the who, what and why of what happened together until later. The one thing she did that made any sense to her was respond to Tiger's voice.

He shouted, "Get down!" And she did.

Hope ducked behind a chair as someone fired a shot. She shouted Tiger's name. A bullet penetrated the back of the chair and she slithered quickly under the table. For some reason she still had the small suitcase clutched in one hand. It wasn't any defense at all, but she held it in front of her all the same. She crawled down the length of the table while people shouted and shot at each other all through the dining room. She heard the fighting spread to other parts of the mansion as well. It was ugly, and she was hardly safe where she was. She had to get out from under the table, get to Tiger.

She managed to make out pairs and pairs of legs from under the edge of the tablecloth. She picked out the longest ones she could find and inched her way out from under the

table beside where those long legs stood, half-crouched be
hind a sideboard.

A dive and a frantic, fast roll brought her up against the
wall next to Tiger. He glanced briefly down, and motioned
for her to back up. She realized that he meant for them to
make a break for the nearby doorway into the front hall.
She hoped that the members of various factions for power
on Isla Sebastian would keep their attention on their fight
with each other while she and Tiger got away. She moved
as fast as she could, bent over, her small suitcase held like
a shield. She followed Tiger, keeping her attention focused
on him, not looking at anything but him. Every thought
was a frantic prayer for the completion of the next step of
the journey. First to the hallway. Crossing the hallway took
a few moments, and seemed like hours. They made a zig-
zagging dash, dodging and sprinting until they made it as
far as the front door.

There was a guard at the door. He leveled a very large
handgun as they approached, but the gun was aimed at
someone behind them and to the guard's left. Tiger shouted
and Hope ducked. Two guns fired at the same time. The
guard went down, blood blossoming onto his white shirt as
his shoulder. Tiger spun around as Hope hurried to tug the
unconscious guard from blocking the exit. She yanked open
the door, but was careful enough not to rush outside. She
bent low and stayed close to the wall as she checked to see
if anyone was outside. Appearing in the center of a backlit
opening seemed like a quick way to get killed by anyone
watching the door to her.

"Clear, Tiger!" She called when she saw no one on the
porch or on the white gravel driveway.

Tiger moved to stand close beside her against the wall.
His gun was in one hand, his throwing knife in the other.
"You sure?"

"Without night vision goggles?" she asked sarcastically. "I've watched too much television," she answered his equally sarcastic look.

"Right." Tiger took another quick look around. There was a thick pillar shielding their position, offering as much cover as possible in the open entrance area.

Quarrels came rushing up from behind them from across the hallway. As Tiger leveled his gun at him, Quarrels shouted, "All right, you two, let's go! No, wait!"

He turned around and took a moment to shoot out the overhead lights. Then he turned his gun on the nearest porch light outside. As the area plunged into darkness Quarrels dashed outside. Hope and Tiger followed swiftly after him.

Chapter 14

Once outside, Quarrels went left and low across the porch, Tiger and Hope went right. Inside the isolated cliffside house the gunfire went on and on. Hope doubted anyone in the resort buildings on the other side of the extensive grounds heard any of the noise. No one was going to call for help. Besides, there was no police force to call and all the private armies on the island were already here.

"Remind me to complain to my travel agent about vacationing in a war zone," she quipped as Quarrels joined them behind a clump of ornamental bushes near the porch steps. She'd learned to handle terror by using brittle, sharp humor to distance herself from the fear that threatened to paralyze her.

"Next time travel first class," Tiger quipped back.

She realized for the first time that he was just as frightened as she was, as mortal. He was dangerous and competent, but no different than her, really. The realization only made her care for him more.

"I did travel first class."

"Oh, yeah. Right."

Quarrels pointed. "My Jeep's that way."

"You offering us a lift?" Tiger asked Quarrels suspiciously. "Shouldn't you be inside trying to kill Cardenas?" he added. "You've gotten rid of Ibarra, now all you have to do is eliminate Cardenas to take over the island."

"I don't want to take over the island. Santiago wants to take over the island. He was shooting at me, too, you might have noticed."

"Sorry, my head was down."

"Only smart move you've made all night," Quarrels declared. "What did you do to get Santiago to make his move before he was ready, Rafferty? Big mistake on his part."

"He tried to steal a shipment for Cardenas from me," Tiger grudgingly told the man with the getaway car. "He sold Cardenas an excuse about a storm screwing up the pickup. For some reason he assumed I wouldn't keep my mouth shut about the—" he almost said *incident,* but for Hope's sake he found himself explaining "—the murder of some innocent people" instead. He put a hand comfortingly on Hope's shoulder as he spoke, and received a nod in response. The small gesture affected him deeply. He kept his attention on the business of survival, though. "Why help us get away, Quarrels?"

"I'm a sentimental guy. Besides, strength in numbers," Quarrels added when Tiger gave him a stone-cold look. "I wasn't expecting this party. I came here alone. Don't think any of us can get out the front way though, do you, Rafferty?"

"Guards on the front gates," Tiger said thoughtfully.

Quarrels nodded. "And we don't know if they're loyal to Cardenas or Santiago."

"What a time for a palace revolution," Hope muttered.

"Don't tell me, they all have cellular phones, so they all know what's going on at the mansion, right?"

"Right," both men answered at once.

"The gate's the only way out?"

"Right," they answered her again.

"Really?" She tilted her head sideways, and Tiger noticed how her hair shone like silver in the moonlight. "At an expensive resort like this? No side entrance for delivery trucks or staff? I know there's a resort helicopter that does tours around the island, I've heard it land and take off."

"Right," Quarrels agreed. "Can you fly a chopper, Rafferty?"

"No."

"Me, either. How about you, sister?"

"Sorry."

"Then why'd you bring it up?"

"I'm only looking for alternatives to trying to ram through a gate manned by armed men, Mr. Quarrels. And I am not your sister."

He snickered. "Too bad, you're a tough cookie."

Hope knew she was no such thing, but she also knew this was no time to engage in bickering. She looked confidently at Tiger. "How do we get out of here?"

Tiger was elated to have Hope look at him like that. "We get to Quarrels's Jeep," he told her decisively. Tiger wished the sky hadn't cleared. The moonlight was bright and the white stones of the drive were very reflective. The drive wound before them like a silver ribbon; anything on the road would be easily seen. He swore silently about this as the three of them rushed single file across the lawn at the edge of the drive, coming to a halt behind a bush near where several vehicles were parked. Night-blooming flowers scented the air. Quarrels's white Jeep shown like a beacon in the moonlight. Tiger made out the shadowy outlines of several men in among the cars. Others who had decided to escape the fighting, or guards set to make sure no one left? There was nothing to do at this point but confront them. There was no way to take anyone by surprise across that white expanse of gravel. He exchanged a look with Quarrels. The other man gave a slight, grim nod.

"Stay low, stay behind me," Tiger warned Hope. "Get to the Jeep."

He gave his instructions then threw his knife as far as he could beyond the parked cars. As the men by the cars turned at the noise from the blade landing on gravel he ran forward, crouched over to offer as small a target as possible. Quarrels flanked him. He heard Hope's footsteps on the gravel right behind. People turned toward them, but the distraction had gained them time. Someone shouted. No one shot at them, yet. Time stretched out as their feet ate up the distance.

Hope didn't think as she moved swiftly behind Tiger, but all her senses were hyperactive. Quarrels tackled one of the men by the cars and they rolled into the darkness of the lawn. Hope heard each distinct sound, each grunt, groan and meaty slap of fist against muscle of the short, nasty fight that followed. It was punctuated at the end by what could only be the sound of heavy metal crashing against the thin bone of someone's skull. She could almost feel the impact as Tiger shot up forcefully out of his running crouch and landed a fist into a man's jaw. The man went down, and Tiger kicked him to keep him there. A third man got off a shot, but it went wild. Tiger's return fire dropped the man to the ground.

"That's all of them," Quarrels said, emerging from the side of the drive. He swiped mussed hair out of his eyes.

"Not quite."

Hope heard the voice, recognized it, began to turn, but

Santiago's arm came around her throat from behind before she could move. She didn't know why she hadn't heard his approach from behind her. She felt the hot tip of the gun barrel pressing against her side, smelled Santiago's sweat as he pulled her harshly backward. Heard Tiger breathe out a word that was a combination prayer, curse and self-recrimination. Quarrels simply swore. Hope didn't know what to do, but she stood very still, fighting to keep the spike of terror from paralyzing her.

"I know you now," Santiago whispered in her ear. "You were on that boat. Good thing I didn't kill you then."

Anger filled Hope as he spoke. She might have spat out a retort, but his arm against her windpipe effectively kept her quiet.

"Let her go."

Tiger spoke with a cold calm he didn't feel. In fact, worry and boiling rage warred inside him and threatened to make him do something foolish that could get Hope killed. He wanted to put a bullet between Santiago's eyes, and not just to get Hope out of the man's clutches. He wanted to prove to her that there was justice in the world, revenge for her family's deaths. She deserved justice, and Santiago more than deserved to die.

Before Tiger could do or say anything else Quarrels drawled, "Looks like you lost the power struggle with Cardenas. You cut your losses and left your own men to die, I suppose." He shrugged unconcernedly. "Too bad. But you're going to have to be more polite if you need our help to get off the grounds."

"Let her go," Tiger repeated.

"We don't have time for this," Quarrels agreed. "Let her go and get in the Jeep."

Santiago showed no trust in this offer. "The woman is my hostage."

Quarrels swore again. "You don't need a hostage." He yanked open the driver's side door of his Jeep. "I'll leave without you if you don't let her go."

Santiago edged closer to the Jeep, still using Hope as a shield. Tiger carefully stepped to the side. He noticed that Quarrels now had the heavy Jeep door as a shield. Santiago had said nothing about either of them dropping their weapons. The man was nervous to the point of panic, which made him sloppy but very very dangerous. Tiger knew there wasn't much time to resolve this. People were running up the drive from the house. Santiago had to get away or he was a dead man. He'd be sure to take Hope down with him since Cardenas's men would hardly hesitate to shoot through her to get to the man who'd tried to kill their boss.

With only moments to spare, Tiger made a desperate decision. Gun raised, he rushed forward.

Santiago turned quickly to keep Hope in front of him. As he did, Hope brought the bag she still grasped in her hands up and hit Santiago in the forehead with it. He grunted, and let her go, just as Tiger ran into him. The two armed men tangled, went down, struggled.

Quarrels grabbed Hope and dragged her behind the shield of the car door before she could throw herself at Santiago in the effort to help Tiger. The men rolled into the shadows just as they finally shot at each other. She screamed. And struggled, but there was no getting away from Quarrels's harsh grasp.

"I have to get to Tiger!" she shouted at the man as Cardenas and a half dozen of his people came pelting up to where they were.

Quarrels faced Cardenas, ignoring her while she squirmed in his grasp. He pointed his chin toward the spot where Tiger and Santiago lay in the darkness. "We did your job for you."

"So you did," Cardenas said as he knelt beside the prone bodies. "One of them is still breathing," he added. He got to his feet. "Rafferty, fortunately for you."

At this news, Quarrels finally let her go. She was praying and crying as she rushed to kneel beside Tiger. He was unconscious, his weight heavy and slack as she took him in her arms. His shirt was covered in blood. Her first impulse was to rock him in her arms while she wailed with grief. Impulse be damned, a saner part of her snarled at this dramatic longing. The man was alive and she had every intention of keeping him that way.

She looked up at Cardenas and demanded, "Help me! Right now! We have to get him to a hospital."

"There is no hospital," Quarrels answered. "We have to get him off the island."

"Then we'll get him off the island. You have a helicopter," she reminded Cardenas. "Don't you have a nurse at the resort?"

He was looking down at her with a look that was half amused, half concerned. He wasn't used to being given orders, but she was used to giving them when she had to. This wasn't the boardroom of her family's bank, but she called on management skills she'd learned there with surprising ease. She didn't have time to put up with anything from anybody right now.

"Call the nurse," Cardenas ordered. "I have a helicopter," he answered Hope. "But it won't get you to the mainland."

Tiger groaned. She felt blood pumping through her fingers. She didn't know when she'd found the wound in his chest, but her hand was covering it, trying to staunch the flow of blood. "Someone hand me some clothes out of that bag," she said. Quarrels handed her cloth to use as a bandage a moment later, and knelt beside her to help. "You've got an airport," she reminded him. "Tiger left an airplane there." She looked imploringly up at Cardenas. "We'll take your helicopter to the waiting plane. Please?"

Cardenas nodded as his men gathered around him. One of them was already speaking on his cell phone to the medical staff at the resort. "Yes," Cardenas agreed to Hope's request. "Good idea. Tell the nurse to meet them at the landing pad with every emergency supply she has. Call the pilot of the chopper," he ordered another man. "Have him standing by. The rest of you help get Rafferty into the car."

"Hurry," Hope whispered. She shared a grim look with Quarrels. Her heart was breaking and panic trying to set in. She was covered with Tiger's blood, and the world was going dark around her. "There isn't much time."

He's going to die, the fatalistic part of her screamed inside her head. *People you love always die.*

"Who are you?" Hope asked, as a way to pass the time. "Really?"

The man sitting beside her hunched forward tiredly on the hard plastic hospital chair and rubbed the back of his neck. "My name's Steve," he told her. "I don't think you need to know much else."

They were the only people in the waiting area of the hospital's emergency room, for the moment, anyway. Somehow, and thankfully, they seemed to have washed up in this quiet spot out of everyone else's way. There had been a lot of people here a few minutes before, some of them medical personnel, others had been officials of a different sort. While some people had been in green medical scrubs, some had been in military uniforms, some in dark, conservative suits. It had all seemed thoroughly complicated and confusing, but really quite peripheral to Hope. With her entire attention focused on Tiger, all other noise and confusion had swirled around her without her taking much notice. Tiger was in surgery. She couldn't be with him now; all that she could do was wait to hear on the outcome. In this quiet lull she let the images that had meant nothing at the time float into her awareness because she couldn't bear the endless replay of the image of Tiger's pale face and bloodstained body for the moment.

My name's Corbett, Tiger told her every time he fought his way back to consciousness. She couldn't stop hearing his weak voice insistently whispering over and over to her. *Michael Corbett. My name's Michael Corbett. You have to know my name's Mi—*

She found that her hands were clasped together in her lap, white-knuckled and aching with tension. Her shoulders burned from strain as well. Hope slowly made her body relax. He gave her his name—gave her his secrets. A final act of trust.

No! Not final. *Please,* she prayed. *Let him live.*

At some point not too long ago she had been marched into a bathroom and someone had helped her wash blood off her hands and face and given her a green cotton tunic to replace the stained blouse she'd been wearing. There was still dark, crusted blood under her fingernails she noticed now.

She'd almost forgotten about Quarrels, until his big hand covered hers. "He made it this far, Hope. He's tough. You won't lose him now."

The words were meant to bring comfort, but only brought the bleak thought, *He was never mine to begin with.* Then she remembered, *We made love. He told me his name.*

What mattered, though, was that Tiger was still alive. Cardenas's well-supplied and trained medic was to thank for that, and the speed at which everything had moved.

Time had gone by in a blur to Hope, both swift and endless. She had no idea how long the trip from Isla Sebastian to the mainland had taken or what time it was now. She wasn't even sure where they were. Florida, perhaps?

"You made calls while we were on the plane," she recalled as she looked at Steve Quarrels. "Made things happen. I don't think you're a drug lord at all. You're some sort of government agent, aren't you?"

He frowned, then ducked his head. When he looked at her again his face had changed somehow. The cold-eyed, cynical criminal was gone and there was a half-shy, boyish grin on his face. "Guilty," he responded. "I'm with the DEA. And you," he continued as she tried to take this information in, "are responsible for my blowing my cover tonight. Cardenas is too smart not to suspect my motives for helping you tonight."

Hope rubbed an aching spot in the center of her forehead. "But—Ibarra?" She closed her eyes and pictured Cardenas's dining room when Quarrels came in. She remembered the conversation. She made herself look at him as she spoke, somewhat accusingly. "You killed Ibarra tonight. To be in complete control of his operation."

He shook his head. "Ibarra's not dead. He's in an American jail. I shipped him off a couple of days ago."

"But—you told—"

He stroked her hands as he explained, "I needed a reason to visit Cardenas. So I faked the news that Ibarra was dead, even called Father Felipe to the house for last rites to make it more believable. Then I showed up to negotiate with Cardenas. I couldn't just break in and grab you. Nobody was supposed to get hurt. The last thing we want is to jeopardize Cardenas's position. While much of his business is illegal, the government sometimes finds him useful. If he falls, then someone worse will take his place. And I shouldn't be telling you most of this,'' he added.

Hope stared at the man, while her head throbbed and her mind reeled. She wanted to be with Tiger, but since that was impossible right now she'd thought conversation with this man would distract her from nagging, aching worry. Conversation, however, was proving almost as traumatic as simply stewing in her fear and dread. Nothing in her world had made sense for a long time, no one was who they seemed, everything was complicated. That Quarrels was yet another masked man with a hidden agenda didn't surprise her, but the knowledge did add to her confusion. It also added to her desperate need to escape this world of masks to find out if Hope Harrison existed at all.

Since running away wasn't an option right now, she tried to get more facts from Quarrels. ''You said something about grabbing me. Why would you want to 'grab' me?''

''Because some Navy honcho who knew about the DEA operation on Isla Sebastian called my boss and he contacted me. Until I got the message to look after you I had no idea Rafferty wasn't some small-time gunrunner. He had no idea who I was, either. And I figured you for some bimbo Rafferty'd picked up—a smart one,'' he added with an amused sideways look at what must have been an outraged expression on her face. ''I liked how you handled the fight with Ibarra when neither Rafferty nor I could manage to get out of it without bloodshed. Anyway, I figured I could go in, tell Cardenas that Rafferty had split on the deal with him, leaving you high and dry. I would then declare my lust for you and get him to give you to me rather than kill you.''

''How romantic.''

''I thought so. Cardenas would have gone for it. He doesn't kill anyone he doesn't have to. I was just following orders when I came to rescue you, sweetheart. Which your boyfriend wasn't, I might add. Let's just say that I was a touch put out to find that Rafferty had ridden in on his white horse. I could have stayed home and gotten a decent night's sleep." He yawned as though he really meant it, and rubbed the back of his neck.

Hope couldn't let her own exhaustion matter. In fact, she was barely aware of it as a tingling buzz of excitement shot through her. She found that she was on her feet, looking down at Quarrels. "Tiger was ordered *not* to come back for me? He came back anyway?"

Quarrels nodded. "Don't know what his exact orders were. All I know is that the mission was handed off to the DEA from Naval Intelligence. NI was officially out of the picture, but Rafferty didn't seem to care. Probably get his ass busted, but..." He stood up and shrugged eloquently. "What the hell? I wouldn't trust somebody else to get my woman off a place like Isla Sebastian, either."

Someone in a suit appeared and gestured for Quarrels to come with him before Hope could respond. Quarrels touched her shoulder, and walked away without another word or glance back. Alone in the waiting room, Hope sank back into the hard plastic chair and hugged herself tightly, trying hard to hold emotion and reaction inside to keep from breaking down completely. After a while the lights of the room faded around her, as did the sharp smell of disinfectant and the cold tang of air-conditioned air on her skin. She was back in the dimly lit cabin of the small private jet rushing over the dark ocean with Tiger's body, slack and heavy, pressed to hers. She felt him stir, coming half-awake. His voice whispered, hoarse and desperate, in her ear.

"I won't die on you," he promised. Over and over. Or, perhaps he spoke the words only once, but she heard them tolling like a mantra over and over in her mind as time bled away. "I won't die, I promise. Promised I'd come back. Trust me, Hope. Always trust me. I won't die. Couldn't leave you. Couldn't let Santiago get away. You deserved justice. Deserved. I won't—"

"Hope Harrison?"

Hope started as a hand touched her shoulder, as the man spoke again. "May we talk, Ms. Harrison?"

"I don't want justice," she said, though not to the man she looked up at. "I want Tiger."

A brief look of puzzlement flashed in his eyes, but he was expressionless when he said, "Come with me, please."

The polite words were no request, and Hope responded automatically to the authority the man exuded. He was wearing a Navy uniform, one with several gold stripes on his sleeves. She let him take her arm and lead her to an empty hospital room.

"Will Michael be all right?" was the first thing she said when they were alone in the room. His eyes narrowed at the use of the name.

The Navy officer touched a thumb to his jaw, and said, "Well, I've decided not to court martial him, if that's what you mean, Ms. Harrison. Please sit down," he added. "I figure it's my fault he got himself shot. I'm sure he'll be fine," he added. The words sounded like an afterthought.

Hope barely heard them anyway. She was thinking that what had happened to Tiger was her fault. It always was. She sighed, and sat on the narrow bed, and wiped tears away.

"I'm Commander Corrigan," the officer introduced himself. "Lieutenant Corbett is under my command. Unfortunately for everyone involved I gave him the impression that I wasn't going to make an effort to retrieve an endangered civilian when I had every intention of getting you off the island. When he left my office he had orders from me not to interfere, but not the assurance I should have given him that you would be fine.''

'' 'Need to Know?' '' she heard herself ask. ''That was the excuse he gave me for not explaining who he was sooner.''

Corrigan nodded. '' 'Need to Know.' Yes. Sometimes we forget that people have a right to know information that will keep them from acting stupidly, despite security procedures. Since I didn't want to jeopardize a DEA agent's cover, I, unfortunately, did not disclose my plan to Lieutenant Corbett. So he disobeyed my orders to stay out of the situation. Fortunately for him he was officially on leave when he decided to take a trip to Isla Sebastian. Of course the DEA is very unhappy with him, but I'll deal with them.'' He put his hands behind his back and leveled a austere gaze at her. ''But first things first.''

She, obviously, was up on his busy agenda right now. All she wanted was to find out about Tiger. As for everything else, well, she'd had quite enough.

''Sir,'' she said. ''All that matters to me is Tiger—Michael. I don't want to be dealt with, or lectured, or comforted or explained to. If you're going to debrief me, or offer me counseling for all the trauma, forget it.'' She rose to her feet, squaring off against the stern, official, steely-eyed military man. ''Tell me that Tiger's going to live, let me see him. That's all I want.''

''Tiger Rafferty does not exist,'' he reminded her. ''He never has. No matter what he told you, no matter what dangers you shared, you don't know Lieutenant Corbett.''

''He risked his life for me.''

''He did his duty.''

She wanted to protest that Tiger—Michael—had saved her life more than once because he loved her. She vividly remembered their passionate lovemaking; those snatched hours defined everything she was right now. She would never forget the touch of his hands on her, or the heat of his mouth covering hers. They'd made love but she didn't know for certain that he loved her. She knew that he liked baseball, and that his sister was getting married, and that he'd wanted her to know who he really was, but she didn't know that he loved her.

"You'll be debriefed and then returned to your home, Ms. Harrison. There are nondisclosure documents you'll have to sign, as well."

"I want to see Tiger now." As she spoke nausea began to build in Hope, and a wave of dizziness hit her. When was the last time she'd slept? What did it matter?

"I won't allow that."

What did he mean, *allow?* Why didn't this man leave her alone? Why was he making her life difficult? Wasn't worrying about whether Tiger lived or died enough to try to deal with right now? Her eyes were closed, but the room still spun around her. She wanted to faint, and thought she would.

She couldn't stand any longer. She couldn't think to answer any questions, either. She vaguely felt Corrigan helping her onto the bed, but she couldn't actually feel the bed beneath her once she was lying down. All she was aware of was the dizziness, the encroaching darkness, and the overwhelming sense of guilt and doubt that came with her into troubled sleep.

Chapter 15

"She's gone?"

"It's for the best, Lieutenant," Commander Corrigan answered Tiger's question. "Don't take it hard, young man. When you're feeling better you'll see that the intensity of what the pair of you experienced clouded your judgment and emotions."

Tiger didn't pay much attention to what Corrigan said. He was too bereft, too devastated, at the news that Hope had returned to Baltimore. He lay propped up in the bed in a private room with a pleasant view, and felt like a prisoner. "She didn't say goodbye."

"She did," Corrigan corrected him. "You were only half-awake at the time, still full of painkillers, but she did say goodbye. She wouldn't leave until she was sure you were going to recover, if that's a consolation." His tone clearly implied that Tiger shouldn't need any consolation.

What Tiger knew was that she was gone and he wanted her to be here. More than life itself he wanted—

"You all right, son? Want me to call the nurse?"

Tiger shook his head. "No. That isn't... No." He closed his eyes and turned his head away. He wanted to be alone, but he could sense Corrigan's presence over the hum of the bedside monitoring units and noise that filtered in from the hospital corridor beyond the room's open door.

After a long silence, Commander Corrigan said quietly, "You really care for this woman, don't you, Michael?"

There was nothing of the sternness of a commanding officer in the man's concerned tone. Tiger responded to the concern, hungry for the compassion he saw in the man's eyes when he turned his head to look at him once more. "I love her more than my life."

Corrigan bit back an immediate answer, and put a hand on Tiger's shoulder, careful not to touch any of the bandaging. "Do you?" he asked earnestly. "What you went through was intense, but did it have anything to do with reality?"

Tiger knew what the man meant; he didn't want to think about it, though. "I know what I feel."

"Feeling and thinking are very different things sometimes. You can't stop your feelings, son," Corrigan advised. "You have no right to act on those feelings."

"You sent her away."

Corrigan nodded to Tiger's accusing glare. He wasn't going to talk about it anymore. "You need to get some rest. I want you back behind a desk at the Pentagon. You've had enough vacation time in the tropics, don't you think?"

"Enough for a lifetime," Tiger managed to answer. He wondered if he truly meant anything to her. He'd risked everything for her—and she was gone.

Maybe Tiger should let her go. Michael Corbett's heart told him he couldn't. His head whirled with so many conflicting thoughts it made him dizzy. Or maybe it was the medication. Either way, he barely noticed when Corrigan left and his tangled thoughts turned into even more tangled nightmares. In the nightmares she didn't love him, she never had, never would.

If she didn't love him, then what the hell did he have to live for? He knew he had to find out. He couldn't let a critical injury and his commanding officer's direct orders get in the way of finding Hope Harrison again. If his sister Julie hadn't arrived at the end of his third day in the hospital he would have worked out an escape plan on his own.

The house she came home to was empty, though the media that gathered outside the walled lawn gave Hope a certain amount of unwanted company. She had several days of being a tabloid sensation. She was the heiress returned from the dead! Again! Old stories about the plane crash she'd survived as a child were dredged up. There were questions and speculation, some of them on evening news broadcasts. She barricaded herself in the too big, empty house, spoke only to her lawyers and rode it out. It all died down quicker than it might have if Commander Corrigan hadn't somehow managed to fulfill a promise that his people would make sure she only had to put up with a "token amount of fuss" to use his words.

It rained for days. It was nothing like the rain Hope had experienced on Isla Sebastian. There was no wildness to it, no hint of danger in the wind or ragged clouds. It was just dull, gray, monotonous and tedious. Cold, too, permeating down to the bone and further down into the soul. Of course, she didn't suppose she could blame the weather for the empty coldness inside her, but it made a convenient enough scapegoat at first. People talked about the aptness of the dark weather to her when they offered their condolences, and Hope went along with the easy pathos of the subject.

She would have liked to have sat at home and stewed in her own misery, but that would have been futile and foolish. She had to find a way back to Michael Corbett, a way to get around government security regulations and his commander. While she fumed and schemed, her family lawyers went to work on wills and the estate and the process of defining her place in the hierarchy of the family's banking business.

It turned out her place was quite easily defined: she owned the place, lock, stock and vault. A month before she would have found such responsibility impossible to assume, would have run to any authority figure she could find to tell her what to do. Now, taking over the reins of the business seemed like the logical thing to do. It gave her something to do while she bided her time. Besides, how hard could running a large business be? It wasn't as if people at board meetings would arrive packing guns now, was it, she asked an attorney at one point. Even if they did, Hope thought she'd be able to handle them. Tiger would be proud.

She held a memorial service for her aunt and uncle. She did slightly regret laughing in Mark's face when he showed up to offer not only condolences but also his strong shoulder to lean on. She didn't regret laughing, just that the sound had been so loud in the relative quiet of the chapel. The look on Mark's face as he backed away from her was priceless. She wished Tiger was there to see it.

When she came home from the service she couldn't sleep that night. Or the following night. The next night, by way of distraction, she turned on her desktop computer and logged onto the Internet. She not only had mail, she was both amazed and skeptical to read a message from someone who said her name was Julie Corbett. ''I work for the

FBI,'' Julie Corbett's message explained. "I can find any-body.''

After she thought about it for a long time, Hope finally moved the mouse to the button marked "Reply.''

The ice-blue shantung silk suit fitted her to perfection, the heels of her pumps added an extra two inches to her five-foot-nine-inch height, her makeup was exquisite, as was the light floral scent of her perfume. She wore a pair of simple pearl earrings and a strand of matched pearls that had come down to her from a great-grandmother. It was the sort of outfit in which a woman could feel well armored to face the world.

"Armed to the teeth, metaphorically speaking,'' she muttered to the mirror. "And scared out of my wits.'' The fact was, she wasn't at all sure she should be doing this. But if she didn't go through with it she knew she'd regret it the rest of her life. What if he didn't really—?

Taking a deep breath, she steeled her resolve and picked up her purse off the hall table. As she was checking within her purse one more time to make sure the heavy parchment envelope was inside, the doorbell rang. She was half relieved at the interruption, half annoyed. "Ambivalent, aren't you?'' she asked herself as she moved to the door.

She stared at the man standing on her front porch. He stared back. Neither spoke. For a while she actually forgot to breathe. The day was bright and sunny and beautiful and the light that shone down on the sight of Michael Corbett dressed in a white naval officer's uniform was the brightest of all. Their gazes met and locked, blue to blue. Time stood still, and every thought in Hope's head fled in the rush of panic, joy, fear, longing, and uncertainty. Her muscles froze; her brain went into overload. If hours past or seconds

or complete geological ages, it didn't matter; she was unaware of the passage of time.

The first thought that worked its way through the shock
was *He's not as tall as I remember.* He was handsomer,
though. She didn't know how that could be, but it was so.
Maybe it was the way he looked in the white dress uniform.
It showed off his broad shoulders and long limbs to perfection. His dark-brown hair was neatly trimmed, without
a strand out of place. Then Hope recalled that she was
wearing heels, so of course he wouldn't *seem* as tall to her.

She finally remembered to breathe, and took a step back.
Tiger took this as a tacit invitation to come in. After he
closed the door behind him he looked her over head to foot.
He made an awkward gesture. The words came out awkwardly, as well. "You're going somewhere. Maybe I
should…"

Hope put up a hand. "No, no. That's all right." Her
mind and heart raced, but her words were strained and
clumsy, her tongue felt like a lead weight. "You look—
wonderful," she told him after a strained pause.
"Healthy." She put a hand out, wanting to touch him, but
stopping just short of contact. "You're feeling all right?"

"Fine," he said. "I—that is…" His voice trailed off. He
went back to staring at her while the air around them sizzled with all the things he wanted to say and do. He wanted
so desperately to touch her!

She was even more beautiful than he remembered. Perfect, and so very poised. Hope was every inch the cool
aristocrat, dressed in a tailored suit. Despite her polite show
of interest and concern she couldn't want him here. He'd
told himself that she would, but maybe he'd gotten caught
up in the fantasy of romance to the point that he was going
to make a complete fool of himself!

Hope didn't know what to do. No, she knew what she

wanted to do, but… She finally made herself say, "Hello, Michael. I've missed you." That was putting it mildly. The truth was she'd missed him so much that she wanted to drag him down on the cool marble tiles of the floor and make love to him right here and now.

"Michael," he said, and rubbed a finger along his jaw. He canted an eyebrow at her. "Not Tiger?"

She put her hands behind her back to keep from putting them around him and drawing his head down into a kiss that might not interest him. She didn't know why he was here, after all. Maybe to tell her that her presence wasn't wanted where she'd been intending to go this morning. "I like calling you Michael."

He took a step closer. He couldn't help needing to be near her. He couldn't keep his hands off her, either. "Michael," he said as his fingers brushed ever so gently across her cheek. She didn't flinch away and his fingertip traced the expertly painted outline of her lovely, lush lips. They parted ever so slightly at his touch. He felt as much as heard her breath catch. "Michael," he said again, as though he were a stranger to the name. "Sounds so different coming from you. Don't you want to remember the tiger?"

"Do you?" was her soft response, though it took her a long moment to get the words out. "Didn't the psychological counselors advise you to put the past behind you?"

"Oh, yeah." He put his hands on her shoulders. "They advised a lot of things."

"Like taking time to think through what had happened? Put some distance between what you thought you wanted and what you really wanted?"

He nodded. "They tried to do that number on me."

"That's why I skipped the posttrauma counseling session your boss wanted me to go to."

"I didn't have a choice."

She sighed, and looked at him anxiously. "Did you learn the error of your ways?"

"No. Do you know what you want now?" he asked, voice hoarse with the effort to control—his need, his pain, his temper. "Do you, Hope?"

"Yes." She sounded so calm, and felt nothing at all like she sounded. She knew she was trembling, at least on the inside. Her knees were weak, and her heart pounded. Excitement raced through her from the spots where his hands rested close to her skin. She felt the weight and the warmth of him, and longed for him to draw her closer. "Yes," she repeated and took her hands from behind her back. Why the devil was she waiting on him? She was brave and resolute and strong these days, wasn't she? He'd helped her become those things, hadn't he? Taught her to trust again, too. She decided to trust her instincts as well as him.

With a sigh of longing, Hope reached up and drew Michael's mouth down to hers. Her lips brushed gently across his at first. For a few moments they lingered close to each other, breath and sensation mingling, relearning the taste and texture of each other. Then his hand cupped the back of her head, drew her closer, and the kiss deepened and became fierce. As their tongues teased and danced together their bodies melded closely, fitting perfectly. Her hands brushed through his thick, soft hair and down, across his wide shoulders. She traced the smooth hard lines of his back. The kiss was paradise, and went on and on. When it ended Hope found that her back was pressed against the floral-patterned wallpaper on the stairwell wall several feet from where they'd been standing when the kiss began. Her perfect hair was mussed, her skirt was wrinkled, Michael was leaning most of his considerable weight against her, and she didn't care one little bit. She was breathless and happy despite her utter confusion.

Their gazes met as he came up for air, and he said, "Woman, this is worse than I remembered!"

She pushed ineffectually against his shoulders. "Worse?"

"Stronger," he corrected. "More devastating. Wonderful. Better than I remembered." He straightened up, but kept his hands flat on the wall to either side of her, pinning her in place while he looked around. He looked back at her with a twinkle in his bright-blue eyes. "I don't suppose you have a bedroom anywhere nearby?"

Hope couldn't help but laugh at his brazenness. "Michael Corbett," she declared firmly, though she wished there was time to take him to her bed. "If you think I'm going to let you miss your sister's wedding, you are sadly mistaken."

Michael's hands dropped to his sides as he took a quick step back. "My sister's wedding?" He eyed her suspiciously. "How'd you know about Julie's wedding?"

Hope took a moment to straighten her silk jacket. "Where do you think I was going when you showed up at my door?"

He spread his hands out in a confused gesture. "But I came here to invite you to my sister's wedding!"

"Julie invited me first," she told him. She smiled at him. It was a wicked smile, but she still felt a great deal of trepidation. "I was hoping you wouldn't mind seeing me again if I came to the wedding today. You—don't—mind—seeing me again—do you?" She squeaked the last words in a near whisper. She rubbed her hands together nervously as he looked on, openmouthed, eyes wide. She couldn't tell what he was feeling as she rushed on, "I couldn't bear not seeing you. I didn't know what you felt about me, didn't know if you cared, but I..." Hope swallowed hard, and fought back the threatening tears. "I left my heart in the hospital room with you, Michael Corbett. I don't want it back, but I was hoping to at least see it again today.'' She wasn't quite sure what she was saying, she only knew she meant every word.

He was half smiling, yet looking thoroughly puzzled as she stopped talking. His hands were back on her shoulders, as well. ''You know, I bet Julie thought I might chicken out about coming here.''

''So she invited me just in case?''

''She should have trusted me. Do you trust me, Hope?'' Before she could answer he went on angrily, ''The counselor told me that I couldn't be in love with you. That everything we went through obscured reality. That it was intense but that it wasn't love. I trust what I felt. What I feel. It hurt to wake up and find that you weren't there.''

''I wasn't given a choice.''

''I know how you must have loved that.''

She sneered. ''Oh, yeah.''

''I had to wait until I could transfer from Corrigan's command before I could get to you. I'm sorry,'' he apologized. ''Hope, I didn't give you too much time to 'get perspective'. I hope that you're still interested in me.'' He looked boyish and hopeful, and scared in a way Tiger Rafferty never would have. It was more endearing to her than anything Tiger Raffety had ever done.

She laughed, a soft, bittersweet sound. ''I don't want perspective—I want the man who taught me to trust again. The man who risked his life to save mine. The man who made love to me. I want him to make love to me for the rest of our lives.'' She blushed at such a bold declaration. ''That's what I want,'' she stated. ''I didn't know what you wanted or felt. But I started out today intending to find out.''

His response was long in coming. Finally he said

thoughtfully, "I see. No, I don't." He touched her throat, her cheek, with his gaze burning into hers all the while, the blue as intense as the Caribbean in the noonday sun. "Of course you know I love you. You. The strong woman who emerged from the hell I helped put you through. I watched you change and grow—and save my butt a few times—and I fell in love with the essential, elemental *you*. I'm through having adventures," he added. "No more undercover assignments, I promise. So you won't have to worry about my getting killed on you, if that's one of the reasons you're afraid to love me."

"I'm not afraid to love you," she told him. "Not now. Not since you helped bring out the strong woman you just mentioned. But I'm glad you're at a desk job. I'm really quite civilized, you know."

"Me, too." He crossed his heart. "Please believe that I love you," he added.

Hope blinked, nodded. Her heart suddenly ached with more emotion than she could express, but not all of it was pain. A tear rolled down her cheek. He brushed it away with his thumb. "You never said— You came back for me, you made love to me, but you never—"

"I never exactly told you I loved you." The words weren't a question. And he didn't sound like he was talking to her. For a moment his gaze was very much directed inward, as though remembering every moment of the time they'd spent together.

All those images flashed through Hope's mind, as well. "I never told you I love you, either. I was afraid to, I think."

He looked back at her. "Because the people you love die?"

She nodded, and blushed hotly. "Stupid superstition on my part?"

"Maybe," he conceded, and his smile returned. "But look at it this way, maybe I broke your string of bad luck by staying alive. I intend to stay alive a good, long time." His hands came up to cup her face. "I promise you that. On one condition."

She turned her head to kiss his palm. "Condition?"

"Actually on several conditions." He looked both playful and thoughtful. He stepped back and made a show of straightening his crisp white dress uniform. "First, I would like you to accompany me to my sister's wedding. And how is it you know my sister?"

"Ever heard of the Internet?"

"Ah." He nodded. "Quite the little webmistress, is our Julie. In more ways than one, it seems."

"She wants her big brother to be happy."

"She believes me when I tell her I need you to be happy."

"Me, too."

He leaned back against her front door, and looked her over in a way that sent fire through her, weakened her knees and set her to trembling with anticipation. "I want to make love to you right now, Hope Harrison."

"Julie will kill us if we're late." It wasn't that far between Baltimore and Washington, but they had no right to waste any time for their own purposes on Julie Corbett's wedding day. "You have to be there to give the bride away, Michael."

"I know." He held his hands out and she rushed to take them. He squeezed. "Tonight." His eyes held a world of sensual promise in their deep-blue depths.

"Tonight," she responded with equal fervor.

"Tonight and forever, Hope Harrison." He took her into a swift embrace, whispering in her ear before they had to leave, "You'll be Hope Corbett soon enough."

"Then Julie can dance at my wedding," she said, adding, "but we won't be honeymooning on any tropical paradise."

"I promise," he replied, stroking his hands through her hair. "And you know I always keep my promises."

* * * * *

MONTANA MAVERICKS
Big Sky Brides

Legendary love comes to Whitehorn, Montana,
once more as beloved authors

Christine Rimmer, Jennifer Greene and Cheryl St.John

present three brand-new stories in this exciting anthology!

Meet the Brennan women:
SUZANNA, DIANA and ISABELLE

Strong-willed beauties who find unexpected
love in these irresistible marriage of
covnenience stories.

Don't miss
MONTANA MAVERICKS: BIG SKY BRIDES
On sale in February 2000,
only from Silhouette Books!

Available at your favorite retail outlet.

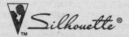

If you enjoyed what you just read,
then we've got an offer you can't resist!

Take 2 bestselling love stories FREE!

Plus get a FREE surprise gift!

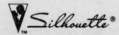

Don't miss Silhouette's newest cross-line promotion,

Four royal sisters find their own Prince Charmings as they embark on separate journeys to find their missing brother, the Crown Prince!

The search begins in October 1999 and continues through February 2000:

On sale October 1999: **A ROYAL BABY ON THE WAY** by award-winning author **Susan Mallery** (Special Edition)

On sale November 1999: **UNDERCOVER PRINCESS** by bestselling author **Suzanne Brockmann** (Intimate Moments)

On sale December 1999: **THE PRINCESS'S WHITE KNIGHT** by popular author **Carla Cassidy** (Romance)

On sale January 2000: **THE PREGNANT PRINCESS** by rising star **Anne Marie Winston** (Desire)

On sale February 2000: **MAN...MERCENARY...MONARCH** by top-notch talent **Joan Elliott Pickart** (Special Edition)

ROYALLY WED
Only in—
SILHOUETTE BOOKS

Available at your favorite retail outlet.

INTIMATE MOMENTS®

Silhouette®

SUZANNE BROCKMANN

continues her popular,
heart-stopping miniseries

TALL DARK & Dangerous

*They're who you call to get you out of
a tight spot—or into one!*

Coming in November 1999
THE ADMIRAL'S BRIDE, IM #962

Be sure to catch Mitch's story,
IDENTITY: UNKNOWN, IM #974,
in January 2000.

And **Lucky's story** in April 2000.

And in December 1999 be sure to pick up a
copy of Suzanne's powerful installment
in the **Royally Wed** miniseries,
UNDERCOVER PRINCESS, IM #968.

Available at your favorite retail outlet.

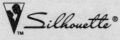

Silhouette®